To Carolyn -
Happy reading!

THE SOLOIST

Anne Wedgwood

Anne Wedgwood

The Book Guild Ltd

First published in Great Britain in 2022 by
The Book Guild Ltd
Unit E2 Airfield Business Park,
Harrison Road, Market Harborough,
Leicestershire. LE16 7UL
Tel: 0116 2792299
www.bookguild.co.uk
Email: info@bookguild.co.uk
Twitter: @bookguild

Typeset in 11pt Adobe Garamond Pro

Printed on FSC accredited paper
Printed and bound in Great Britain by 4edge Limited

ISBN 978 1915122 155

British Library Cataloguing in Publication Data.
A catalogue record for this book is available from the British Library.

*Not many authors are lucky enough to have live music playing all day,
so this is for my very own soloist, supporter and husband – Bruce*

ONE

I couldn't kill Max Silento. He was already dead.

I was nervous enough when I knocked on the door, and it didn't help when there was no answer. I stood in the corridor for ages not knowing what to do before remembering what Ada had said about the terrace and the back door. I was pleased with myself for this, but it didn't stop my heart pounding. I don't like problems. I don't like the unexpected. It was all planned out and he was supposed to answer the door. It had been hard enough working myself up to do it in the first place without it all going wrong from the start.

I took a deep breath, counted slowly to ten and went back down the corridor, through the restaurant and into the courtyard. Even though it was late, there were plenty of people sitting around drinking. I pretended I was a Russian spy escaping with secret papers, sticking my chin in the air and walking carefully so as not to trip over my heels. No one looked at me, so it must have worked. His room was at the end of the corridor, so now that I was outside it would be at the end of the building. I checked for cameras as I approached, and, seeing none nearby, stuffed my baseball cap into the backpack and smoothed down my hair. Hesitation wouldn't help; I marched straight onto the little porch and up to the door, my hand ready to knock. It was open. Just a crack, but open, and swaying ever so gently. It was a still night – I'd noticed on my way, because I'd been worrying about the wind messing my hair, but it hadn't. Had someone else just gone in? Or left?

Paralysed by uncertainty, I hesitated. Stick to the plan, Scarlet, stick to the plan, Ada's words echoed in my brain. Whatever happens, she'd said, stick to the plan. OK, the plan was to knock on the door. Not this door, but it would have to do. I held onto the handle with one hand and knocked with the other, feeling pretty stupid but not knowing what else to do. There was no answer, and I couldn't risk anyone asking what I was up to, so I stepped inside. Despite everything, I couldn't help noticing what a gorgeous room it was. It was just like the pictures on the website, only better. Except for the mess. And the dead man on the bed.

The relief of knowing I didn't have to do it after all allowed my heart to stop thumping, but blind panic wasn't slow to fill the gap. What was I supposed to do now? Ada had sent me to kill him. Stick to the plan, she'd said. Stick to the plan, no matter what. It's foolproof, remember. We'd planned for all sorts of eventualities. What to do if someone else was there, if he was in the bar, if it was raining, if he came on too strong. You name it, we'd planned for it. But not for this. And I couldn't ask Ada for help this time. I had to work it out for myself.

Stick to the plan. The bed was on the other side of the room, and I thought I'd better check to see if he were really dead and not just asleep. I pulled on the thin gloves ready in my jacket pocket, slipped out of my heels and went to the bed. He was a horrible waxy colour and his chest wasn't moving but I needed to be sure. A pair of reading glasses lay on the bedside table and I held them over his mouth and then his nose but they didn't steam up. He was definitely dead. I stood still, listening to the thrum of the air conditioning and the voices of the drinkers outside, considering my options. I could just leave everything as it was and creep away. Max was dead after all, and that's what Ada wanted. Maybe he had died of natural causes after all.

But she'd told me to stick to the plan and I knew she'd grill me on every detail. I'm no good at making stuff up, and I was pumped full of adrenaline, knowing I *had* to do what she'd told me. I'd gone over it so many times in my head, I couldn't walk away now without carrying out Ada's instructions, even if they weren't needed. I slipped the backpack off my shoulders and removed the contents. I couldn't get Max to drink the champagne but I could still get the morphine into him. It was in a tiny bottle, ready for me to add to his glass when I got the chance. I took out the syringe and filled it with the surprisingly clear liquid. I pulled off his soft leather slip-on shoe, eased off the silk sock and checked the syringe was primed. I'd never used a syringe like this before, but Ada had made me practise with it when it was empty so I had an idea of what to do. And he was dead anyway, so as long as I got it into him my injection technique wasn't too important. It was easier than I'd expected. It went straight in, the pinprick hidden between his toes.

I rinsed out the syringe in the sink and repeated the injection, this time with the air that Ada said would go to his brain and kill him. He couldn't have been dead long because his feet weren't stiff, but it still took some fiddling to get the sock back on, and I was glad not to have to tie any laces. The champagne was still cold; wrapping a towel around it while I opened it muffled the pop, and it went straight down the plughole, just like it was supposed to.

Glasses next. Now that I was carrying out the plan, even with variations, I felt calmer. I had to wash the glasses out and put them back in their places. But there weren't any glasses – we'd not drunk the champagne. Thrown by this problem, I decided to tidy up instead. We hadn't expected a mess like this one, and I knew Ada wouldn't want me to leave it. The seating area looked like a bull had been charging around, and as soon as I picked up the side table the smell hit me, making me feel small and scared and nauseous. A whisky bottle was under the toppled chair, minus what I reckoned to be two generous slugs. The top was on so it hadn't spilt on the carpet, but it doesn't take much to set my mental alarm bells ringing. A glass lay close to the table and another had rolled under the built-in desk, each containing a few drops of amber liquid.

This wasn't in the plan either, but I decided it wouldn't hurt to put the whisky bottle and one of the glasses by the bed. I wiped them clean and pressed Max's fingers around them, leaving the dregs where they were in the glass. The second glass could have come from the tea tray or the bathroom, and I picked the latter, rinsing it out and popping his toothbrush and paste inside. Washing a glass was part of the plan and I felt I was back on track. And I was proud of myself for thinking to put the bottle by the bed. It would help it to look like natural causes after all.

It was surprising what a difference the tidying-up made. It really looked as if Max had gone to bed with a nightcap and died in his sleep, which wasn't much different from the original plan. Perhaps everything would be all right. It didn't matter how he'd died; the important thing was that he was dead and I'd done what Ada told me to do. I looked around the room before leaving. A man asleep on a bed. A tidy room. A clean sink. It should have been reassuring but something was off. My nerves were screaming at me to leave now, before anyone could come in and find me there, but I made myself wait until I could work out what was wrong. The lights; why would they all be on if he were supposed to have died in his sleep? Sighing with relief, I crossed to the bed and fiddled with the three switches set into the wall, leaving just the lamp by the bed on. Much better. I picked up my shoes, slung the bag back onto my shoulder and eased quietly out of the door.

A couple strolled into the car park just as I stepped outside the room, holding hands and laughing. I held my breath as they walked to their car, glad to be wearing a black dress. I waited until they drove out before shutting the door, not wanting to make even the smallest of movements while there was a chance they might see me. I pulled off the gloves, put my shoes back on and dumped the champagne bottle with the hotel empties by a bin in the corner of the car park, just as Ada had told me to. I was terrified of having forgotten something important, but I'd attract attention if I hung around any longer. No one saw me as I walked out of the car park and into the night.

Once clear of the hotel, I stepped into a doorway and took off the heels. It had been fun to wear them, it was all part of the 'killing Max' plan, but there was no way I was going to walk home in them. As soon as the thin ballet pumps were on my feet the adrenaline started to drain away, leaving me so faint I had to crouch down to stop myself from passing out. I put my head between my knees and counted to ten, and that was enough for me to get going again. The last thing I needed was to be hanging around in a doorway on a Friday night. I knew I couldn't go straight home. If everything had gone to plan it would have taken well over an hour, and a glance at my phone told me I'd barely spent half that time in the hotel. I didn't like the idea of walking around on my own at this time of night so I went to the bus station and sat on a bench near the stop for Hull. The last bus leaves after midnight, so I reckoned I'd be safe until then. Waiting on the bench gave me time to think, to go over everything I'd done. The important thing was, I'd stuck to the plan. I could go back to Ada with a clear conscience and say that I'd done what she wanted me to and Max was dead. Well, not quite what she wanted, but nearly everything, and he was still dead.

I didn't know why Ada needed him dead, but if he was a threat to the Rosewoods that was good enough for me. Nothing good ever happened to me before I met Ada, and nothing good would ever happen again if I had to leave her house. The way she'd explained it, I had no option, and I was looking forward to seeing her face when I told her Max was dead. She'd be proud of me, and I'd be able to plan properly for the future.

For the first time, I wondered how he'd died and who'd done it. It could have been a stranger but people don't get murdered by complete strangers. Perhaps he was threatening other people as well as us? No, he was a pianist, not a gangster, and anyway, that would be much too like an Agatha Christie novel – it must have been someone in the family. Perhaps they put poison in his whisky, although that didn't explain the mess. Maybe they'd not had time to tidy up. I realised with a jolt that I must have interrupted whoever it was and that was why the outside door was open. The realisation that I'd probably only missed the real murderer by a matter of seconds took me completely by surprise. Ada liked to say that truth is often stranger than fiction, and I thought this might prove her right, although I could hardly tell her about it. I decided it didn't matter who did it. All that mattered was Ada thinking it was me. And keeping to her side of the bargain.

* * *

Ada was supposed to be asleep so I tiptoed into her room and sat in the chair beside the bed to tell her all about it. A fancy fire escape led from Ada's room to the garden below but it had never been needed before, and I could see she was tickled to see it put to good use at last. She was sitting up in bed reading her book with no apparent sign of anxiety, but she put it down as soon as I was in the room and reached for her hearing aids, eager to hear my story.

'Done?' Ada's never been one to waste words, even at a time like this.

'Done.' I matched my whisper to hers and sank into the chair, putting my bag and shoes on the floor.

'Any problems?' If only she knew... but I had my story ready, as close to the truth and the original plan as possible, rehearsed in detail in the bus station.

'No, it worked perfectly.' There was no way that would be enough, and I knew it. She looked at me expectantly, and any hesitation would have made her suspicious. I leant back in my chair in genuine exhaustion and took a deep breath.

'It was easy to get in the room, you were right about that.' Ada nodded with satisfaction; there's nothing she likes better than being told she's right. 'The dress helped, and the makeup of course. I said I was a fan and I'd been plucking up my courage all day to talk to him but was too shy in front of other people, and would he like to share a glass of champagne. He said it was a bit late but why not and he let me in.'

'Did you manage the morphine?'

'Yes, I did what you said and asked to use the bathroom. I took my glass with me and put the morphine in while I was there. Then I told him to dim the lights and swapped the glasses while he was fiddling with the switches. There was a big sofa so I sat on that and tried to look inviting. It worked perfectly.'

'I knew it would. You're more attractive than you realise, Scarlet. At least you are when you make the effort.' She didn't mean to be rude, and I didn't mind her saying it. It was perfectly true, and being able to switch from mousy and dowdy to glamorous was always going to come in useful.

'Thanks,' I whispered, giving her a smile.

'Did it take long to work?' she asked. 'I hope you didn't have to put up with his unwelcome attentions for too long.'

'No, I swigged my champagne back a bit and he copied me like we hoped he would. I kept him talking for as long as I could and he started to get drowsy pretty quickly.' I was getting into my stride despite my lack of experience in lying; perhaps it's like murder and all it takes is preparation. 'I said I needed to use the bathroom again to get ready. He asked what I needed to get ready for and I said I thought he might have worked that one out and maybe he should make himself comfortable.'

'And did he? Make himself comfortable?'

'He tried. I heard him getting up and bumping into stuff. He was calling for me at first but I didn't answer. I locked the door and kept quiet. I heard him knocking some furniture over but then it went quiet. I waited for a while and when I came out he was on the floor. He'd knocked a table over, and a chair, but he was out cold.'

'Excellent. Although I'm surprised he could move around so much. Never mind, what did you do next?'

'I pulled him onto the bed and injected the air bubble. Between his toes, like you told me to. Then I tidied up the mess and got out.'

'What about the bottle? And the glasses?'

'I washed the glasses and put them in the bathroom. They were just the hotel water glasses, nothing special. And the bottle with the hotel empties. And yes, I was wearing the gloves, you don't need to ask.'

'I wasn't going to,' she said, although I was sure that wasn't true. Ada leaned back on her pillows, apparently satisfied. 'Thank you, Scarlet. And well done. I can sleep much better now, knowing that man's dead and the family's safe. And admit it, Scarlet; it will have been good practice, don't you think? For when it's my turn?'

'I guess so,' I said. 'Although that's a long way off, Ada, let's not think about it now.'

'I think about it more than you know,' she said, relaxing at last. 'And so would you if you were in my position.' I was pleased to see her eyelids drooping because I didn't think I could carry on lying to her much longer.

'Time to sleep, Ada. Let me help you to lie down properly.'

'Thank you, dear.' Sleep was coming, but she was fighting it. If Ada's got something to say, she won't stop until she's said it. 'You know, Scarlet, I wasn't sure you could do it. I wasn't sure you'd have the nerve when the pressure was on. But I am now. I know you'll be able to help me when I need it. It's a great comfort. And we'll go to the solicitor soon. Get those papers signed.'

'All in good time, Ada. Go to sleep, I'll see you in the morning.' I turned out her light and tiptoed to the door, not wanting anyone downstairs to know we were still awake. In my own room at last, I lay on the bed in my posh dress and stared at the ceiling. She believed me. She believed I killed him. As long as the police didn't find out, she'd never know the truth. And I'd be safe.

TWO

It's a Saturday morning when they come. A woman and a man, and I don't realise they're police at first. We laugh about that afterwards, Ada and me, despite everything. After all those TV shows we've seen, you'd think I'd be able to spot a detective a mile off, but I had no idea. I'm thinking it's a good thing I'm in, since no one else is, and I'm a bit breathless from running down the stairs and wondering who's gone out without telling us there's a delivery due. They don't always wait when I have to come from the top floor, so I give them a big grin, even while I'm wondering in the back of my head why it needs two of them to bring a parcel.

'Oh, good, you're still here. It takes a while to get down from the top floor. Do I need to sign something?' There's a slightly awkward silence and then the woman speaks.

'I'm Detective Inspector Ronnie Twist and this is my sergeant, Luke Carter. We need to speak to Mr and Mrs Rosewood. And anyone else who lives here. Does that include you? Are you their daughter?' She's holding out a laminated ID card, but I can't look at it properly because I'm concentrating on not letting my knees fold under me. They say everyone gets nervous when the police talk to them, even when they've not done anything worse than jaywalk, but I know this isn't about crossing the road without looking.

'Um, no. I'm Scarlet. I'm the carer. For Ada. That is, Mrs Rosewood, the older Mrs Rosewood, not Emma. She's upstairs but everyone else is out. What's it about?'

'I'd rather not say until the owner of the house is present. Do you know when they'll be back?' Now I think about it, there's no way she could be delivering parcels. She's wearing a navy linen jacket with a white shirt, open at the collar, and a thin silver necklace. Matching earrings, subtle but smart. Hair swept back in a bun, fair and a bit wispy. I can't tell if it's deliberately done or come loose in the wind, but it looks good. My hand goes instinctively to my own hair, wondering how to achieve the same effect. She catches me looking at her and clears her throat to remind me she's still there, and I pull myself together enough to talk sense.

'Emma's out, she usually goes for a run on Saturday mornings. She shouldn't be more than an hour. Daniel's picking Theo up from a sleepover so he'll be home soon. I don't know about Polly. She didn't say what she was doing. Do you want me to ask one of them to give you a call to arrange a time later on?'

'No, we can wait in the car if it's only for an hour. We'd like to see as many of you as we can as soon as possible. We'll catch up with Polly later if she doesn't turn up soon. Maybe you could try calling her to see if she can come back sooner rather than later?' It's put as a suggestion, but it doesn't feel as if saying no is an option, so I say I'll give it a try and watch as they walk back to their car, a nondescript vehicle parked neatly to one side of the turning circle. They turn round when they get there and look up at the house. Most people do, but these two resist the temptation to comment and open the car doors after just a moment or two of admiring glances. Once they get inside, I close the door carefully and walk slowly up the stairs. It gives me a minute to think and to steady my nerves, although I can't say I make much use of it.

Ada's doing the crossword when I return to the sitting room. She doesn't look up; her hearing aids are on the table beside her and I don't even know if she's aware I'd left the room. I touch her gently on the shoulder and mime a letter 'C' with my hand. She smiles and nods, and I go into the kitchen to make the coffee. We like our routines, Ada and me, and it will help to stick to them, even if the police have been knocking on the door. I put the cup down on the table and hand her the little buds. She looks up quizzically, but sets her newspaper aside and puts them in.

'What's up?' We usually read the paper in silence with our coffee on a Saturday, and she knows me well enough to be able to tell from my face when something's wrong.

'The police were at the door just now.' If I wanted to give her a shock I've succeeded, I can tell from her eyes, but she's as calm as always. It must be all those years on the bench, not letting criminals and their lawyers see what she was thinking.

'Oh, were they indeed? And where are they now?'

'Waiting for Daniel and Emma to get back.'

'Not in the house, I hope?'

'No, they're in their car. It's on the drive. You can see it from the kitchen window, but you can't see inside.'

'And did they say what they were here for?' She's sipping her coffee, not wanting to meet my eye. She doesn't want to know if it's upset me. She won't like it if I'm upset. She's better at handling people who can keep it together, and I know I'll have to stay cool.

'No.'

'Ah.' We exchange glances, but she's clearly decided to bury her head in the sand from the start.

'They said they want to talk to everyone. I told them Emma and Daniel will be back soon, and Theo as well. They said to call Polly and tell her to come back too.'

'Well, you'd better call her, hadn't you? Thank you for the coffee, Scarlet. I'm going back to my crossword now. There might not be much time for it later on. And maybe you should get some work done while you can. Bring it in here; we can't have you escaping to the library, can we?' She gives her version of an encouraging smile. 'Don't worry. I'm sure there's nothing to be concerned about as long as we stick to the plan.' She returns to her crossword, composed as always, back straight in her chair and glasses perched on her nose, looking more like a duchess than an old lady with crippling arthritis.

I'm not falling for her reassurances for a minute, but I do as she tells me and call Polly. She says she'll come home; she's at the leisure centre and has just got out of the pool. I suppose I should have guessed she was there, but my brain froze when they asked. I perch my laptop on my knee as I sit in the comfy chair opposite Ada. We planned what to say if the police came ages ago. We always knew they might, because of Polly's connection to the festival, but that was before. There's a lot more to fear now, but Ada doesn't know that, and I have to look as if I'm calm. But it's impossible to concentrate, and I end up staring out of the big window at the trees and the blue July sky. The word fills my mind. Police. In big capital letters. At least they're not in uniform. I hate that. It reminds me of bad things. I don't know exactly what, but I know it's all to do with them taking Mum away and me yelling and being given a big teddy. They were trying to be nice of course, but I've never liked teddies since that day. Or the police.

* * *

Ada doesn't want everyone crowding into her sitting room, so I get her into the wheelchair, and we go down in the lift to the family room. The detectives are already there, sitting on the big sofa with coffee in front of them on the table, with chairs positioned so as to allow everyone to sit in a circle. They're ogling the room, not knowing whether to look at the state-of-the-art kitchen or the view across the garden and onto the Westwood. Daniel's giving them the short version of how he built the house, and he breaks off as we come in. There's a space for the wheelchair and I push Ada into it, sitting on a dining chair beside her. It feels as if we're about to play a party game. I've never liked those, so the butterflies in my stomach feel oddly appropriate. Emma and Daniel are on the other sofa and Polly's in the comfy chair. There's lots of room on the big sofa, but – not unsurprisingly – Theo has chosen another dining chair in preference to cosying up to the law. Sergeant Carter asks for all our names and notes them down on his electronic tablet.

'Is this everyone?' DI Twist enquires, and Daniel gives her a nod. He's got one of his long-fingered hands covering Emma's smaller one, as if he already knows what's coming is going to upset her. I almost wish I had someone to hold my hand too, but on the whole I'm happier without it. It all feels like a scene from a detective novel, only one from the end rather than the beginning, and if DI Twist doesn't speak up quickly someone will be bound to ask, 'So, what's all this about, Inspector?', but we're spared the cliché as she gets down to business without delay.

'I'm sure you're aware of the death last weekend of Max Silento?' There's a shift in the air, as if everyone's thoughts are rushing out of their heads and colliding in the middle of the room. I can feel it of course, but I wonder if she has time to before Daniel – doing his man of the house thing – speaks.

'Of course we are. It was a terrible tragedy. We were all expecting to meet him at the festival reception, and Polly was due to perform with him in a concert last week. That's why she's home – she came back early from her music college to play in the festival.' He can't help a note of pride creeping in. He's always thought it miraculous, the way she can play the viola.

'Oh, really?' I'll bet she already knew all that, but DI Twist manages to make it sound as if this is news to her. The sergeant is tapping away on his tablet. I'd love to see what he's writing, but there's no chance of that happening.

'It was a heart attack, wasn't it?' Daniel says. 'That's what Maggie told us. Maggie Chapman, she runs the festival.' I'm sure they know this too, but the detective is too polite to mention it.

'Yes, that was the original assumption, but the coroner requested a post-mortem, and the report indicates this may not have been the correct diagnosis.'

'What are you trying to say?' Emma's gone a pasty colour, like she's about to be sick, and I can see Daniel squeezing her hand.

'The inquest was held yesterday afternoon, and the coroner has adjourned proceedings pending police enquiries,' says DI Twist.

'Enquiries into what?' Theo hasn't read many detective novels, or he'd be able to work out what she means.

'The post-mortem suggests Mr Silento may not have died of natural causes. The coroner has instructed us to carry out a murder investigation.' Now there's no mistaking the reaction, a restrained but audible range of gasps and sighs from the family, myself included, and a low whistle from Theo, whose insensitivity can be excused by his teenage condition. My heart thumps so loudly I can't believe no one can hear it, but everyone's too busy being shocked to look at me.

'But how?' asks Theo, only just getting in before Emma, who starts to speak and quickly shuts up.

'We're not able to discuss that at this point in time,' says DI Twist. She's using what Ada likes to call police speak, but it sounds all wrong coming out of her mouth. She's got a calm face, almost distant, and her pale blue eyes are ranging around the room, even while she's speaking. It looks like she's talking to the furniture, not the people, and I wonder if it's because everyone thinks this room is amazing or if she does it all the time.

'But why are you here?' Theo persists. 'What's it got to do with us? Or are you visiting everyone who took part in the festival? It was only Polly who was in it, you know. The rest of us were just dragged along to listen to her.'

'Be quiet, Theo, that's not what the inspector wants to hear,' says Daniel.

'Theo's right to ask, Daniel. Why are you here? What has this death got to do with us, other than Polly's connection through the festival?' I thought Ada was keeping unusually quiet, and it will have been deliberate. She's never minded being overlooked because of her age and the wheelchair. She says it gives her an advantage, lets her have a good look before she's properly noticed, but she's certainly been noticed now. DI Twist turns to face her as she speaks, and I can see her baby blue eyes narrowing slightly, as if recognising a potential adversary.

'Our preliminary enquiries have included a forensic examination of Mr Silento's mobile phone. One of the apps has recorded his movements over the past month, and it would seem he visited this area on the day before his death, soon after his arrival in Beverley. It also indicates another visit four weeks previously. The app isn't exact in its location, but it is accurate enough to tell us he was in the close vicinity of this house for over an hour on both occasions.'

'Here? Why?' Daniel is mystified, and everyone else is wearing puzzled expressions, although I have to wonder how many of them are genuine. I'm still in shock, but I know this is important. Ada refused from the start to tell me why she wanted Max killed, but it hasn't stopped me wanting to know, especially since I found him already dead. I've been trying to work out which of them might have done it, and this might be the first hint of a clue.

'That's what we're here to find out. We're talking to other homeowners nearby too, but this is the only house with an occupant with a connection to the festival, so you're our first port of call. I don't suppose you can help us, Polly?' Polly's got a trance-like expression on her face, as if she's a million miles away, but she must have been listening because she answers straight away.

'I don't think so; I didn't even meet him. I was going to be introduced to him at the reception and rehearse the day after with the rest of the ensemble, but that never happened, of course. They managed to get someone else in at short notice, and... oh, sorry, I don't suppose you want to know all this, do you?'

'On the contrary, we're interested in anything you have to tell us.' DI Twist smiles kindly at Polly, her face softening and returning to its previously bland expression. I suppose she wants us all to trust her and tell her things. It's the way these things work in books and on TV. I find myself wondering if the sergeant is the bad cop to her good cop, but he doesn't look the type, and he certainly doesn't sound it either when he asks a question of his own.

'Did you know Mr Silento in some other capacity? Had you met him in London at a performance, or through your music college, perhaps?'

'No.' Polly frowns as she tries to think of any possible occasion that might otherwise have slipped her mind. 'No, I've never come across him, I'm sure. I think I'd remember if I had.'

'Maybe at an event? Like a concert? Or a party? It might be harder to remember that,' Sergeant Carter prompts her. He's a big man; he looks like he might play rugby, in which case he'd get on better with Theo than Polly.

'I don't go to parties much. And I've never seen him perform. I only go to concerts if there's something I specially want to hear, and he doesn't usually play chamber music.' The sergeant looks as if he has no idea why this might be relevant, but he doesn't ask and takes refuge behind his tablet as his boss picks up the questioning again.

'I'd like to talk through everyone's movements on the days indicated on the app and on the evening of Mr Silento's death. It shouldn't take too long, and there's no need for you all to come to the station. We can carry out the interviews here; do you have a room we could use so the rest of you can go about your business while we do it?'

'Are we being formally interviewed? I assume you're not regarding anyone here as a suspect?' Ada can't help an imperious tone creeping in, but DI Twist doesn't rise to it.

'No, of course not. These are just preliminary enquiries. We'll be conducting interviews with all sorts of people connected with the hotel, the festival and in the houses nearby. We'd appreciate your help in getting through this quickly, so we can leave you in peace.' She smiles around the room, but no one looks particularly reassured.

'I suppose we'd better get started,' says Daniel. 'You can use the study; I'll show you where it is. Theo's got cricket practice in an hour, so perhaps he could go first? He's only seventeen; am I right in supposing he should have an adult with him?'

'Yes, it would be helpful if you were to accompany him. Thank you, Mr Rosewood.' The inspector and her sergeant both rise and follow Daniel and Theo out of the room. The rest of us look at each other, not knowing what to say. It's Polly who breaks the silence.

'How extraordinary. Oh well, it's nothing to do with us. I'm going to practise. Call me when they need me, will you?' I almost laugh at her complete lack of curiosity, but it's a typical Polly reaction; if it's not about music, or maybe swimming, she's not bothered.

'All right,' says Emma. She sounds like she's about to say something more, but she doesn't; she just stares into space. Ada holds her tongue for once, and I don't think it's for me to say anything at this point.

Ada looks at me and tweaks her head towards the lift, so we go back upstairs to wait for our turn.

* * *

'I think we need another coffee,' Ada says as we emerge onto our landing. 'With sugar.'

'All right.' I let her wheel herself into the room and put the kettle on. She'd never admit to being shaken, but she's told me as much by asking for the drink, and I'm simmering with pent-up anger and exasperation. It wasn't a routine visit, and it's frightened me. Ada knows I'm going to ask questions, and she's ready for me when I join her in the sitting room. She's wheeled her chair over to the window, and she's looking out over the Westwood as if engaged in scientific study of the cows. She lets me turn the chair round, and I sit opposite, our mugs on the table between us. I've been thinking hard about what to say but she interrupts me as I open my mouth to speak.

'I know what you're going to ask, Scarlet, and the answer's no.'

'No what?'

'No, I can't tell you what Max Silento was doing outside our house.'

'He obviously came to see someone in the family. And caused trouble of some kind. More than trouble, or—' She cuts me off before I can finish the sentence.

'Or I wouldn't have asked you to kill him?'

'Maybe you should keep your voice down, Ada. The police are still here, remember.' It's the closest I've ever come to correcting her but she can't argue with me. She frowns and lowers her voice.

'What he was here to do and who he was here to see are none of your concern, Scarlet. And from a police point of view it could be nothing to do with us. Maybe he knew someone else living nearby or wanted to stretch his legs.' She can make up all the stories she likes, but I can't believe she thinks I could be so naïve as to believe this.

'Ada, there's hardly any houses on this road. And he might have been out for a walk on the day he died, but what about the other time? He wouldn't come all the way here from London just to walk down our road for fun. You can try that theory with the police but you know as well as I do that it isn't a coincidence. You've got to tell me what's going on.'

'On the contrary, I don't have to tell you anything, and you know I don't like you asking personal questions.' It's true, and I have always trusted her in the past, so maybe I should do now, even though every bone in my body is telling me not to. I sip my coffee to stop myself saying something I might regret later, and I can see her shoulders relax as she watches me.

'Stop fretting, Scarlet,' she says, her voice gentler again. 'You're overthinking it. The police are speaking to lots of people, don't forget, and I'm sure they'll decide it was natural causes. They said a heart attack before, didn't they?'

'That's what Polly said Mrs Chapman told her,' I admit.

'And there's not much else that looks like a heart attack as you well know. I'm sure there's nothing to worry about. It all went to plan, and as I keep telling you, it's a foolproof method.'

'But what if—' She stops me with a finger to her lips. She can hear well enough when her hearing aids are in, and I realise there's someone coming up the stairs. It's Theo, clumping about like a herd of elephants as usual, which is a good thing for once.

'The police lady said she'll see you next, Gran, so you don't have to delay your lunch. I told her how you like your routines and she said there's no need to disturb them.' He gives me a wink which I know Ada can see, but she'll forgive him anything, even a bit of cheek at her expense.

'Thank you, Theodore,' she says, and she wheels her chair towards the lift. 'Help me in with this, will you? And Scarlet, why don't you make yourself a sandwich? I'll eat downstairs with the family when I've finished with the detectives.'

'All right,' I say, and I'm glad I'll have something to do while she's downstairs. It might help take my mind off the awful prickling feeling in my head that everything is not going to turn out all right after all.

* * *

I don't see much of Ada until dinner time. She spends the afternoon downstairs with the others and doesn't invite me to join them. I know she's avoiding me – and my questions – and I don't want to antagonise her so I spend the time doing coursework. Or trying to. The longer I'm on my own, thinking about it, the more scared I become. My thoughts are chasing round my brain, and I'd give anything to be able to talk to someone about it. I've never seen the point of friends, which is just as well, as no one ever seems to want to be one. I can always talk to Polly and Theo, but I can hardly confide in them about this.

The post-mortem must have revealed something. Something that I couldn't see. The whisky will have shown up – and so might any poison that was in it. Have they found the morphine? It would have left his system in time for the post-mortem if he'd been alive when he took it, but would it work the same way if his blood had stopped moving? And is there a difference between morphine you drink and the sort you inject? I can't believe I was so stupid – I was too busy making sure I followed Ada's precious plan to think straight. I won't make a very good spy if this is how I react when something goes wrong. I look up morphine on the internet, but I can't find a conclusive answer, and I realise I should never have injected it in the first place. If it's still in his system it could be traced back to Ada and then to me. I don't suppose Ada would hesitate to make up some story about me killing Max for my own reasons; she'd say anything to protect her family. What was I thinking of? Ada's promises won't be worth anything if I end up in jail. And who would they believe? A respectable retired judge or a school dropout with a dodgy past?

By the time Ada comes back my thoughts have cleared sufficiently for me to know that I have to protect myself. I've got to work out who killed Max Silento, and the first step will be to find out why Ada wanted him dead in the first place. She comes back upstairs in time for the evening news and tells me we'll eat together, just the two of us. It's Saturday, so Emma and Daniel have gone out with friends and the children have ordered in pizza. Ada can't stand pizza, so I make us a risotto instead. She likes my cooking, which is no surprise since it was she who helped me learn and bought the cookbooks. I don't suppose she'd have taught me to make food she didn't like. I put her after-dinner glass of port on the side table and go to turn the TV on when she stops me.

'Leave that for now, Scarlet. You've been very good, not bothering me about today's events, but I understand you wanting to know more.' I can't believe it – this morning she said she wouldn't explain anything – what's changed?

'I've asked everyone what was said in their interviews, and they've told me, so now I can fill you in too.' Ah, so she's not telling me everything at all, just the select details she wants me to know. Which is a different thing entirely, and not at all unexpected. I sit down and wait.

'You'll know from your own interview that the police are interested in the days when Max Silento appears to have been near the house. As well as the night he died, of course.'

'Yes, the morning of last Saturday and another date a few weeks before. I told the police that I was at home both times, like we planned. And then they asked if I knew him or if I knew of a connection with anyone else in the house. And I said no. Because it's the truth. I didn't and I don't.'

'Exactly. They asked everyone the same questions, which is only to be expected. I gather they got similar answers from the others. There was a lot of coming and going last weekend, and they've got those details now. It was harder to remember further back to the previous occasion, but they all managed it. The police appeared to be happy with everyone's answers. They didn't say they'd be back, and I'm sure there's nothing for any of us to worry about.' She looks at me meaningfully as she says this, and there's a hint of warning in her voice.

'That's good,' I say. 'But Ada, what's really going on? I did what you asked, and I've put myself at risk of going to jail for you. It was one thing not knowing why before, but things have changed now the police are involved. You have to tell me why Max Silento was such a threat.'

'I don't *have* to tell you anything. And you'll be well rewarded for your efforts, don't forget. In any case, you won't be going to jail; this post-mortem is a formality, nothing more. Given his age, if there were no underlying health conditions, it was bound to happen.'

'But they said they had reason to think it wasn't natural causes!' I can't help feeling exasperated. Can't she see how frightening this is for me? Even if she doesn't care about me going to jail, she could at least pretend to show some concern.

'Yes, I know, and I can't understand why; our method won't have left any traces, so I can only think that someone with a personal connection has got involved. Maybe his family is kicking up a fuss, or the festival organisers. For whatever reason, the police are having to investigate, but I'm sure it's just a case of their going through the motions. You know as well as I do that they won't find anything. We just need to sit tight and wait for it all to blow over.'

'But they came here – they found a connection to this family. Aren't you worried about that?'

'No, Scarlet, I'm not worried about that. But I am concerned about you working yourself into an unnecessary state. You've got to stop this. All you need to know is there's nothing to worry about. I've told you that all along, and nothing has happened to make me think differently.' That's all very well, but she doesn't know what really happened, does she? She doesn't know that someone else – someone in this family, I'm sure – has interfered with our plans, and there's no way of knowing if they were as clever as us.

I open my mouth to argue but I shut it again when I see her face. She's looking at me with her fiercest expression, and if I'm not careful I'll end up telling her more than I should.

'All right, Ada, I'll trust you. I'm sorry, it's just been a shock, the police coming, you know.'

'I know,' she says, and her face softens again. 'Now, why don't you put the television on, and find an episode of *Spooks* on that new streaming service? We could both do with a bit of distraction.' I find the controls and put on the programme she wants. But I'm not distracted. I'm planning. Ada might think there's nothing to worry about, but she'd feel differently if she knew what I do. I've watched enough spy programmes on the telly over the past two years, and I've got what they call 'previous experience'. If she won't tell me what was going on with Max Silento, I'll find out for myself.

THREE

We always have Sunday lunch together. It's one of our family times. When they all moved in fifteen years ago, Ada set down her famous ground rules. She could do that because if it weren't for her they wouldn't have the house in the first place. She said they must live independently as well as together and the only meals they would share on a regular basis would be Sunday lunch for fun and Wednesday evening for organising. Wednesdays have often been a moveable feast – they've had to adapt for Polly and Theo's clubs and so on, but it's always worked well. Anything's on the table on Wednesdays, from planning holidays to booking the chimney sweep, and we all have to be nice to each other on Sundays. I was invited to Sunday lunch as soon as I moved in and Wednesdays soon afterwards. Daniel said if I was going to put up with them all long term, they'd better include me in the family planning. I wrote that in my diary. It was nice the way he said it. And I was glad to be included properly, even though I'd been listening in from the start.

This Sunday's a muted affair. Ada's rattled, although I know she's trying to hide it. She's deliberately kept to herself this morning, and I've taken the hint and got on with some coursework in my room, only coming out to make coffee. We go down at midday as usual, and Daniel's ready with Ada's nicely chilled white wine and a Coke for me.

'Here you go, Mother. Scarlet.' He gives me a smile, as if nothing out of the ordinary has been happening. I'm working hard on trying to behave normally whilst watching for any signs of nervousness. It's strange to think that someone's hiding as much as I am – more than I am, I suppose – but I guess a visit from the police is enough to unsettle even the most innocent of people, and it'll be hard to spot anyone behaving differently from the rest of us.

'Thank you, Daniel.' I let go of the wheelchair and Daniel pushes Ada over to the kitchen, where Emma's stirring the gravy and Polly's peering into the oven to check on her nut roast.

'Did you have a nice time last night?' A bit of small talk won't hurt, and I don't know what else to say that won't sound all wrong.

'Yes, we did, thanks. Paul and Jenny's daughter was back from uni and she was telling us about her new project. It's in Dorset, even though she's studying in Edinburgh, and she's made a real feature out of the landscape's natural porosity.'

'Daaaad!' Theo's on the big sofa and turns to pull a face at Daniel. 'Scarlet doesn't want to hear about porosity. Can't you talk about something the rest of us can understand?'

'Like what? Cricket? Or would you prefer politics? Much safer to stick to architecture, I'd say, don't you agree, Scarlet?'

'Definitely,' I say, and plonk myself down next to Theo. Once he gets going on the relative merits of socialism and communism there's no stopping him, and even though I don't understand much about concrete, I always find talk of perspectives and plans rather restful. My mission today, however, is to find out who knows more about Max's death than they want to let on, and Theo could be a good ally.

'D'you think the wind will be OK this afternoon?' Theo asks, turning around again. 'You said we could go out on the boat, remember?'

'I checked the forecast an hour ago, and it looks all right to me,' says Daniel. He goes to the window and assesses the sky. 'They said there might be a shower later on, but that won't stop us. Do you want to come along for the ride, Scarlet?' It's sweet the way he always invites me, even though I know it's his 'boys' time' with Theo.

'No, thanks, I need a nice calm lake, not a choppy sea, if I'm going to enjoy sailing. And I've got a lot of coursework to do.'

'No problem. It's very impressive the way you keep your nose to the grindstone with your studies in between looking after Mother.' He looks meaningfully at Theo, whose nose has never been anywhere near a grindstone.

'You can nag me when my grades drop and not a moment sooner,' he says, and Daniel has to concede defeat. Theo will have to work hard at some point, but that day appears to be a long way off at present.

'Daniel, I need you,' Emma calls, and he hustles off to pour more drinks or see to the carving or whatever it is she wants him to do. She's a good cook who seldom asks for help, and there's a note of tension in her voice, which might have more to do with the police than the dinner. She's been edgy for some time now, and I wonder if she's less surprised by the arrival of DI Twist than she made out. I'd put it down to nerves for Polly in the festival, but now I'm not so sure. I turn to Theo, confident there's enough distance between us and the others for privacy.

'So, what's the news on this murder business?'

'I dunno. No one's talking about it down here. Has Gran said anything to you?'

'No, she doesn't want to talk about it, so I thought I'd ask you. Have your parents said anything about it?'

'No, they're really wound up by it all. It's a waste, it's the most exciting thing to have happened around here for years. Everyone's been going on about that boring festival for ages, but it'll have been worth it if something exciting comes out of it now. I've tried to ask what they think, but they keep shutting me up. They might be less stressy about it if you ask them. What do you reckon?' Perfect. I knew he was the one to help me.

'Sure, I'll give it a go. What about Polly? Is she OK?'

'I think so, why shouldn't she be?'

25

'Well, she was supposed to be playing with him, wasn't she? She was upset when he died, I remember her being in a right state.'

'Yes, but only because she thought the concert would be cancelled. And someone from a quartet in London was coming to hear her. She thought she'd lose her chance if they didn't come. She wasn't fussed about Max whatever his name is.'

'Silento.'

'Yeah, that's it. How come you remembered?'

'I'm good at names. Especially unusual ones.'

'Hmm. Like you're good at coursework.' He punches me on the arm. I like it when he does that, like he's my brother.

'So, what do you want me to say?'

'Dunno. Anything you like. Just ask what they think – I'd like to find out how he died for one thing.' I'm delighted he wants to talk about it, but I remember Ada's comments yesterday and I'm not convinced it's a good idea for me to be the one to bring it up.

'I'm not sure. I don't think Ada would want me to talk about it. I'll try, but it might be better if you start and I back you up.'

'Chicken.' He rolls his eyes at me. 'I'll ease them in gently with random stuff and then strike when they're least expecting it.'

'Food's up!' Emma calls, and we grab our drinks and go.

* * *

Emma's cooking often stops conversation. We're all too preoccupied with the first delicious mouthfuls of lamb – or in Polly's case, nuts and lentils – to say much, but you never get much of a silence when Theo's in the room, and he doesn't waste any time in getting going.

'Can I have some mates round for a barbecue next weekend?'

'Theo, how can you possibly think about more food with that enormous plateful in front of you?' says Daniel.

'I'm thinking about friends, not food. Anyway, why shouldn't I? Good food makes me think about more good food, what's wrong with that?'

'Nothing, except you're eating your poor parents out of house and home,' says Ada. 'Am I invited, Theodore?'

'Sure, Gran, if you think you can cope with our not-so-elevated company.'

'You're very kind. I'll let you know if I'm free.' Ada likes to tease him, and he loves it too, I know. 'Will you be joining us, Polly? Polly? Are you with us?'

'Oh, yes, what?' Polly's been in a complete dream, picking little bits off her nut roast and turning them into tiny skewers with cubes of carrot on her fork.

'A barbecue,' says Theo. 'D'you want to have one? With me and the boys?'

'Oh, no, thank you. I don't think so. I might be going back to London soon, anyway.'

'But you've only just got here!' Emma looks up from her plate. 'I thought you were staying for the holidays. Why would you go back to London?'

'Oh, I thought… some of the others have season tickets for the Proms. I thought I might go to some concerts with them.'

'Really? I thought they played orchestral works at the Proms. Isn't chamber music more your thing?' Emma prides herself on knowing all about Polly's musical preferences, which Polly usually likes, but not today.

'It does me good to listen to all kinds of music, Mum. The teachers are always nagging us to go to orchestral concerts.'

'If you say so. It would be a shame for us to have you leave so soon, that's all.' Emma gives Polly a little smile.

'Have you heard from that woman – what was her name? You know, the one from the quartet who was coming to listen to you?' Daniel's always good at changing the subject, and he was excited about Polly's chance to join a professional ensemble.

'No, she didn't come after all. She was only interested because Max was playing, so when he died, she decided it was too far to travel.'

'How disappointing,' says Ada. 'I hope there'll be another opportunity for her to hear you play.'

'I doubt it.' Polly's in a real gloom. 'It was stupidly bad luck.'

'Worse luck for Max Silento,' Theo says, clearly pleased to get a chance to bring up the subject at last without looking too obvious.

'Theo!' The word comes out of Daniel's mouth, but it's Emma who looks as if she's seen a ghost. Theo doesn't notice, though, he's too busy with his roast potatoes.

'Oh, come on, it's only a joke. I know it's all very sad, but can't we talk about it? It's weird not to.' No one's rising to the bait, they're all clattering their cutlery around on their plates, and I decide I need to show willing, especially if I want to learn anything.

'It's certainly a strange thing to have happened.'

'Yes, and many strange things happen in life, as well you know, Scarlet. I'm sure nothing will come of it. It seldom does in these cases. They'll talk to lots of people, find no evidence and call it a heart attack after all.' Ada's got her lecturing voice on, and even though I know she's reprimanding me, I find it reassuring. Theo, however, has barely hit his stride, blithely unaware that he might have been told off as well.

'It's weird though, isn't it? Are you sure you didn't ever meet him, Polly? In London?' I have to admire Theo's tenacity; he's not about to let it go without a fight.

'No, she didn't.' Emma's not usually snappish, and Theo's fork stops half way to his potato. 'I mean, she said she didn't, so leave her out of it.'

'All right, Mum, but even if she didn't, it's odd his coming to our road, don't you think? And if it is a murder, what d'you suppose the cause is? It can't be a gun or a knife or they'd never have thought it was a heart attack in the first place. I reckon it's poison. Isn't poison supposed to be a woman's method? Do you reckon he had a lover who got mad at him? Or maybe it was an overdose? What do you think, Scarlet? And you, Gran? You watch enough detective series on the telly, don't you?'

'I think this is all highly inappropriate and unhelpful speculation. As I said, in my experience, death from natural causes is far more common than murder, and I have no doubt the police will be back soon to tell us this was the case with Mr Silento.' Ada seldom uses such a sharp tone with Theo, and it brings him up short. Despite wanting to find out more, I'm relieved she's brought this train of thought to a halt, even while I'm shooting Theo a sympathetic glance.

'Sorry, Gran.'

'Apology accepted. Emma, that was delicious as always, might I have a few more carrots, please?'

'Of course.' Emma looks relieved to have an excuse to leave the table, and as seconds of gravy and vegetables are handed round, talk turns to the weather and whether Daniel and Theo will have time to sail to Bridlington and back before it rains.

* * *

It's Polly who lets some information slip while we're stacking the dishwasher. Theo and Daniel have escaped to the coast, promising to do everything at supper time, and Ada has gone to lie down. Emma's done the same, saying she has a headache, so there's just the two of us to clear up. We're close, Polly and me. We weren't at first; she'd already left home to go to a music school in Manchester when I first came and then she went to London, so we didn't spend much time together at first, not like I did with Theo. Then when she was home for the summer Ada suggested we go for a swim together, and by the time we'd walked to the leisure centre and back we'd found we had more in common than we realised. She's only interested in music and my head's full of computing and cyber-crime, but we had fun moaning about Theo and I found myself telling her more about my life than anyone who's been paid to listen to me. Her life's been completely different from mine and she has terrible taste in clothes, but we like the same movies and books, and it's been enough to make us friends. I never had a sister, but I think this is what it might feel like to have one.

'Mum and Dad are seriously stressed about this whole police thing,' she says as she runs water into the sink for the glasses. Emma doesn't like them in the washer; she says they're too delicate.

'Why? I thought it was only a formality, all those questions yesterday.'

'Yes, you'd think so, but apparently not. They were arguing last night when they came back. They thought I was in bed, but I was in the study on the computer so I heard it all.'

'Really?' I have a feeling she'll tell me a lot if she doesn't think I'm probing, which I am of course, so I have to be careful.

'Yes. It was about the night it happened. The night he – Max Silento, that is – died. Dad was saying he didn't like lying and he wished Mum hadn't made him.' This is more like it. I control my excitement and take care not to look at her. Polly's like a deer sometimes, easily startled.

'Oh?'

'She was shouting at him. It was almost like she was drunk, but she was driving last night, so I know she wasn't. She was saying, "It's only a bloody run, Daniel, don't make such a fuss," and he said, "If it's only a bloody run, why couldn't you tell them about it?" and she shouted at him. Something about never understanding, and he said how could he understand if she kept him in the dark, and then she ran down to the bedroom and he followed. I couldn't hear any more and then I had to stay up here for ages so they wouldn't hear me go down and know I'd been listening.'

'It all sounds a bit dramatic,' I say, hoping a lighter tone will help her to keep going. The washer's stacked so I put the kettle on and reach for the green tea bags which I know she likes.

'It was a bit,' she says. 'The thing is, I don't actually have a proper alibi for that night either. I was feeling wound up about the festival, and I went for a long walk. I don't know what they think the time of death might be, but no one can vouch for me for those two hours.' She hunches into her cardigan as if needing protection from suspicion. I get the feeling she's hiding something, and I wonder what it is.

'And you think your mum might have a similar problem?'

'Yes, and she's asked Dad to say she was at home with him the whole time.' Polly picks up the kettle and fills our mugs. We take them over to the sofa and sit side by side, looking at the view.

'But why would she do that?' I ask. It's always been our favourite place for heart-to-hearts. I find it easier to talk when I'm not looking at a person, and I think Polly's the same.

'I don't know. I think she must have panicked. I've been working it out, and she must have asked Dad to do it while Gran was being interviewed. I was practising, and I know Theo went straight out when they finished with him. She must have been waiting to ask him as soon as they were alone.'

'Maybe she didn't want the hassle of being questioned about it again. Maybe she thought if we all had alibis they'd go away quicker.'

'Maybe. She forgot about me and my walk, though, so it didn't help much.' Polly sips her tea and blinks hard before turning to me. 'What about you, Scarlet? Do you have an alibi?'

'Me? Oh, yes, I was here with Ada. We were watching television.' I wondered if she'd ask. She's as curious as Theo, even though she might not show it.

'Some spy thing, I suppose? Or detectives?'

'What else?'

'I don't know how you put up with it – it would drive me nuts watching that sort of thing all the time.'

'I don't mind. I like those programmes.'

'Who knows, maybe you and Gran will solve the case between you. She'd love it if you did.'

'Now wouldn't that be clever? Talking of which, I'd better get upstairs. She'll be waking up soon and it's time for our Sunday afternoon game of chess.' I put my cup in the sink and climb the spiral stairs to Ada's floor. With luck, she'll sleep a bit longer and I can use the time to plan my next move.

* * *

'Don't do it, Scarlet.'

'Do what?'

'Probe.' Ada looks at me over her reading glasses. She's marking all the programmes in the paper that she wants to watch this week while I try my hand – without much success – at the cryptic crossword. I know what she means, of course.

'I need to know what's going on, Ada. And if you won't tell me I'll have to find out for myself.' I can see she's surprised. She's used to getting her own way, and it's taken me the best part of the afternoon to work up the courage to challenge her.

'Why can't you trust me, Scarlet? You know the only important thing in my life is this family, and that includes you. I thought you felt the same way. Can't you leave it alone and let it take its course? It would be far better for you if you did.'

'I do feel the same way, and I did what you asked me to, even though I didn't know why. I have trusted you, but the police are involved now and if I'm going to end up in prison I think I deserve to know why I'm there. Why don't you just tell me? It would save a lot of hassle.' I try a meaningful look of my own, in the hope she'll realise I'm serious.

'I daresay it would, but it's not going to happen.'

'I have to know, Ada. You think you're protecting me, but you're not. I'm scared, and the only thing that will make me feel better is knowing the full story. If you won't tell me, I'll prod and poke and probe until I do, and you won't be able to stop me, no matter how much you want to.' It's a long and rather dramatic speech for me, and I can see she's shocked, even though she's trying to hide it. She looks at me, tapping her pen against her teeth, the way she always does when she's thinking hard. I wonder if she's on the verge of saying she understands how I feel, but no, true to form she's not going to give an inch.

'Scarlet, I'm sorry. I know I've asked a lot of you. And I'm still asking a lot of you, and I'll ask a lot of you again in the future, but no. We have an agreement. Maybe not an entirely legal one, and not signed and sealed, but an agreement, nonetheless. We've both got a great deal at stake and if you want me to keep my side of the bargain, you'll have to keep yours. The whole arrangement's based on trust. On both sides. I promise you, I'll not let you down, but your whole future could be in jeopardy if you don't do as I say. Please don't ask any more questions about this. I can't answer them, and the sooner you stop asking, the better.'

'Can't or won't, Ada?' Her face is set, but she gives me a smile.

'All right, won't. You've always had an ear for detail, Scarlet. You'd have made a good barrister.'

'And "could" be in jeopardy? Or do you mean "will"?'

'I'm sure you can work that one out for yourself,' she says. The smile's starting to fade and I know I mustn't push her any further.

'If I didn't know you better, I'd say that sounds like a threat.' I can't afford to give in too easily or she'd smell a rat.

'It's a good thing you do know me better, then,' she says, going back to her paper. 'It's all right, Scarlet, you don't have to say you're backing down. Just stop asking questions and let us all get on with our lives, that's all I'm asking. Now I'm sure it's time for a cup of tea, and then you can let me help you finish off that crossword.'

* * *

The family are up late watching a film and I stay in the sitting room to listen after Ada's gone to bed in case there's another argument. There isn't, so I go to my room to start writing. I begin by noting down everything Polly's told me. I was going to use my book, but after the conversation with Ada I know I need something else, even though it's the place I go to instinctively. It's not a diary – I keep that separate. My book is where I write about things I see, people I watch, decisions I make, plans for the house I'm going to live in, clothes to buy. Ada's not the snoopy kind so she'd never come looking for it, or for my diary, but I keep them hidden just in case. It feels more private, and it's what I've always done.

I've got a new notebook already. I like to be prepared, I don't like running out in the middle of things, and I got this in the Paperchase sale a few weeks ago. It's got a map all over it, like the ones you see in school atlases, and I expect it's for people to write their travel journals in. I'm not likely to go travelling but I like the smooth feel of the cover and the thin silky ribbon for marking your place. It can be my investigations log. There'll be more in the future, and I can look back on this one nostalgically one day and remember my very first case. I start with a list of everyone in the family. At least one of them is connected to Max Silento, and I'll need to consider everyone carefully, Ada included. She knows everything that goes on in this house. She hasn't always been in a wheelchair, and she has extremely well-developed lines of communication. Sitting up here like a queen in her castle or a spider at the top of its web, there's not much that happens without her knowing it. She's not going to tell me anything of course, but there might be some papers or old letters tucked away in her belongings, if I can only get the chance to look for them. It's a pity I didn't use the time she was downstairs yesterday to have a look, but maybe I could sneak back in one day while she's out with Emma and the house is empty.

There's not much to suspect about Theo or Daniel yet, although that's not to say there won't be by the time I'm finished. Polly and Emma look more interesting, and there's always reason to suspect Ada herself of more than she gives away. I wonder if Max Silento was blackmailing someone? It's thanks to Ada's money they can live such a nice life in this house. What would happen if she had to give it away? Or maybe he was after Emma or Daniel? What would there be to blackmail them about? They don't seem to have much to hide. That's what I need to find out; everyone has something to hide, even when there isn't a murder to solve. That's where I'll start.

FOUR

It seemed like an ordinary job at first. Just another name on the list and a new address to put into my phone. It was in Beverley, and I wasn't too pleased at first as it would mean getting a bus there and back, and I knew Mrs Davis wasn't about to pay for that. I'd been lucky to get the job in the first place, what with being asked to leave Sunnybank. Mind you, she's nice, Mrs Davis. She told me she didn't think it was my fault and she was sure I'd be happier working one to one. She was right about that: I like the old ladies well enough; it's the other girls I have problems with.

I'd only been to Beverley once or twice before and it was further from the station than I'd thought. I was planning on telling Mrs D to find someone else but I changed my mind as soon as I saw the house. I'd never seen anything like it in real life; it was like something out of Grand Designs. *I knew it would be amazing inside and well worth the journey. Mrs Davis had said the old lady – Mrs Rosewood – was very particular. I'd to be sure to ask before using her first name, and I'd need to listen carefully to everything she said.*

'She knows her own mind, if you know what I mean,' she'd said. 'And I don't think she'll be the patient sort. But I have the feeling she'll be good to work for if she likes you. So be nice to her.' She looked at me in a funny way when she said that, as if she were trying to tell me

something without saying it. I reckon she knew all along that it was a competition. Well, not a competition exactly, maybe more of an audition. Whatever it was, I know Ada would have sworn her to secrecy, and you don't cross Ada if you can help it. I reckon Mrs D's done very well out of the whole arrangement. She must have negotiated a nice bonus once it was all sorted.

It took me a while to find the doorbell. It wasn't where you'd expect to find it, and it made me wonder how anyone ever managed to deliver a parcel. I found it in the end, set into the smooth dark wooden doorframe with a tiny camera just above it. It was a while before anyone opened the door; I suppose it can take a long time to answer when your house is that big.

'Hello, you must be Scarlet?'

'Yes, that's me.'

'I'm Emma, Ada's daughter-in-law. Come in, I'll show you up.' Emma looked like someone out of Grand Designs too – smart, efficient and very purposeful. She had a shiny blonde bob that must have cost a fortune to maintain and the sort of makeup that doesn't look like you've got any on. Her clothes were sharp-edged and colour-coordinated; she looked to be about my size, and I wondered where she got them. There was no messing around with cups of tea and small talk, or unnecessary explanations of how the house worked. Emma led the way up the stairs without bothering to check if I was following her, so there was no time for gawping at the jaw-dropping living space on the way up. After the clean lines and light of the first floor, it was a surprise to find myself, slightly out of breath, on the much cosier and more conventional top floor where Ada lived.

'This is Scarlet. From the agency. I'll be downstairs if you need me.' Emma didn't wait for a reply, but she gave the old lady in the wheelchair a smile that was totally at odds with her cool image, so maybe she wasn't a complete ice-queen after all. Ada was by the window in what I was to learn was her favourite place. She had a small table beside her with a coffee cup on it and a newspaper folded to what I could see was the crossword page. The light was behind her so I couldn't see her face properly and it felt a bit like something out of a film where the vulnerable young orphan meets the grumpy but kindhearted benefactor for the first time. I suppose it wasn't that far from the truth, but I didn't know that at the time. Ada was peering at me as if I were a specimen so I decided it was up to me to start the conversation.

'Good morning, Mrs Rosewood. How are you today?' Old ladies like you to ask this; it gives them an excuse to tell you all their woes.

'Very well, thank you. Come and sit down and let me tell you how I'd like this carer thing to work.'

That was Ada all over. She was never one to waste time on pleasantries; she preferred getting to know people in her own time and she never told me more than I needed to know about anything. So I knew she'd had an accident, but not what it was. And she had to tell me about the arthritis, but that was only to make sure I didn't treat her like an invalid. I knew she'd paid for the house and Daniel designed it, and about her grandchildren, but not until much later on. That first conversation was more about time-keeping than anything. And cleanliness, tidiness and the importance of proper coffee. I didn't ask if I could call her Ada; I knew what she'd say.

She wasn't like the other old ladies I looked after, but I liked her. She was clever and quick and she was interested in me. She didn't pry, but I found myself telling her more about myself than anyone since the last counsellor they made me see. And I didn't mind. She never commented on any of it, even the bad stuff. There was only the one time, when I'd been working with her for a few weeks.

'You can't change the past, Scarlet, but you're the one in charge of your future.' It didn't quite come out of the blue, but it took me by surprise. Ada had never offered me anything close to advice before. Unlike most older people, who seem only too keen to tell me what's wrong with me and how to live my life. How I should talk to people, what I should wear, where I should live, and – most of all – what I shouldn't do.

'I suppose that's true,' I said. We were sitting by the window with our coffee and I was reading a book she'd lent me. It was about spies in the Cold War, which I didn't know much about. It was more interesting than I'd *expected. I'd got used to reading every morning instead of doing jobs. Ada said it disturbed her concentration if I was fussing about when she did the crossword and she liked to have something to discuss that wasn't the weather.*

'Don't suppose. It is true. I didn't start out with a lot of money, you know. I got where I am through hard work and determination. I'll admit you've coped with more troubles in your life than I had at your age, but that shouldn't stop you.' It was nothing new; people had said things like that to me before; teachers, social workers, you name it, every adult in my life seemed to think they had the right to tell me what to do. But this was different. Ada wasn't telling me what to do, but how to do it. I put my book down and looked at her. She didn't sound as if she'd finished, and I was right about that.

'You're a bright girl, Scarlet. You're good at your job, but is it your long-term plan? To work in care?'

'I'd not thought about it.' Which was true. I was grateful to have a job and a place to live and no one breathing down my neck all the time; I hadn't thought beyond that.

'Well, you should. There's nothing wrong with care work, and you're good at it. But you're clearly intelligent, and it's not too late to pick up your education again. There are all sorts of courses available these days. You don't have to go to college; you can do it all part time while you're working. But you don't need me to tell you that. You're more than capable of finding out these things for yourself.' She picked up her crossword, bringing the discussion – if you could call it that – to a close. She'd planted a seed, though, and when I told her a few weeks later about the course I was applying for she smiled. She didn't say I told you so, or well done for taking my advice, or anything like that. She just said she knew I'd go far and she wanted to know all about it when I started.

'The best way to learn is by telling others about what you're studying,' she said. 'So I'll want to know everything you're doing.' I knew I'd done the right thing when Mrs D called me the next day.

'You've made yourself popular with Mrs Rosewood. She wants you as her regular carer.' She sounded surprised, as if no one would want to see me more than they had to.

'Oh, okay.'

'Is that all right with you, Scarlet? It'll mean going to Beverley more than you have been. Will you manage the travelling?'

'Yes, I guess so.' It would stretch my budget, but I was excited; Ada was much more interesting than the other ladies I worked for, and a lot less fussy, now that I knew her ways.

'In that case, she'll pay extra. For the travel. She said not to tell you until you'd agreed. She didn't want you just doing it for the money, she said.'

'That sounds like Ada.' I couldn't help smiling. 'She likes to be the one in charge.'

'Jemma will do weekends and she'll cover for you if you're ill or need a break. Just say if you want a holiday or anything.'

'Okay. I don't mind doing weekends if Jemma can't.' I'd have worked every day; I'd nothing else to do with my time. Although my course materials had already come through and I'd need to get started soon.

'And Scarlet?'

'Yes?'

'Let me know if it doesn't work out. If you're not happy with anything. She's a strange one, Mrs Rosewood. I can't put my finger on it but there's something odd about her. Don't let her boss you around too much.'

'I'll be fine. We get on. I like her.'

I knew what she meant, though. Ada was strange, but I thought it was in a good way back then.

FIVE

When I wake her the next day, Ada behaves as if nothing has happened. There's always a lot to do in the mornings; it takes ages to get her up and washed and dressed, but we keep ourselves entertained with a mixture of Radio Four and Classic FM. When we get fed up with politicians we switch to music, and when we've had enough of the adverts, we go back to the talking. By the time *Woman's Hour* comes on we're done, and I make coffee. We never talk between ourselves until this point, so it's only when we sit down by the window with our mugs that I realise the only subject I can think of is one I can't discuss with Ada. I'm sure it's filling her thoughts too, but we can't talk about it now, and the silence starts to weigh heavily while we both rack our brains for something to say. I reckon it's best to let Ada take the lead. She likes to be in charge of conversations; perhaps it makes up for having so little control over her body. Despite her dislike of trivial topics, she finally resorts to the obvious, although she does at least manage to avoid the weather.

'What are your plans today, Scarlet?'

'I thought I'd go to the library. If you need anything, I can pick it up on my way through town.'

'No, I'm fine, thank you. It's bridge club this afternoon, I'm sure you haven't forgotten?'

'No, I'll be back for lunch at one. We'll be there on time, don't worry.' It's stilted and awkward, not at all like our usual conversation, but it will have to do. Perhaps we'll get back to normal once I've been out and there's something new to talk about.

'All right. I'll see you later.' She's picking up her paper and writing in the first clue of the crossword before I've left the room. I don't know how she can do it so quickly – if I get more than half a dozen answers I call it a good day. I've got my backpack ready, and I turn to give her a wave as I head down the stairs, but she's immersed and her hearing aids are out, so I don't disturb her.

As I'd hoped, everyone's out. Emma and Daniel are at work and Theo's at school. Polly likes to swim in the mornings, so I reckon I've got an hour to make a start. It's a long time since I've snooped. I've not done it since I moved in here, but I know it'll come back to me quickly. I reckon I'll be better at it now after picking up tips from spy dramas. I know about only moving one thing at a time and putting it all back exactly as it was. I was thinking about it last night in bed, and I'm going to take photos first, to make sure I replace everything perfectly. I don't stop on the first floor, but head straight down to the bedrooms. People think it weird when they first come here, and so did I, bedrooms at the bottom. But it works – all the best views are higher up, so why wouldn't you make use of them? Ada has the nicest one, but then she would, wouldn't she? I can't complain, mine's pretty awesome, even if I don't have a balcony to myself.

Who should I snoop on first? Emma. She's been acting more strangely than anyone else; she's nowhere near as good as I am at hiding her feelings. It makes sense to start with her. The door's shut so that's easy to remember, I won't need a photo yet. I step inside and look around, using my phone to take a video of the whole room first, in case I move any furniture.

I don't come in here much but I've seen enough to know that I'd do it differently if it were mine. Modern houses need modern furniture, but Daniel let Emma have her own way with this room and it's posh oak, with comfy chairs and floral curtains pulled back from the sliding glass doors which open out into the garden. I know where I'm going to look first: Emma's walk-in wardrobe. I've always wanted a proper look at her clothes, but it's taken a murder to give me the courage to do it. I've got into trouble in the past for snooping and I've not wanted to wreck everything again. It's funny, but I haven't felt the urge for a long time. Not since the first Sunday lunch, when Daniel introduced me to Theo and Polly.

Emma has what fashion experts call an 'understated sense of style'. I don't know how she does it, but she always looks smart, even when she's in joggers. When I worked in the care home, I heard one of the girls there, Kelly, telling her friend about her trick of picking four colours and sticking to them. You buy fewer clothes, but good ones, and everything goes with everything else, so you've got lots of outfits. I tried it for a bit, and it worked really well. I used red, white, blue and black, but then Kelly noticed and gave me a hard time for copying her and eavesdropping. Then she told her friend and they said I looked like the Union Jack so I stopped.

The sliding doors are already open, as if inviting me in. I stand on the threshold and sigh at the sheer pleasure of it. Emma's wardrobe is perfect. She's got sections for T-shirts and blouses, jeans, running clothes, jackets, everything. The shoes are on little racks, jumpers are neatly folded on open shelves and there are drawers for undies, socks, bras, the lot. I photograph everything and check every drawer, shelf and rail, but there's nothing out of place. After all this time of not letting myself come in here, a wave of desire almost overwhelms me. It's like my mum and the first drink after a month on the wagon, and despite my best intentions I can't keep my hands off Emma's stuff. I find the silk shirt she had on when she went out at the weekend and the polo-necks she wears for work. There's gorgeous silky underwear and matching bras, snugly fitted into little compartments in the drawers. Her posh frocks are in plastic dry-cleaner bags, and I lift one out to feel the stiff, shiny fabric. She wore it to an awards dinner last year with Daniel. She doesn't like to socialise much, but he persuaded her, and she said she enjoyed herself when he teased her about it afterwards. My fingers are reaching for the zip when I hear a bump overhead. I freeze, hand in mid-air. It can't be Ada; she'd never come down in the lift on her own. Who's in the house? Was I so preoccupied I didn't hear someone come in?

I stuff the dress back in the wardrobe and go back into the bedroom to see a ladder outside the French doors. It's the window cleaners. My heart stops racing, and I'm furious with myself for letting down my guard. I pull the curtains, hoping they won't have noticed they weren't drawn before, and go back to rearrange the dress, making sure the wardrobe is perfect before carrying on. Fear has jolted me back into efficiency and I tell myself I have to be finished in ten minutes.

Emma's dressing table's the same as the wardrobe – everything in its place and perfect. She'd get on with Kelly – there's not much makeup, and only expensive brands, and with so little of it, it's easy to check for hiding places. It's the same with the jewellery; it's all beautifully neat, and I can't help wondering if she's got that book about sparking joy and rolling your T-shirts. I check my phone. I've five minutes left; what shall I do with it? The bedside table. I should have looked there first but the pull of the wardrobe was too strong. I know better than to put important stuff there, but Emma doesn't watch the same TV programmes as me, so she might think it's OK. Daniel wouldn't ever think to snoop or suspect she has anything to hide, so I don't blame her.

I like the way you can always tell which side of a bed belongs to who in couples' houses. I've been in enough in my time, and no matter how much people shout at each other, I always feel a pang of envy when I see matching bedside tables with their little lamps, books, tissues and phone chargers or whatever. When there's no one in the room you're free to imagine the occupants as a perfect couple with perfect lives, reaching to turn off their lamps in unison and wishing each other a loving goodnight. It doesn't last long, mind. As soon as you look in the drawers all sense of romance shrivels and dies, and this one's no different.

Emma's reading a novel called *Birdcage Walk*. I have a look at the blurb and decide it's not very interesting. Daniel's got a pile of architecture books which I bet he's been meaning to read for ages on his side, with *I am Pilgrim* on the top. He was talking about it the other day, and I was teasing him, wanting to know if he'd like a spoiler or two. There aren't any lamps, just little switches on the walls which turn on the lights set into the unit above the bed. It's all beautifully neat and organised, but in my experience it's the tidy ones who have the most to hide, and I turn to Emma's drawers. There are three of them, and the contents of the top one aren't worth the bother of disturbing. Emma's 'ladies' items', as Lena used to call them, are lined up next to a packet of tissues and some throat pastilles. No pills, they're probably in the bathroom. I'll check for them later.

The middle drawer has a pile of letters and cards. The birthday card on top is from Emma's mum and dad. There's a letter underneath, and it's from them too. You don't expect letters these days; people use emails and messaging apps, don't they? It seems Neville and Barbara aren't very computer-savvy, which is no surprise. I've never known them to use Zoom or Skype; Emma says they prefer phone calls. It must be hard for her, having them live on the other side of the world, but at least they have nice holidays together. My time's nearly up; I put the letter and the card back, checking their positions on my phone. There's just time to look in the bottom drawer and then I'll have to go.

I pull open the bottom drawer, not expecting anything more exciting than a pile of handkerchiefs, but I'm wrong. There are hankies, which almost makes me laugh, but I lift them, just to be sure, and there's something underneath. A phone. It's an old-fashioned mobile with a flip top. It looks about ten years old, maybe more, and there's a charger too. I know lots of people have a pile of old phones lying around, but not Emma. She always passes hers on to Polly. Theo would never take them, he likes his tech to be up to date, but Polly doesn't care. So what's this one doing hidden in the bedroom?

I drop the hankies quickly and take a picture, then lift them carefully and photograph the phone and charger. When I turn it on, the phone's almost fully charged. I have to think for a minute about how to navigate around it. I've never had one like this, although I remember adults having them when I was younger. I got my first phone when I was fourteen, and it looked nothing like this. I find the messages first, but there are only reminders from the phone company to top up. It must be pay as you go, which is interesting in itself – who doesn't have a contract these days, except for criminals? Either she doesn't use it for messages or she's deleted the rest.

The call record hasn't been deleted though. There's only one number, and the calls stretch back for years, few in number until recently. Then there are half a dozen, in and out and close together, over the past two weeks. I hold the phone in my hand and think. If this were a movie and I was a proper spy or a detective, I'd call the number. But I'm not stupid. I know that if I call and someone answers I'll have to hang up. And whoever's on the other end will call Emma back later to ask why she did that, and then she'll know someone's been looking through her drawers. I get out my phone and add the number to my contacts. I'll think about what to do with it later.

Checking the photos on my phone, I replace the contents of the drawer. I'm out of time but it would be silly not to check Daniel's side of the bed while I'm at it, and a swift look through his drawers tells me I was right not to have any suspicions about him as yet. It's time to go. A peek round the curtains confirms the window cleaner has moved to another part of the house, so I pull them aside and finally escape from the room. I let myself quietly out of the front door and head into town.

* * *

Despite everything, I'm shocked. I know Emma's been acting strangely, but I didn't really expect to find anything in her room. I need time to think about it; I know I won't be able to focus on my work, so when I get to the library I go up to the café and get a coffee.

45

Sitting by the window, I pull out my laptop and open my emails. I'll send one to myself and then copy the notes into my book this evening. I know it seems daft, but I like to write things down properly, not just electronically. Maybe it's because handwriting was the only thing I was any good at when I was little. I couldn't concentrate on much at school, but the teachers always said my writing was beautiful. I buy special calligraphy pens, and my diary and notebook are a work of art, even though I say so myself. I'd love to look through the photos of Emma's clothes, but I'll save them for bedtime.

The big question right now is the phone. Who does that number belong to? I could call it and pretend to be a cold caller. I'll have to block my number or whoever it is might ask Emma if she knows it, and even in her current state she might recognise it as mine. I'm glad I didn't do it when I was in the house. Polly might have come back, and it would have been difficult enough explaining what I was doing in her parents' room without having to come up with a reason for making a phone call while I was in there. I can't do it here, and someone might overhear if I do it in the toilets. I'm thinking of possible places when I'm rudely interrupted by Polly.

'Hey, Scarlet,' she says, sitting down in the chair opposite me. 'You look a million miles away, didn't you hear me calling you?'

'No,' I say, managing to sound casual, even though I realise she must have been doing so at the exact moment I was thinking about her. Weird. I close my laptop without haste, not wanting her to see the notes I've made so far. 'Have you been for a swim?'

'Yes. Mum asked me to pick up some recycling bags on my way and I was hungry, so I came up here for something to eat. I've not got anything yet, do you want another drink? Or something to eat? My treat – go on, I won't feel so greedy if you have a cake too.'

'All right, thanks, I'll have a black coffee and a scone, please.'

'Won't be a minute.' She puts her bag on the chair and turns towards the counter. Her wet hair's made a dark patch on her T-shirt, but she doesn't seem to care. I open my laptop again to send the email, and then open some coursework. I don't suppose Polly will be interested enough to look at the screen, but you can't be too careful. She comes back with the tray as I'm writing a spreadsheet calculation.

'Oh, I'm sorry, Scarlet, am I interrupting your work?'

'No, I was just finishing this spreadsheet, I could do with a break.' It's a good thing she's not into spy shows, or she'd be wondering how I could be nearly finished when my first coffee cup's still warm.

'Do you come up here a lot?' she asks.

'No, I usually work downstairs – it's cheaper for one thing.' I don't want her thinking I've got cash to splash on cafés every day or she might tell Ada she's paying me too much. 'I fancied a change of scene today.'

'Yes, it's nice up here, isn't it? A lot quieter than most other coffee places in town.'

'Mmm,' I say as I spread butter and jam on my scone. I'm not sure what we're going to talk about, now we're here. I can't tell her what's uppermost in my mind, and I rack my brains for something harmless to say.

'So, are you planning to go back to London soon?'

'I am thinking about it, yes. How did you know?'

'You said so at lunch yesterday.' For goodness' sake, doesn't she remember anything about our conversation? Am I so forgettable? Or invisible?

'Oh, yes, sorry, I'm a bit distracted at the moment.'

'I suppose we all are. With everything that's going on.'

'Everything? Oh, yes, the Max thing.' Either she's brilliant at hiding things or she truly has no connection to the man at all. I can't ignore her lack of an alibi for the night of the murder, though. Or her eagerness to get away, which is suspicious in itself.

'Is that why you want to go back to London? To get away from the Max thing?'

'It would be nice to get away from it, but I was planning to leave soon anyway.'

'So you can go to the Proms?'

'What?'

'The Proms, you said you wanted to go, with your friends. You said your teachers think it's good to listen to lots of different kinds of music.' I can't help a note of exasperation creeping into my voice.

'Oh, yes. I do need to listen to as much as I can, and promming is so cheap, it's silly not to take the opportunity. I didn't go last year, and everyone said I'd missed a treat.'

'What about your holiday? Aren't you due to go to Scotland soon? Or aren't you going this year?'

'Not for another month. I can get a train from London; it'll still be worth it for a few weeks of music.' She takes a bite of her flapjack, having seemingly forgotten it so far, even though I've nearly finished my scone. 'Will you be going to the summer school again?'

'Yes, it's in Bath this year, I'm looking forward to it.'

'I guess it's a good opportunity to meet other people doing your course. Is it fun?' I can see she's trying to show an interest, and it's nice of her.

'It's more about hard work than having fun, really. There's a lot to squeeze into a short space of time, but I do enjoy it, yes. It's nice to have lectures in a real theatre, with other people. And it's easier to ask questions than online. Somehow I don't feel so stupid asking them out loud rather than on a screen.' None of this is true – I'd do the whole course online if I could, but it's a requirement of the course to attend, and I know it's what I'm supposed to say, about wanting to see other people. Polly's opening her mouth to reply when her phone pings. She takes a quick look at it in her bag, and a smile flits across her face.

'I'm sorry, Scarlet, I'm going to have to make a call. Do you mind?'

'No problem, I'd better get back to my spreadsheet anyway. Thanks for the scone.' She's already half way out of her seat and tapping at the phone before I finish my sentence, and she gives me a wiggle of the fingers clasped round the phone as she weaves her way through the tables and out of the café. I look out of the window and see her emerge from the door below a few seconds later. She crosses the road and sits on the bench opposite to talk. She looks happy enough to start with, but as she listens to the other person, a change comes over her and she hunches over the phone as if she wants to make sure no one will hear what she's saying. She's trying to hide behind her hair, but it's still damp so I can see through the strands. There's a tight sort of look on her face as she listens, talks and listens again. The growing tension in her body tells me more than any grand gestures might have done, and it's at least ten minutes before she finally ends the conversation and stalks off, a grim expression on her face. It's all been rather dramatic, and I've a good idea what the problem might be.

* * *

On the way home I plan what to say to Ada. I need to prepare because I know she'll want to know everything I've been up to, even though I've only been to the library. Telling Ada about my day is like breathing. I've been doing it for so long I hardly know it's happening. She hasn't needed to ask for ages now; I just tell her. I used think it was because when I'm not with her she's lonely, and it's nice for her to have some news, even if it's only about who I've met or what work I've been doing. I wonder about that now, though; maybe it's more to do with checking up on me. I've never told her anything but the truth before and I'll have to be careful not to blurt out my findings in the bedroom. I decide to focus on Polly. The expression on her face when the text came through looked exactly like Lena's when Oskar used to message her from the night shift. He'd call her too, from the ambulance station, but he didn't like to have to break off suddenly when a shout came in so he usually texted. We'd be watching television and her phone would beep and she'd look at it with that special smile, exactly like Polly's. She never looked like Polly did when she was on the bench, though. I reckon Polly's got a boyfriend and he's dumped her.

I deliberately arrive just in time to make lunch before we go out to the bridge club, so there's not time for too much detail. Ada's looking at me closely; perhaps she's wondering if I'm going to stick to my word after all. I suppose a certain amount of tension would be natural, especially since I've gone on about it so much, and I need her to be convinced I've backed off. It gives me a buzz to be keeping a secret from her, and I tell her about Polly and my suspicions about her with more animation and detail than I might normally have done, high on the success of keeping my bedroom search from her. Only then does she bring me back down to earth with a crash.

'You know, Scarlet, you may be right about Polly,' she says as I get up to clear away our plates.

'Will you say anything to her?'

'I don't think so. She'll tell us about it in her own good time. If she tells us at all, of course. She'll have to say something if she doesn't manage to hide her feelings, but I expect she'd rather keep it to herself. She's not had a boyfriend since she went to college, at least not one she's told us about, and it will be a shame for her if it's not worked out well. I always thought it a pity she stopped seeing that nice boy from the school. What was his name? James? Jacob? I'm sure it started with a J.' Ada stops, disconcerted to find herself forgetting.

'I think it was just Jay,' I say. 'It could have been short for either of those names. I'm sure one of them is right.' It's the right thing to say. I can see her face relax again, and I change the subject.

'Do you want coffee, Ada? Or will you have some while you're out?'

'I'll have a small one, thank you, Scarlet.' As I go to the kitchen and put the kettle on, she calls through to me.

'I'm glad you've found something to occupy your mind, Scarlet. I knew you'd feel better once you'd stopped fretting about that other business.' It's a good thing I've got my back to her, or my face would be sure to give me away. I've been so pleased with myself for finding the phone and keeping it secret, I've completely overlooked the fact that Polly's boyfriend might have some bearing on the case. Why hasn't she mentioned him? Why is she making up reasons to go back to London? What has she got to hide? I can't believe I've been so stupid, and it takes me several seconds to pull myself together. I open the fridge for the milk to give myself time to answer.

'Yes, I suppose I do.' I take my time stirring the coffee and adding the milk, then bring it through and set it on the table beside her.

'There's a good girl,' she says, glad of the opportunity to be patronising. 'Now, since you've spent all morning working hard, maybe you should take a walk on the Westwood while I'm playing. They say exercise is a good stimulus for the brain.'

'Good idea,' I say. Anything for a quiet life.

* * *

Ada's bridge club is a select affair. I don't know how it first started, but it's not in a draughty church hall, which is where I've always imagined such things might take place. It's in Felicity Grainger's house, a big Edwardian place not far from ours, a little bit closer to town. We don't bother getting the car out unless it's raining, and it only takes twenty minutes or so to wheel Ada down the road. Ada taught me how to play a long time ago. She said teaching me was good for her brain and learning to play was good for mine. We play online together at least once a week and I reckon I could hold my own now in her group, although she'd never invite me, and I'd rather not spend all afternoon with her friends.

'Ada! How are you?' Felicity ignores me as usual, as Ada wheels herself into the hallway. She likes me to push her most of the time, but not in front of her friends.

'I'll see you at four thirty, Scarlet,' she says over her shoulder, and I let myself out, since Felicity's not likely to.

I usually go back home while Ada plays and make the most of being able to work in the sitting room, but I think she might be right about having a walk, and I turn towards town instead. I'm not a fan of healthy walks, or exercise in general, come to that. I don't see the point of exhausting myself for no good reason, and I spend enough time pushing Ada around. But the sun's shining and there's a light breeze, enough to stop it getting too hot, and it might be nice to get some fresh air. I go round the racecourse first, then across to Burton Bushes and towards the golf course. The cows are mooching around the verge, and I enjoy watching a small queue of motorists waiting for half a herd to cross the road. I can't avoid the pull of the Black Mill, and I sit on the curved bench which hugs its walls, looking towards the Minster below.

I know I should be focussing on my discoveries this morning, but the clouds and the cows have distracted me, and I find I've been thinking of nothing much at all. I scold myself for wasting the opportunity and turn my thoughts to Polly. Is her return to London important? Is hiding a boyfriend relevant to the case? It's fun to think about who he might be and what reason she could have for keeping him a secret, but I can't see how it could be relevant to Max's death. And she wasn't at home the first time he was hovering about the house, so it can't have been her he was coming to see. On the other hand, she doesn't have an alibi for the night of the murder, so I can't dismiss her entirely. I'll have to keep an open mind.

Emma is much more interesting. Polly's love life has got me thinking, and if I didn't know Emma better, I'd think she was having an affair. I can't believe it of her, though. She's devoted to Daniel, and the children. I can't imagine her seeing someone else. Or having the time to, come to that – she's always dashing around and saying she's run off her feet. But how else to explain the phone? And she's got no alibi for that night; she could easily have visited Max when she was out for her run. I've got to question all my past assumptions, even where she's concerned. It makes me sad to have to think like this. I always thought I'd found the perfect family at last, and it's hard to accept something nasty's been lurking beneath the surface. I'd never been able to trust people properly before I came to live with the Rosewoods, and even then it took a long time. It was Ada who taught me that families can be kind, and reliable, and calm. Happy, even. When you're used to chaos and uncertainty, it's hard to get used to what she'd call normal, and I thank her in my head every day for wanting me to be a part of it.

My phone beeps, reminding me to pick Ada up. I've been sitting here for ages; I must have lost track of time. As I head back down the hill towards town there are grey clouds moving in from the east, sharpening the sunlight and turning the grass and trees a deeper shade of green. The still-blue sky behind me and the dark clouds in front feel like two halves of a life. I've allowed myself to think the dark times are behind me, with sunnier days ahead, and I find myself fearing I've got it the wrong way around.

* * *

I love my bedroom. I remember when I first moved in, the biggest wonder was the little en-suite shower room. I had to stop myself going into it every half hour, to admire it and relish the fact that it was mine. I've got used to it now, but it still gives me a thrill to see my toothbrush and shampoo and everything all neat and tidy, with no one else's stuff there to mess it up.

The bedroom's the best bit, though. It's in the eaves, with a dormer window looking out over to the Westwood. It tickles me to be able to look out and see the spot where I was sitting earlier today, and to see my window when I'm out there. I've always liked looking at places where I've been and imagining what I looked like sitting there. It makes me feel more alive, as if confirming I was really there.

My room's all slopy ceilings so Daniel had special fitted wardrobes and shelves put in, and I love the way they fit perfectly into the space. It's the same in Ada's room, only bigger, and she's got a balcony as well. The sitting room's in the middle, so we can't disturb each other, although neither of us makes much noise. I keep my room spotless. Ada's too, come to that. She likes things to be as orderly as I do. Maybe it's why she chose me in the first place to come and live here. She knew I'd keep the place just the way she likes it.

I've been saving this up for bedtime, so I can be sitting in the little chair by the window, looking at the sunset. I get out my phone and upload the photos to the cloud so I can see them on my laptop where they'll be bigger. I've not put the light on, and the room's dim, so it almost feels as if I'm back in Emma's wardrobe. It's easy to forget it's only two floors away, and I wonder if she's in it right now. But not for long. I let myself get sucked into the room on the screen, and move around the shelves with the camera, taking my time now I don't have to worry about window cleaners or anyone else. It's as gorgeous as I remembered, and I linger over her perfectly arranged shelves and rails, and those little rolled-up socks in their special spaces. It makes me want to go back and photograph the dresses properly, maybe try some of them on, but I know I can't. I force myself away from the wardrobe and on to the rest of the photos. They're not as enticing, but they're interesting, nonetheless. She has some nice jewellery, and I bet I could get something similar to her bangles in the shops in Beverley.

I'm about to close the computer when I scroll onto the last pictures. The ones of the bedside table. And the phone. How could I have forgotten the phone? I was supposed to call that number and find out who it is. I only ever use my phone to call Ada, so I have to search on the laptop to find out how to hide my number. It's easy enough to do, but I can't do it at ten o'clock at night if I'm going to pretend to be a cold caller. I'll have to wait for a chance during the day. I'll do it tomorrow.

SIX

There's something soothing about routines. I like them. People used to ask me how I could stand looking after old people and getting them washed and stuff, but I've never minded. Not when it's part of knowing what's going to happen every day. Knowing I'm safe. So even though things are strange, and I know something's not right with my world, my morning jobs with Ada keep me calm. I go to the library again before lunch. I work hard this time; it's easier not to have to pretend when I get back, and I know I'll have some time to myself this afternoon.

Ada likes to get out and about, and it's the U3A quiz on Tuesdays. She's into her U3A groups. University of the Third Age, that's what it means. She explained it all to me the first time I took her to a meeting. Ada likes explaining things to people, and I like learning new things, so we make a good pair, she says. The third age is what they call your 'golden age'. I call it being old, but I don't say so to Ada. She says it keeps her mind active and stops her losing her marbles. She didn't say that exactly, but it's what she meant. It hasn't done that too well today, though. She reminded me about bridge again this morning and I had to tell her it was Tuesday, not Monday. We managed to laugh it off, but she won't have liked making the mistake.

It's a long trundle through town to the Tiger Inn where they hold the quiz, so we go in the car. I like being able to drive; it's not something I ever thought I'd learn to do, but Ada paid for me to learn so I can take her places. I get nervous, because I don't do much of it, but it's better than bumping the wheelchair all the way through town, and we never go far, so I don't mind it. The pub's got a car park so I leave the car there and push Ada to the door.

'See you at four, Ada,' I say, but she's already half way down the corridor. She likes to look down on some of the people who come to these things, saying she's cleverer than the lot of them put together, but I know she loves to come. I suppose it makes a change from hanging out with me all day.

I often go back to the library when she's here, but I've got other plans today. I'm going shopping. I don't earn a lot; most of my payment is what Ada calls 'in kind', which means I get my room and all my food. But I do get some money, and it's easy to save when you never go out. I wear practical clothes most of the time; it's easier when I'm helping Ada. But I like to dress up, and I always make sure I look nice for family meals and for the university summer school. I like to think my wardrobe is small, simple and stylish. I read the style section in Ada's Sunday newspaper, and I once saw an article that said it's more economic in the long run to buy a few quality garments than lots of cheap rubbish. Maybe that's how people like Emma always look so good. I hadn't thought of that before, even though it's a bit like what Kelly was saying all those years ago. Polly definitely hasn't read that article, but maybe Emma has. Although she's got masses of clothes. She's probably been doing the small, stylish thing for a long time. You'd be bound to build up a big wardrobe in the end, because good stuff lasts longer.

I only read the article a few months ago so I've not had much of a chance to do anything about it, but I've decided to start today. I'll look for bangles and a silky shirt. I've never bought real silk before, but if I only get one shirt and don't buy another one for a while, I'll be able to afford it. I've always used cheaper shops in the past, so I don't know where the nice ones are. I decide to walk up to the North

Bar and start there. I can work my way through the town and check out all the shops I've not been in before.

I don't want to look out of place in posh shops, so I've dressed more smartly than usual. I'd have liked to borrow one of Emma's tops, but I didn't dare: Ada would be bound to notice. I'm wearing my newest white T-shirt and some black jeans. They look better than blue ones, I don't know why. I've put on a lightweight, tailored jacket that I got it in a second-hand shop, after reading an article about how a navy jacket is a 'must-have' item for the smart-casual look. I've never worn it, but it's come in useful today. I've put my hair up in a loose bun with some wispy bits at the side. I've got some pearl earrings that Lena gave me, and I think I look quite good. Ada noticed, of course. She always does. She didn't say anything, but she looked me up and down quickly in that way she has. She knows I'm up to something, but she's too proud to ask what it might be.

As I walk towards the Bar I remind myself to keep my chin up and my back straight. They told us that once at school, when they were doing 'preparation for work' sessions. Look like you own the place and you're more likely to get the job, they said. It's good advice. I've used it lots of times and it's got me into all sorts of places I'm not supposed to be.

I turn round when I get to the memorial gardens, where the shops end, and I realise I've never explored this section of town before. There are signs up telling me I'm in the Georgian quarter, and I remember reading about it now in the local paper that comes to the house. The Beverley Arms is here, of course, but I've never looked properly at the shops, and I wasn't thinking about clothes when I came to kill Max. There are some lovely little boutiquey places, and no one seems to mind me browsing. I thought I'd have to go to a jewellery shop to get the bangles, but they have some in the first place I go into. Nice, heavy silver ones like Emma's, and not too expensive. I try them on, and the shop lady's unexpectedly friendly.

'They look lovely on you. We have them in gold as well, if you prefer?'

'Oh, no, thank you. The silver's fine.' She's startled me. I'm not used to this kind of attention. I suppose it's to get me to spend money, but I don't mind, it's nice anyway.

'We have matching earrings, if you'd like to look at those as well?'

'Um, all right, I will, thank you.' I won't be buying them, but I'm enjoying being made a fuss of, so why not have a look? She brings them over, and a hand mirror too, which she holds up to my face.

'They look lovely, don't they? I think silver's your colour. These pearls are nice, but the plain earrings would go better with the bangles, don't you think?'

'Well, I'm not sure,' I say. Despite my best intentions, they do look nice. 'How much are they?'

'Tell you what, I'll give you a discount if you want them both. Our sale's starting tomorrow so it won't hurt to reduce them a little today. Why don't you come over to the till and I'll see what I can do for you?'

As I walk out, swinging the tiny pink bag, I realise this is how Emma must feel every time she goes shopping. Important, pretty, cherished. I think that article was right. Less is best. Thanks to the discount I've still got enough for a blouse, and I head into the next shop along to see what they might have inside.

* * *

Ada's tired after her meeting and when we get home she wants a lie-down before dinner. This isn't like her, and I think she might be up to something when she suggests I go downstairs to see if Polly would like some company. I don't expect she will, but it's best not to argue, so I go down and find Polly in the family room, curled up into herself on the sofa and watching a film. I thought there might be a hint of yesterday's upset in her face, but she looks perfectly normal. Maybe it wasn't a serious boyfriend after all. Perhaps she was cross to be dumped rather than distraught. And I suppose I can hardly blame her for keeping it secret from a family which has Theo as a member.

'Hi, Scarlet,' she says. 'Is Gran all right?'

'Yes, she's fine. I think she wants to be on her own, though. She suggested I come down here for a bit to keep you company. D'you mind?'

'Of course not. It's just something I found on the iPlayer.' She tips her head towards the television. 'I don't know if it's any good. Have you seen it before?'

'I don't think so.' I drop into the comfy chair and pull up my feet like Polly's. She looks a bit like a cat, and I wonder if I do too.

'It only started a few minutes ago,' she says, pressing the pause button. 'That girl's called Anna. She's moved to California to go to uni and she's just met the guy with ginger hair. We don't know his name yet, but—' Polly's interrupted by the doorbell.

'Are you expecting someone?' I ask her. 'Shall I go and get it?'

'No, and yes. Thanks, Scarlet.'

Ada won't have heard if she's taken out her hearing aids, and I know she wasn't expecting a visitor. It's probably another delivery for Emma; she doesn't always remember to tell us when they're coming.

It's not a delivery. It's those detectives again. I'm better prepared, but not much. I really need to get it into my head that it's not just me trying to work out who killed Max Silento; there's a murder investigation going on and this household is part of their enquiries, as they put it.

'Good afternoon. It's Scarlet, isn't it?' I've got a sense of déjà vu, except my legs don't go so much to jelly this time. DI Twist is wearing almost identical clothes, but she's got pearl earrings on this time instead of silver. The sergeant's still looking like an American student – preppy, I think they call it. He looks a bit like the actor frozen on Polly's film only ten years older.

'Yes. Emma and Daniel are at work and Theo's at school. They'll be back at about six. Do you want to wait? Or come back later?'

'No, it's Polly we've come to see,' she says. 'She's in, I take it?'

'Yes, of course. Come on up.' Polly? Why Polly? What's she got to do with it? I know she's hiding a boyfriend, but I can't see why it would have anything to do with the murder. Maybe Ada was right after all and it is suspicious. I lead the way upstairs to where Polly's waiting, the film still frozen on the screen behind her.

'It's the police. They want to talk to you.'

'Me?' She switches the TV off and unwraps herself from the sofa, standing up in a swift, graceful movement that's all at one with the cat look.

'Good afternoon, Miss Rosewood,' says the detective. 'We have a few questions to ask you. Is this a good time?'

'Um, yes, I guess so.' Polly looks completely mystified, but I can't help wondering if this has something to do with the secret boyfriend.

'Should I have a solicitor with me? Is it that sort of questions?' Polly must have been watching some of the same TV programmes as me and Ada after all.

'No, if it were, we'd be asking you to come to the station. There's no need for alarm. Although you're welcome to have someone with you. Would you prefer to wait until your parents come home?'

'No, it's all right.' Polly's pulled herself up and put her chin in the air, like Ada tells me to do. 'Can Scarlet stay, though? In case I forget anything afterwards? Would you mind, Scarlet?' DI Twist nods, and I do too, surprised and pleased to be asked. It'll save me listening in by other means.

'Shall we sit down?' Polly suggests, and for a moment she sounds exactly like Emma. 'Would you like coffee or tea or something?'

'No, thank you, we won't take up more of your time than necessary.' DI Twist makes a beeline for the big sofa and nods to her sergeant to sit beside her. Polly and I take the smaller one opposite, and we wait for Sergeant Carter to get out his electronic tablet and switch on the screen.

'We've been looking into all aspects of Max Silento's life,' DI Twist begins. I know why that is. Whenever someone's killed, the police focus on their life and everyone who knew them to see who could have had a motive. I can't wait to hear what Polly's might be.

'You're a student at the London Music Conservatoire.' It's not a question, but she looks at Polly as if expecting her to confirm it.

'Yes,' says Polly. 'I've just finished my second year. I came home for the festival and it's the holidays now, so I'm staying at home for a while.' She's not mentioned her plans for going back to London. Interesting. Why doesn't she want the police to know about them?

'In which case I'm surprised you didn't mention it when we spoke to you at the weekend.'

'Why should I?' Polly's looking puzzled, but I'm starting to get the glimmer of an idea as to what might be coming next. I know how to put two and two together as well as anyone, unlike Polly, whose head is full of viola music and not much else. Maybe her mysterious boyfriend has some space too.

'Because Max Silento has been teaching there for the past year. As a visiting professor. I gather there was quite a fuss when he was appointed to the post.'

'Was there? I wouldn't have been aware of it. He's a pianist and I play the viola. String players don't have much to do with the pianists. They don't play in the orchestras, and my chamber music units haven't involved pianists yet.'

'But you were due to play with Mr Silento in the festival?' DI Twist is looking at the shelves behind the sofa. They're mostly full of books about architecture, so I hope she's interested in buildings.

'Yes, but only because it happened to be in Beverley and they needed an extra viola. I'd never have played with him at the college. We play with other students, not professors.'

'What about your friends? Were any of them taught by him?'

'No, my friends are string players, not pianists. Like I said, we don't tend to socialise with them much.'

'What about Jessie Morton? Isn't she a friend of yours?'

'Jessie? Oh, yes, I suppose so. We lived together in our first year. We meet for coffee sometimes, but not often. We hung out a lot in first year because of living in halls together, but we moved into different houses in September and I don't see so much of her now.' It all sounds very pat to me. Has she been expecting these questions? Is it really likely Polly wouldn't know about Max teaching at her music college? There's nothing in her voice to suggest she's anything other than genuine, but I can't help wondering.

'What do you talk about? When you meet up?'

'The usual things. The course, performances which are coming up, concerts we've been to, gossip about other students.'

'What about relationships? Would you tell each other about your boyfriends? Or girlfriends, perhaps?' Polly's sitting next to me so I can't see her expression, but I can feel the heat in her body now, and I'm sure she must be blushing. I can't let myself look at her, but I don't need to. I can hear it in her voice.

'Boyfriends? Well, yes, I guess we would. If we had any, that is. But we don't. I mean, I don't at the moment, and I don't think Jessie has either. At least, if she has, she's not told me about it.'

'If Jessie had a secret, would she share it with you?'

'A secret? What do you mean? What sort of secret?' Now she's definitely nervous. I don't know if DI Twist can hear the tension in her voice, but I can.

'A secret relationship. One with an older man. Perhaps a married man, or one who was engaged to married. Perhaps a professor at the college.' I knew it. Polly's friend was having an affair with Max Silento. And Polly knew about it. But what's it got to do with his death?

'You think Jessie was having an affair with Max Silento? That's ridiculous!'

'Is it? Why do you think so?'

'He's old enough to be her father! I mean, he was,' Polly corrects herself.

'I think you'll find an age difference is no barrier to attraction,' DI Twist says, and I wonder if she's speaking from experience, but I don't have time to consider it properly right now. 'Please think carefully, Polly. If Jessie asked you to keep a secret for her, it's no longer appropriate for you to do so. We have reason to believe she was seeing Mr Silento, and, given his position and his engagement to another woman, it's not unreasonable to suppose he had asked her to keep it secret. If you have any information for us about how Jessie was feeling about the situation the last time you saw her, you need to tell us about it.' Polly pulls up her legs under her again and hides her hands in her cardigan sleeves as if trying to make herself disappear. There's almost a minute's silence while she considers the detective's request, and I look at DI Twist while she waits. She's got her usual vague expression on her face, and I reckon she keeps it there so as not to frighten off people like Polly.

'All right,' Polly says at last. 'Jessie is seeing someone, at least, she was the last time I saw her. And she did tell me he's older than her, but she said he was married, so it can't have been Max, can it? She was always saying how he'd promised to leave his wife, and I told her not to be stupid, people don't do that.' I'm surprised at this. Polly's never struck me as the sort of person to be so direct, but maybe she's more like Ada than I realised.

'It's possible Jessie described Max as married in order to protect his identity,' says DI Twist. 'Can you tell us more about what she said? Even small details could be helpful.'

Polly fidgets with her fingers while she thinks about it.

'I'm sorry. I can't think of anything. I don't even know what you mean. What sort of details?'

'Maybe references to when she saw him? Times when he was away? We'd be able to cross-reference those with dates when Mr Silento was on holiday or on tour.'

'I told you. I don't see her much. Not enough to know things like that. I only know what I've already told you. There must be other people who know Jessie better than I do. Why don't you ask them?'

'We are asking them. Officers are in London right now, doing precisely that. But those friends don't live in the town where Mr Silento was murdered, and you do.' There's not much Polly can say in response, and I'm alarmed to hear her calling it a murder, not a death, and I wonder what has happened to make her so certain.

'What about Jessie? Isn't she the one who can tell you the most about it? Why aren't you asking her all these questions?' Polly's sounding more sure of herself now. Maybe she genuinely doesn't have anything to hide.

'We've not been able to locate Jessie,' says DI Twist. 'In fact, we wondered if you might have any idea of where she is. Do you know if she was planning a holiday?'

'I keep telling you, I don't see much of her nowadays. The last time must be, what, a month ago?' Polly's sounding exasperated now, and she's looking towards the door as if hoping Daniel will return and put a stop to all the questions. DI Twist must have noticed, as she nods at the sergeant to take a turn. He must be the good cop.

'A month isn't so long ago, is it?' he says, leaning forward and smiling at Polly. It works; she relaxes a bit and I can feel her leaning back beside me. 'It must have been coming up for the end of term. A time when people start planning their holidays. Think carefully, Polly, take your time. I expect you told her something about the festival? It must have been an exciting time for you, coming home, and with an opportunity to perform professionally. Did you talk to Jessie about it?'

'Yes, I did.' He's clever. This sounds much more inviting than DI Twist's barrage.

'Perhaps you talked about the piece you were going to play? It was by Mendelssohn, wasn't it?' Top marks to Sergeant Carter. He's done his homework, and this has certainly worked on Polly.

'Yes. The piano sextet. The Harlequin quartet were doing a concert and they needed an extra viola and a pianist. My old music teacher from school is on the festival committee and she suggested me.'

'It must have been exciting for you,' he says. 'Did the concert go well?'

'Yes,' Polly's leaning forward now, excited to tell him all about it. She's putty in his hands, as they say. If it were me I'd be shutting up sharpish, but she's not me and she obviously hasn't watched enough of those programmes, I'm pleased to say. 'We had a last-minute replacement, of course, but she was great, and the audience loved it. I was hoping an agent would come to listen, and she didn't in the end, but it's still something to put on my CV.'

'Of course.' Sergeant Carter smiles again, but he has to get back to the point, and he doesn't waste any time in doing so now Polly's loosened up. 'You were asked to take part through your old music teacher?' Polly nods. 'What about Mr Silento? Do you know how he came to be involved? He's a big name for a music festival in a town of this size, I'd have thought.' He's been doing his research, and I can see he's gaining more and more of Polly's confidence by the minute.

'Yes, he was a big name for Beverley,' she agrees. 'Although we've had big names here in the past. You'd be surprised at the connections the organisers have. But no, I've no idea who asked him. It was a late addition to the programme, though, the piece, that is. I was only asked to do it about a month ago, which is very short notice. They usually fix the programmes at least six months in advance, and they often announce the performers much earlier. You'd have to ask Maggie about it, I suppose.'

'Thank you, Polly, you've been very helpful.' I can't help jumping when DI Twist speaks. She's been in a daze, gazing out of the window while Sergeant Carter was talking, but she seems to have decided she's got what she wants. As she rises, she looks at Polly sideways.

'So there's no chance Max Silento was loitering round your house because he thought Jessie might be here?'

'Here? Jessie? No, why would she be?' Polly is either genuinely bemused or an accomplished actress, ready to bat away random questions designed to trick her into giving herself away.

'So as to meet secretly with her lover while he was safely away from London and the watchful eye of his fiancée, perhaps.'

'Well, she wasn't. She's never been here, OK? And I don't know where she is now.' Polly's losing patience at last. 'Are you going now?' It's politely put, but they realise they won't be getting any more from her, and they let her show them to the front door. I wait upstairs and put on the kettle. I think we're both ready for a cup of tea.

SEVEN

It's not easy finding a quiet time and place to make a fake cold call. I've worked out what I'm going to say, but I've received cold calls myself and I know they don't have the sound of shoppers or birds and cows in the background, so I can't do it outdoors. I need somewhere inside where I won't be interrupted, and I can't bank on it in the house. I've resigned myself to the fact that I may have to do it in the garden shed and hope for the best, when an opportunity presents itself.

It's Wednesday, so I'll have the afternoon to myself while Emma takes Ada out. It's their weekly date, and Emma has time off every week for it. I've been planning to go into York on the bus and look for a silk blouse. I tried on a few in Beverley yesterday but I didn't find one I liked, and they have more shops in York. If it weren't for Polly I'd stay home and make the phone call, but there's no point with her around.

As I'm getting ready to leave I overhear Polly and Emma talking. Emma's taking Ada to visit a stately home and she's suggesting Polly join them as there's a musical link of some kind. A connection to the Queen as well, apparently. I can't hear the details, but I can hear Polly saying all right, she fancies getting out of the house for a bit. Maybe she wants to make sure she's not left here alone for the police to come and question again.

I get my bag and leave as planned, walking to the bus stop where I can watch the drive to see when they come out. I cross my fingers, hoping they'll leave before the bus arrives. My fingers can't be very lucky as the bus arrives much more promptly than usual and I have to get on it or they'll wonder what I'm still doing here when they drive past. I get off at the bus station, have a coffee in a café nearby and then call the house phone. It goes to the answerphone and I know it will show the missed call, so I leave a message, saying I'd forgotten to ask if anyone needed anything from York, just to cover myself.

I'm not often in the house on my own, and it's all I can do not to go back to Emma's wardrobe and try on some of those gorgeous dresses, but I make myself go upstairs where it will be properly quiet. A professional wouldn't allow herself to be distracted by a wardrobe and neither must I. Even though I'm in my own ordinary clothes, I imagine I'm dressed as a cleaning woman, infiltrating someone's house to prepare their murder. It makes me feel nervous, which is no bad thing. I know I'll be able to pull this off better with adrenalin in my veins.

I've written down what I'm going to say, and I pull the paper out of my bag and put it on the table in front of me. I practise reading it out in my best cold-caller voice and check the private number setting on my phone. I've got this. I'm in control, pursuing my investigation with dispassionate calm, as they say in the TV listings. Without even the smallest tremble of a finger, I pick up the phone.

Calm or not, my heart starts thumping as soon as I hear the number connect, and it beats even harder with each ring tone. I can't believe how quickly my mind is working, and a completely different scenario flies through my brain after each vibration. By the time it's rung six times, I've considered the possibility of it being answered by a man, a child, a dotty old woman, a butler and even Emma herself. Despite everything, my nerves are starting to get the better of me, and I tell myself to slow down, fixing my eyes on the paper in front of me and readying myself to speak.

It goes to voicemail. The one eventuality that hadn't occurred to me. I panic; what should I say? I open my mouth to speak, and then remember I have a plan for this. Plan for every eventuality, Ada says, and I did, even if I've nearly forgotten about it. If it goes to voicemail, hang up straight away. It's what cold callers always do, and it won't arouse suspicion. I listen for a bit in case the message says who the phone belongs to, but whoever it is, they haven't recorded their own message and it's the same impersonal voice Ada has on her phone. I suppose it's on mine, too. Feeling proud of my efficiency, I gently press the little picture of a red receiver. I've not learnt anything, but at least I've not given myself away either. I'll be more confident next time, whenever that is. My heart thuds back into its normal rhythm and I feel an unexpected sense of anti-climax.

I let a deep sigh out of my lungs and wonder what to do next. It feels like ages since I left to go to the bus stop, but it's actually less than half an hour. I can have a look at Emma's wardrobe or get on the next bus to York. The wardrobe is too tempting to resist. I'll give myself ten minutes. I set the timer on my phone to make sure I don't spend too long in there and go down to the bedroom. The door's shut again, so it'll be easy to get it right afterwards. I step into the room and close it behind me to remind myself this is what I'll need to do when I leave, and head for the wardrobe, thinking I could try on the blouse and take a photo to make it easier to find something the same in York.

I'm reaching for the blouse when I hear someone's key in the front door. I freeze, my heart hammering. I force my shoulders to drop, stand stock still and listen. I know who it is, of course, and I should have remembered before I started poking around. It's Wednesday, and Theo's allowed to come home early if he doesn't have a sports fixture. It's a new thing, now he's about to enter his final year at school. Seniors' privilege, they call it. I forgive myself for forgetting about it; he's never used it before, and it's ages since he told me about it. Anyway, it's given me a new challenge and I like those.

I hear Theo thumping up the stairs to the kitchen where I guess he's getting himself a snack. What next? I reckon he'll be back down soon to change out of his school uniform and then go back upstairs or stay in his room to do some work. Either way, I'll have to be careful if I want to leave the house without him hearing me. I can't use the front door, it would be far too noisy, even if I did it carefully with my key in the lock. And I don't want to risk him coming out of wherever he is and hearing me. I'll have to leave through the sliding doors in the bedroom. They lead onto the lower courtyard, sunk into the ground below the main garden. I can creep round to the front quietly enough for Theo not to hear me but the lock's on the inside of the door so I won't be able to lock it behind me. I'll have to leave it unlocked and hope to get back in the room later on to deal with it.

Theo's coming downstairs again. He goes into his room and shuts the door. I decide it's best to leave now, and I tiptoe out of the wardrobe and over to the door. Theo's room looks over the garden too so I'll have to be quiet. The soundproofing's good in this house, but I'm not sure he won't hear the door sliding. I hesitate; should I wait for him to go back upstairs after all? I wait by the door, looking out at the courtyard on the other side. What would a spook do? What would killer Eve do? My decision is made for me when a sudden gurgling in the en-suite washbasin makes me jump. I know what it is: my shower sometimes makes the same noise when Ada's running the tap in her bathroom. I smile. I know what this means. Theo's having a shower, and when Theo takes a shower, he's in there for at least ten minutes. Daniel's always nagging him about it, saying he's wasting water. Theo doesn't like to admit it, but I know he sings in the shower; he won't hear anything in there. There's no need for caution now. I unlock the sliding door, step onto the deck and close it behind me. I don't even worry about my feet scrunching on the drive as I stride out in the direction of the bus stop.

* * *

York's hot and crowded with tourists, but I find a blouse in a sale that's perfect. I had the photos of the first time I looked in her wardrobe, and this one is almost the same, but different enough for Emma not to notice if she sees me wearing it. It didn't take long to find, and I don't want to stay in those crowds, so I get home in plenty of time for dinner with the family. As the bus turns the corner into town I look down from my top-deck seat and see Theo walking along the pavement. What's he doing? He'd normally be at home at this time, doing his homework or eating something. Emma and Daniel are strict about going out on school nights, and even though this isn't exactly night time, he should be at home. My instincts are telling me he's up to something. Making the most of Emma being out with Ada and not in the house to check up on him.

I zip down the stairs and hop off the bus at the next stop. It's not far, and I backtrack on the opposite pavement until I see him. I stop at an estate agents' window. They're good for this sort of thing – everyone expects people to look at them, not like banks or barbers. The sun's behind me and I can see him in the reflection. He's heading into town. Good, it will make it easier to follow him. Even though it's the end of the day, the pavements are busy with school kids and their mums and people picking up bits of shopping on their way home from work, and this gives me the cover I need. I'm close enough to see Theo's wearing his favourite jeans and the button-down shirt Polly says makes him look like a film star. I reckon he's going to meet a girl.

Theo turns in at one of Beverley's many coffee shops. Most of them shut at four o'clock, but this one doubles as a wine bar so it'll stay open later. I position myself a couple of doors down the street. Not opposite, that would be too exposed, but close enough to see who goes in and out. There's no way of telling who Theo's meeting, and I can't go inside, or even close enough to look through the window and try to see him. I resign myself to a wait, and scout around for a suitable place. There's a bench on the street almost opposite the coffee shop which will do. I don't usually read magazines but they come in useful for hiding your face when you're spying on people so I always keep one or two of Ada's cast-offs in my bag. I take one out, along with a hair band to put my hair in a bun. I never wear it like this in the house, so the top of my head won't look familiar to Theo when he comes out. My jacket's reversible and I turn it round to the black side which I only use away from home. Hidden behind the magazine, he shouldn't recognise me, especially if he's busy trying to impress a member of the opposite sex.

I open the magazine and try not to become too absorbed in an article about someone's renovated home by the Suffolk coast. It looks really good. Nothing like Daniel's designs, of course, but spacious and with lots of light. There are some great interior décor ideas and I might cut some out for my book when I get home. I remember to keep raising my eyes to the coffee shop door and hope Theo didn't change his mind and leave while I was rummaging in my bag. I decide to give it an hour and a half. Any longer and I'll risk being late for dinner. Twenty minutes later, I'm starting an article about herbaceous borders and finding myself surprised by how interesting they can be when I'm interrupted by a loud voice and an equally large body parking itself next to me on the bench.

'Hi, Scarlet. Fancy seeing you here.' I have to look up whether I want to or not, and I hope that when the time comes Theo is thoroughly distracted, since my disguise is clearly not as effective as I'd hoped.

'Hi, Jonny,' I say, my heart sinking. What on earth is Jonny Parker doing in Beverley at this time of day? I thought I'd managed to escape people like him when I came to live here. People are most likely to come up from Hull at the weekend, and I avoid town then. I won't be able to get rid of him quickly but there's no need to encourage him; I turn the page and admire a picture of delphiniums.

'So, how're you doing? Scarlet?' He's not going to go away in a hurry, I can see. I'll have to talk to him in the end, and it might as well be now. The sooner I answer his questions, the sooner he'll leave.

'OK.'

'What're you doing here, then?' He's picking at his fingers. He always used to do that when he was nervous. He'll be rummaging in his pocket next for an old piece of chewing gum. It'll be wrapped up in a scrappy bit of paper. Disgusting.

'Reading.'

'Yeah, I can see. No, in Bev. What you here for?'

'I live here.'

'Nice. You gone posh or what?'

'I work here. I look after an old lady and I live in her house.'

'Sounds nice. Can I come and see it?'

'No. It's not a tourist attraction. She wouldn't want you poking around. What are you doing here, anyway?' I don't really want to know but it might give me an idea of when he's likely to go. I don't want Theo coming out while Jonny's still burbling on at me.

'Meeting someone. Why d'you want to know?' He's looking shifty now, and he pulls out the inevitable screwed-up paper and pries the gum from within. I try not to look.

'Just being polite. Ever heard of that? There's no need to tell me if you don't want to. I was only wondering how long you're going to sit here asking me stupid questions.'

'Ha, you've not learnt any manners since school, have you?' Jonny's leaning back on the bench, and he puts his arm along the back of it so it's resting proprietorially behind my back. 'I might be coming to Beverley a bit more often now. I'm doing some work for a mate of my dad's. Up at the racecourse. D'you go up there often? I could probably get you in for free if you like.'

'No, thanks. I'm not interested in horses. Or racing.' Or you, but perhaps it's better not to wind him up. He always had a nasty streak at school, and I don't want to get on the wrong side of him just now.

'That's a shame. You could have come with me. Have a bit of a night out. I'm coming up in the world, Scarlet. It mightn't do you any harm to come along for the ride. I could introduce you to some important people, you know.' He's puffing out, I can feel it, and I turn to face him so I can tell him straight where to go. It's the first proper look I've had of him, and I'm shocked. He sat down before I saw him coming, and I'd assumed he was in his usual scruffy joggers and T-shirt, but he's wearing dark trousers and a pink striped shirt. There's a tie loosened around his neck and a jacket spread across his knees. Looking down, I can see matching pink socks and shiny black shoes. I can't help it. It's the pink shirt that does it. Pink? Jonny?

'Crikey, Jonny, where'd you get those clothes?'

'Wouldn't you like to know? If you'd taken your snotty nose out of your magazine a bit sooner I might have told you.' I know he's waiting for me to ask again. I didn't want to encourage him, but I'll have to now.

'Well, it's out now, so tell me.' He won't be able to resist showing off to me now he's had the fun of getting a reaction.

'A mate of my dad's has a friend with an uncle who works at the racecourse. He's given me a job. He likes me to look smart, so he bought me this gear. Looks good, doesn't it?'

'I suppose so.' I lean back against the bench again, shifting along a bit so his arm doesn't look like it's around me. I need him to go. Time's moving on and Theo could come out at any moment. 'Don't you need to get going? Aren't you at work today?'

'Na, there's no races on today. Don't you think there'd be a few more people around if there were? I'd have thought you'd know, what with you living here an' all.'

'So why are you here then, if there's no racing on?' For goodness' sake, when will he go? It's complicated enough, trying to hide behind the magazine and look out for Theo without having to think about getting rid of Jonny as well.

'To meet people. Find out what they want me to do. In-service training, they call it.' There's a smirk in his voice, and I bet whatever it is, there'll be something dodgy going on. I try to think what Jonny could possibly do for anyone that would make it worth their while training him and buying him smart clothes and fail miserably. I turn a page in the hope he'll take the hint. He's quiet for a moment. Maybe he's thinking, although that wouldn't be like Jonny.

'You busy tonight, Scar?' I hate, I absolutely hate that name. No one's used it in years, and it makes me prickle all over and want to get up and run. I jiggle my knees in an effort to control the impulse.

'Are you trying to ask me out?'

'I might be. So, are you?'

'Yes.'

'What about tomorrow? Or the weekend? You could give me a tour of Beverley's Saturday night hotspots.'

'I'm busy.' I'm desperate to tell him to go away. Theo's sure to come out soon if he's not going to be late for dinner himself, and I can't hide behind garden articles and talk to Jonny at the same time. There's a long pause and I turn another page.

'Oh, nearly forgot. Here's my card.' He pulls out a creased business card and puts it on the bench. 'Call me if you change your mind, Scarlet. It could be your big chance. I'm going places now and I could take you with me.' Jonny Parker, general assistant, it says. A mobile number and nothing else. Who on earth is he 'assisting'? And why does he need business cards?

'OK.' Maybe if I take it and give him a crumb of encouragement he'll go. 'Thanks, Jonny. See you around.' I turn to give him a smile, but he's clearly decided this is a good parting line. He's already heaving his bulk up from the bench and I watch as he waddles off in the direction of the station. I return to my magazine, remembering to dart a glance at the coffee shop, and I see Theo coming out with his arm around a girl. They're laughing at something on her phone, and he doesn't raise his eyes until they've walked well clear of the bench, but I keep the magazine up and my head down until they've gone past four shops.

It's best to assume you're being watched all the time, so I look at my watch, put away the magazine and follow them at a distance. There are fewer people about now so it's easy to keep them in view. The girl's put her phone away and they're holding hands. I only got a brief look at her when they came out, but it was enough to tell she's pretty. Tall and blonde, nothing like me or Polly, and a short skirt. Looking at her from behind, I have time to take in a pair of long, tanned legs and a swinging ponytail. She's got a little pink jacket on and matching pink sandshoes. A leopard-print bag is slung across her shoulders. She looks like something out of *Grease*. No wonder he's not brought her home for tea.

Despite this, we're heading out of town in the direction of home. Maybe I've got it wrong and he is bringing her back to the house. I can't help grinning to myself at the thought of what Ada will think, even if she manages not to say it. I'm not wrong in my assessment, though, because they stop outside the side entrance to the Beverley Arms for what appears to be a farewell kiss. I turn to look in the window of an interior design shop. They've got gorgeous things in here and I might come back and look round properly one day. For now, though, I sneak a sideways look at them. Theo's facing the other way but I don't want the girl looking at me too closely in case we meet again one day, so I stop to adjust my laces while I'm at it. They say goodbye and she goes in through the side entrance. He leaves straight away, and I follow her under the arch in time to see her go in through the restaurant door.

There's not much more I can do unless I want to stay and buy a drink, so I walk back slowly and take a detour home so as not to arrive when Theo does. I turn over my thoughts as I walk. Who is she? And what's her connection to the Beverley Arms? It's unlikely she's a guest; I can't imagine Theo being in a position to get to know her so well under those circumstances. She must work there. Maybe as a waitress or behind the bar. And if she does, did she meet Max Silento? And what else might she know?

* * *

The first thing I do when I get back is stop in the hallway outside Emma's bedroom and listen. I need to lock the sliding door before anyone notices, and hopefully she'll be upstairs helping Daniel with the dinner. She's not. I can hear raised voices behind the door. I know they're not the perfect couple, but I can't ever remember hearing

Emma and Daniel argue before. The door's thick enough to muffle their voices; there's no point staying any longer, and I go up to my room. Ada's in our sitting room when I get to the second floor, and I can see the crossword on her lap is almost done.

'Good day, Scarlet?' She's got her hearing aids in ready to go down for dinner so she must have heard me coming up the stairs.

'Yes, thanks.'

'Good.' She goes back to her puzzle. Ada's not one for chit-chat, and I'm grateful for it today. So much has happened I wouldn't know where to start if she wanted to know what I've been up to. The others might though, and I sift through the day's events as I hang up my new blouse and change into clean clothes for dinner, reminding myself the focus needs to be a shopping trip to York rather than snooping round the house and making fake phone calls.

As it turns out, there's not much interest in my doings. Emma and Daniel are subdued, and it's left to Polly and Ada to entertain us with stories of their outing to the stately home. Theo's not got much to say, and it's hardly surprising. I wonder if anyone else even knows he came home early from school. This family is simmering with secrets, and although the atmosphere is strained, it excites me to know I might be on the way to unearthing some of them.

Clearing up doesn't take long as Daniel ordered a takeaway. This in itself is an indication of how unsettled things are. He takes pride in his cooking on Wednesday nights, and there's usually banter about the number of pots and pans he uses. He's cagey with his reasons, but I reckon it was his argument with Emma that left him with no time to cook. We settle round the table with our coffee for the weekly round-up, but other than a few dates in the diary and making sure Theo and Ada have the lifts they need for school and appointments, there's not much to say.

I'm distracted by the need to lock that door. The evening is slipping away, and although we often watch a film together on Wednesdays, I'm worried Emma or Daniel might not stay for it. Daniel always checks the outside doors last thing at night. I haven't actually ever seen him check the one in their room, and maybe he doesn't bother if he hasn't used it himself, but I can't take the risk. I'll have to think of something, and fast. Everyone's moving to the dishwasher with their mugs now, and once there's a bit of noise in the room, I take my chance.

'Did I just hear someone at the front door?'

'I don't think so,' says Polly.

'I'm the last person to ask.' Ada fiddles with her hearing aids to check they're working properly.

'I'm sure I heard something. I'll go and check.' I'm half way down the stairs before anyone else can volunteer, and Emma's thanks drift down behind me.

I open the front door and then dash into Emma and Daniel's room, lock the sliding door and come straight back, shutting their door behind me as silently as I can.

'No, they're a little way down the road. Turn left out of the drive and it's about a hundred metres along on your right,' I say to the empty space on the front porch. 'You're welcome.' Back upstairs, a discussion about the relative merits of house numbers and names follows my return, and the atmosphere lightens as Polly and Theo first disagree and then join forces to come up with hilarious alternatives for the name of our house. Even Ada can't help smiling at Daniel's horrified reactions, and it's not long before Polly's making popcorn and Theo's choosing a movie. This is more like it. My family's happy again. For now.

EIGHT

It only took her two months. It doesn't sound long, but Ada's never one to delay taking action once she's made up her mind. It was morning coffee time again, which seems to be her favourite time for serious discussions, and it was raining so there wasn't much of a view, but we were sitting by the window anyway. We were trying a new kind of coffee – Theo had persuaded her to buy it to support some charity at his school – and Ada wasn't sure she approved of it.

'It's not as strong as I'd like,' she said, putting down her mug. 'Perhaps another spoonful in the cafetière will do the trick.'

'Sure, I'll try that tomorrow,' I agreed, picking up my book. 'It would be nice to support Theo.'

'Hmm, yes, but not at the expense of my morning coffee.' I had to smile. One of the things I liked about Ada was her refusal to say anything but the truth. If she didn't want any more of Theo's coffee, she'd definitely let him know.

'Scarlet.'

'Yes?' There was an edge in her tone that told me she had something important to say. My heart dropped into my boots. Was she going to tell me she didn't want me to come any more? Did she prefer Jemma? Had I done something wrong? The certainty that the best two months of my life

were over flooded my brain, but I made myself stay calm and closed my book over my fingers.

'Are you happy working here?'

'Yes.' I could have said a lot more, but I knew it wouldn't make a difference if she was going to sack me.

'Good. Because I've a favour to ask.'

'Oh?' This didn't sound like a dismissal, and I allowed my hopes to rise a little.

'Daniel and Emma are going on holiday soon. They'll be away for a month. They go every year with the children to Emma's parents' house in Scotland. I usually go with them, but I can't now. The house isn't wheelchair-friendly and the journey would exhaust me. They're worried about leaving me here on my own, so I wondered if you'd consider staying here while they're away? You could have the spare room up here. Jemma could still come once or twice a week to give you a break. What do you think?' I couldn't answer straight away. I was too shocked. And something else, a feeling I'd not had before – excitement, delight? I still can't put a name to it, even after all this time, but it felt like a glow inside, like drinking thick hot chocolate on a cold day.

'I don't know what to say, Mrs Rosewood. Are you sure? That it's me you want?'

'Yes, Scarlet, I'm sure. I like the way you work. I like the way you look after me and I enjoy your company. I'd be happy to have you with me for a few weeks, and it would be a great weight off Emma and Daniel's minds. I do hope you'll think it's a good idea.'

'Yes. I mean, yes, I do think it's a good idea. Thank you. I'd love to.' I found myself blushing, which doesn't happen often. I didn't know what to do or say next, but Ada was already picking up her crossword, the conversation over as far as she was concerned.

'Good, that's settled,' she said. 'And if you're coming to stay, I think it's time you started calling me Ada.'

NINE

Emma comes up the stairs as I'm putting on the kettle for Ada's morning tea. I almost jump when she speaks. I hadn't heard her bare feet, and she's usually getting ready for work at this time of day.

'Sorry to disturb you, Scarlet.'

'No worries. I'm just making Ada's tea. Is everything all right?'

'Yes and no. I'm not feeling too well so I'm taking the day off. I'm going back to bed now, but I might get up later. I didn't want you to think I was a burglar. Or to set the alarm if you go out with Ada and Polly's not in.'

'No problem. Can I do anything to help?'

'No, I'll be fine. I think I'll feel better if I can go back to sleep for a while. Are you off out somewhere today?'

'Yes, Ada's going to the silver screen this morning with a friend. It's a film about the war, I think. I was planning on dropping her off and going to the library to work. They're having lunch afterwards so the house should be nice and quiet for you.'

'Great. I'd hoped you might say that. Don't mention it to her, will you? It's nothing more than a dodgy tummy, and I don't want her to worry.'

'Sure.' I fish the tea bag out of Ada's morning china and add the milk. 'Hope you feel better soon.'

'Thanks, Scarlet.' She's off before I can pick up the tray, with a lift in her step that doesn't look anything like an invalid. I take Ada her tea and sit at the table with a mug for myself. Something's going on with Emma. First the argument with Daniel, and now this. What's up with her? Then it hits me. Of course – the phone. I got so tied up with Theo it went out of my mind. The owner of the other phone will have seen the missed call. If Emma's phone only has one number on it, maybe the other one only has hers. If that's the case, they might have called her to ask if it was her. And I bet it will have made her panic. What will she do? What would I do? I can't answer that question, but I do know she was pleased to hear that Ada and I will be out this morning. Polly's pretty regular with her morning swim these days, and Daniel and Theo are at work and school. I reckon she wants time on her own. That's why she's faking an illness. To be home alone.

* * *

I drop Ada off outside the cinema and head over to the multi-storey, considering my options as I park the car. It would be impossible to hear Emma make a call, even if I were in the house, but I don't think she'll be doing that; she could make a phone call at work if she needed to. I can't think of anything she'd need to do at home. I reckon she'll be going out. To meet someone.

I go to the library as planned but instead of settling at my usual place in the computer suite I head for the toilets and change into the short skirt and Doc Martens in my rucksack. My jeans and trainers go inside, and I reverse my jacket, wind up my hair and add a pair of sunglasses. I can't change my height but my slouching skills are well honed, and I'm confident Emma won't recognise me. I leave the rucksack in one of the library lockers, stuff my phone in my pocket and saunter out of the library into the sunshine, another of Ada's magazines in my hand.

It's only a twenty-minute walk back home, and I position myself at the bus stop opposite the entrance to the drive and return to the garden article, peeping over after every sentence to check the house. It's not long before Polly emerges on her bike, a pack on her back, heading for the leisure centre. How long will it take Emma to come out? Not long, I'm sure. I wonder if she'll be wearing different clothes too. If I were her, I'd be wearing joggers or running gear, and I'd go to the Westwood if I needed to meet someone. It's mostly dog walkers at this time of day, and there are plenty of quiet spots if you don't want to bump into anyone you know.

It turns out I'm right. After a quarter of an hour, Emma comes out, dressed in jeans and a T-shirt, a smart pair of trainers on her feet. I breathe a sigh of relief; I'd never have been able to keep up with her if she'd been running. She heads towards the new houses on the site of the old college. There's still a cut-through to the Westwood there, and I expect she comes this way regularly when she's running.

I know I'll be able to see her from a little way off once she enters the estate, so I take my time, looking at my watch, checking the timetable, shrugging my shoulders and tucking the magazine under my arm. I walk, slowly at first but quickly picking up my pace, up the road towards the new houses. I turn the corner just in time to see Emma turning off down the path which leads to the gate onto the Westwood. When I get there, I can see her striding along the edge of the pastures. I have no alternative but to follow her and there's limited cover on the path, but she's got a purposeful air about her and I'm hopeful she won't look back. I don't want to risk her hearing my footsteps behind her so I keep to the grass beside the path.

The track runs parallel to the edge of the pastures, and Emma's pace soon slows. I know there's a pair of benches round the next corner, and I wonder if we're nearing her destination. I thought she'd go somewhere more private – the nearby copse, perhaps – but maybe she thinks there's less risk of meeting someone she knows if she doesn't go too far. When I reach the bend, reducing my speed to match hers, my heart skips a beat as I see there's someone sitting on the second bench. I step sideways into the thin border of trees along the edge of the grass, thinking it will be harder for them to spot me if they have to look sideways in order to do so. I can hardly hide behind a magazine here, so I go for the shoelace strategy, watching them out of the corner of my eye.

Emma doesn't sit down. She turns abruptly off the path and heads towards the racecourse, and the man on the bench folds his newspaper and does the same. They converge after a minute or two and walk on together. They don't appear to greet each other, but there's something about the way they're walking that suggests this is something they've done before. I take a turn on the bench and watch them from behind my magazine. In the short time available, I've clocked him as being significantly older than Emma, and it surprises me to think she'd choose someone of that age to have a fling with. There's no accounting for taste though, and he has a distinguished air about him which I can see might appeal. He's well dressed, in upmarket outdoor clothes I know will have cost a lot, and I'd guess he's a professional of some sort.

There's not much more to be gained now. I could wait in case they come back but there's no chance of hearing what they say, and they'll be walking towards me. It's too great a risk of Emma recognising me, and it means I'll be able to use this disguise again on her. I go back to the cut-through and then along the road into town. Back at the library, I change into my other clothes and go to the computer suite. I've a deadline coming up at the end of next week, and thanks to my investigations I've not got as much work done as I should have.

I make myself switch off from Emma and her mystery man, immersing myself in anti-viral programming for three solid hours and working through my normal lunch hour. At two o'clock my stomach starts to make noises, and I realise if I want to eat it will have to be soon if I'm to pick up Ada on time. I don't want to fork out for food in the library café and it will be good to get some fresh air, so I go to a bakery and sit with a Coke and a sausage roll on a bench by a little patch of grass on the way to the cinema. It's beside a mini-roundabout, and I watch the cars as they slow, clocking their makes and wondering where the people inside them are going. The road leads between the town centre and the new shopping centre where the cinema is, and there are shoppers walking between the two. I suppose some of them are going to the station, which lies in the same direction, and I amuse myself by trying to match potential travellers to nearby destinations. There's a tall girl crossing the road with a little wheelie suitcase. She must be catching a train. Somewhere far enough away to need an overnight stay, maybe London. You can get there in less than four hours, I know, because Polly does it all the time. Or maybe Manchester, which isn't so far. I'm thinking about the best way to pack such a tiny suitcase – I read an article about it once in the travel section of Ada's newspaper – when I see Emma. And that man.

They're on the opposite side of the roundabout, walking quickly and close to catching up with the tall girl. He's got a wheelie case too. He didn't have one on the Westwood, so he must have picked it up from somewhere while I was in the library. I stuff my half-eaten sausage roll into its paper bag and chuck the Coke can into a bin as I cross first the grass and then the road. I keep behind them rather than on the opposite side. It would be too easy for them to spot me if they crossed, and I can see them from a safe distance from here. It's only a few hundred metres to the station and a tiny café on the opposite corner gives me the cover I need as they walk towards the entrance. I get a coffee and sit on one of the bar stools looking out of the window. There are only two platforms and I can see the train as it comes in. It's heading south, towards Hull and then who knows where.

If only I didn't have Ada to collect I'd run across and jump on the train myself. I imagine myself hopping on at the last minute, buying a ticket from the conductor and tailing Emma's man at the other end to see which train he gets on next, maybe even getting on it too and following him all the way to his destination. I can feel the adrenaline running through my veins at the thought of it, but I know I can't stay here much longer. Emma will come out soon and she mustn't see me. There's a tiny loo in the café so I go in and wait for five minutes, which must be enough time for her to leave. It's nearly three – time to collect Ada. I make myself walk slowly to meet her and prepare a suitable answer for when she asks about my morning.

* * *

Ada's usually tired after a long morning out and I'm hoping the rest of the afternoon will pass uneventfully, as I can't stop my head spinning round, wondering what's going on with Emma and that man. But Ada doesn't want to go straight home. She says it's such a lovely afternoon, why don't we go to the nice café by the lake on the way to Skidby for a cup of tea. I'm surprised but I can't say anything, and it's not long before we're sitting under a parasol and looking at the ducks and the fishermen. Ada's in good spirits, telling me about the film and her friend's family.

'They're a real trial to her, Scarlet. She's got four children but they all live hundreds of miles away and hardly ever come to see her. Not that it stops them asking her for money all the time.' Ada sniffs disapprovingly. She's more than happy to give her family money when it's for her own benefit as well, but she likes to see people stand on their own two feet, as she puts it.

'It makes me realise how fortunate I am,' she goes on, sipping her tea. 'I may only have one child, but at least he's always been able to look after himself without any help from me.'

'You're lucky with your family, aren't you?' I say.

'Yes, I am. And so are you now, Scarlet, don't forget.' She turns her eyes from the ducks to me, and there's something indecisive about her gaze. I'm suddenly sure she wants to check I've given up asking questions; perhaps that was why she wanted to come here, to give herself the opportunity to talk about it without any of the family walking in. I've had to hold my tongue to stop myself asking again, and now I'm pleased I have; it's been worth it just to see the look on her face as it dawns on her that by raising the subject she could put the idea back into my head herself. Despite everything, I can't help wanting to laugh, and I have to take a sip of tea to cover my smile. I can't think of a suitable answer, though, so I say I need to use the ladies and leave her to ask for the bill.

* * *

We don't talk much on the way home, and by the time we get back to our sitting room Ada's energy is finally waning.

'I think I'll lie down for a bit, Scarlet. I won't need much for supper after my lunch out. A boiled egg will do me nicely, and an early night.'

I help Ada into bed and make the most of having the sitting room to myself by making a coffee and sitting in Ada's favourite chair, the one looking over the Westwood. I let my mind wander where it will while I drink my coffee, but all I can think about is Ada. She wasn't herself today. It's not like her to suggest unplanned jaunts to tea shops, and I'm sure she wanted to check up on me; something must have happened to rattle her. Is it to do with Emma? Or Polly? Or even Theo? It looks like they've all got something to hide, but which of them is connected to Max Silento?

My brain's tying itself in knots and I decide I need to write down the day's events if I want to untangle it. It's lovely sitting here but I don't want to risk Ada seeing my book so I retreat to my room and my investigation log. I was late to bed last night after the movie so I've still got my notes about Theo to write as well as everything from today. I know getting my observations down in order will help me to work out what it all means and it gives me a sense of calm to get out my pen and read over what I've got so far. I'm half way through yesterday's notes about Theo when I hear the doorbell ring. I assume someone else will answer it. I was preoccupied with Ada when we got back earlier and Emma's bedroom door was shut. I guessed she was there, lying down, perhaps – our going out for tea would have given her plenty of time to get back before us. And Theo and Polly must be in by now. I listen out for the bell ringing again but it doesn't and I go back to my notes.

It's not long, though, before I hear footsteps on the stairs and there's a soft knock on my door. Polly's standing on the threshold, looking nervous.

'Are you OK, Polly?'

'Yes, I'm fine. You're needed, Scarlet. Downstairs.'

'Needed? What for?'

'It's that woman again. You know, the detective woman. And her sergeant. I can't remember their names, but they're here again.' She looks as if she's seen a ghost, and I wonder if she's told her parents about Tuesday's visit.

'And they want to see me?' My legs suddenly want me to sit down, but I hide it by leaning on the doorpost in what I hope is a nonchalant manner.

'Yes. I don't know what it's about. But Scarlet...' She breaks off, biting her lip and looking embarrassed.

'What?' I keep my voice low, knowing how easily voices can drift up and down the spiral staircase, and Polly unconsciously follows suit, as I hoped she might.

'I haven't told Mum and Dad about Jessie. You know, about her and Max Silento. They're not in right now, but if they come back while the police are here... I guess I can't help it if they mention it now, but if they don't...'

'You'd rather I didn't either? Sure, although I don't know why it matters.'

'I don't want them worrying about me, and they might if they knew Max had been teaching at my college.'

'Okay, but I think you should tell them, Polly. If it doesn't come out now it's bound to later on. The police will delve into everything, you know, even stuff which might not seem relevant to us.'

'I know.' She's looking miserable at the thought of it. If there's one thing Polly hates, it's a fuss.

'Do they need to talk to your gran as well?' There's no point dwelling on what we can't change and we don't want them chasing up here, wondering where we are. 'She's having a nap at the moment.'

'They didn't say so,' says Polly. 'And I'd like to see them try to interview her when she's tired and cranky.'

'Me too.' I smile at the thought as I close my bedroom door behind me and we make our way down the stairs.

DI Twist and Sergeant Carter are back in their customary places on the big sofa. I wonder if they claim a regular patch in everyone's home. I think I would in their shoes; it must save the bother of deciding where to sit each time. I notice they've managed to find a spot where the sun's not in their eyes, and perhaps it's another strategy. There's no one else in the room. Daniel won't be home yet and Theo's probably out playing some sport or other, I don't keep track of what he does. No Emma either, so maybe she's feeling 'better' and has gone out – she usually does a big supermarket shop on her way home from work on a Thursday.

'Hello,' I say, and sit down on the comfy chair. I make myself sit right back in it. I don't want to perch on the edge and look nervous.

'Hello, Scarlet.' DI Twist's looking friendly enough, but it doesn't stop my nerves jangling. Sergeant Carter's tapping away on his little screen as usual, and with such efficiency I can't help wondering if they teach them touch typing at police training school these days.

'Do you need me as well?' Polly asks, edging towards the door.

'No, not unless Scarlet wants you to stay,' says DI Twist, looking towards me. I shake my head and give Polly a smile, and she retreats quickly. If I know Polly, we'll be hearing scales any minute now. It's what she always does when she's stressed.

'What did you want to talk to me for?' I can't help asking, although I know they'll tell me soon enough. 'It won't take long, will it? Only Ada's having a nap and I'll need to wake her up soon to give her some supper. She'll find it hard to sleep tonight if she doesn't get up soon.' I realise I'm making Ada sound like a toddler, and even though I've not said anything which isn't true I'm glad she's not here to witness it.

'No, it won't take long. We can go somewhere more private if you prefer not to risk being disturbed? We may be talking about matters which you'd prefer to keep private.' Okay, I think I know what might be coming next.

'No, let's get it over with. I'm sure you're busy too, Inspector.'

'Very well.' DI Twist consults her notebook for a moment and then appears to be distracted by the painting on the wall behind me. She carries on talking, sounding as abstract as the art itself, but there's no avoiding the content of her words.

'We've been looking into the backgrounds of the people who may be connected to the death of Mr Silento. We're casting a wide net at the moment so the investigations are at a preliminary stage, but one of the first things to yield results is always a search of criminal records. I expect you know what I'm going to ask you next?'

'I might.' Give as little away as possible. Name, rank, number and no more. I know I can't afford to antagonise her, but there's no need to make it easy for them. I don't think I'm reacting any differently to how anyone else would in my position.

'In that case, you won't be surprised to learn that we've uncovered your history of harassment and stalking.'

'Alleged. It was alleged. It was never proved. And I wasn't arrested or anything like that.'

'No, but it sounds to me as if you were lucky there,' she says. 'It seems the care home took your circumstances into account when dealing with the matter. And Mrs...' she consults her notebook, 'Mrs Davis was of the opinion that without her help you'd have found it hard to get another job in the care sector.'

'Okay, so I did some bad things once. But I've changed. I got some help and made a new start, all right? And Mrs Davis has always said what a good worker I am. Did she tell you that too? I'm good at my job. I always have been. It's not my fault if the only people who like me are all old enough to be my grandma.' I stop myself abruptly. Allowing myself to get agitated won't help. I realise I've worked my way to the edge of the chair, and I make myself sit back again and ask a sensible question. 'Anyway, what's it got to do with this Mr Sil... whatever his name is?'

'In a murder investigation we look at anyone who is or might be connected to the crime. People with any previous history of contact with the police must expect to come under particular scrutiny. I'm sure you understand, Scarlet.' She looks straight at me now, and her expression isn't so friendly any more. Those baby blue eyes are boring into me like Jedi lightsabers, and even if I'd never done anything wrong in my life, I'd be feeling nervous now.

'Yes, I do understand, I'm sorry. It's just… I thought I'd put all that behind me. Made a new start, you know? It's not nice to be reminded of the stupid things I did back then when I've worked so hard to make a new life for myself.'

'I'm sure it's not.' Sergeant Carter's taking over now, leaning forward and looking sympathetic. 'Can you tell us more about that? When did you decide to make a career for yourself in caring for others?'

'I don't know if I'd call it a career. It's a job. My social worker suggested it when I was coming up to doing my GCSEs. My foster mother said I was good with her mum when she came to visit. She said I was more patient with her than anyone else, and I should think about working in a care home. They found me a course to do at the college, and I thought it would be better than staying on at school, so I did it.'

'Where did you work first?' It's starting to feel like a job interview, but it's better than talking about the murder, so I won't object.

'At a care home in Hull. And then Sunnybank, in Cottingham.' Where the trouble started, but they know that already so I don't mention it.

'Did you like it there?'

'I liked the residents. I don't mind old people. They've often got more to tell you than you'd think if you give them time. It was the other care workers I couldn't get on with.'

'Hmm, yes.' There's a pause, but I'm not going to bring it up if he doesn't.

'So you moved on to your job with the agency?'

'Yes. I preferred being with the old people in their own homes. It was easier to get to know them properly that way.'

'And you couldn't stay at the care home because of the allegations made against you.' He's trying to be nice, but there's no easy way to put it.

'No. They didn't sack me, but the girls were horrible to me so I left.' It's true; they were. And I was less likely to get into trouble when I wasn't working with other people my own age.

'Where were you living at this time?' Sergeant Carter asks. 'You must have had to move out of your foster home by then. Were you in social housing?'

'No. I didn't want to live with that lot. I'd saved up from delivering newspapers while I was at college. I had enough for a deposit and I got a room in a house. A Polish couple who needed a lodger.'

'And how did that work out?'

'It was OK. I liked living there.'

'No more allegations?' He smiles encouragingly at me.

'No. Lena was nice to me. She lent me stuff, gave me some of her old clothes. She taught me to cook a bit as well.'

'So what led to you working here?' It's DI Twist's turn again. How can her words sound so suspicious when Sergeant Carter's felt so innocent, even though they're asking about the same things?

'Ada was one of my clients. That's what the agency calls them – clients. She said she liked the way I worked so I started coming regularly, then later on she asked me to live in so I could look after her properly.'

'Did she know about your history?'

'Yes, she did. I told her myself when she asked me. I didn't want it coming out later and her thinking I'd hidden it from her on purpose. Ada knows everything about me.'

'She must have liked you a lot.' DI Twist sounds as if she thinks this is surprising, but I hold up my chin and look her in the eye.

'Yes, she did... does. She said I was the best of the bunch. She said I got on without a fuss or unnecessary chatter and I had an intelligence unusual in people in my line of work.'

'You've remembered her words very clearly,' says DI Twist. 'I expect you were pleased to be so highly thought of.' There's no sense of irony in her tone and I decide there's no harm in being honest for once.

'Yes, I was. It's the nicest thing anyone's ever said to me.' There's a moment's silence as she takes this in, and I wonder if I've said too much as Sergeant Carter picks up the questioning before his boss has a chance to get going again.

'I think you mentioned you're studying, Scarlet. What course are you on?'

'It's maths and computer programming. I'm doing it through the Open University, and I'll have a degree by the time I've finished. Ada encouraged me to do it. She said it was a shame to let my natural aptitudes go to waste.' I can't help it. I'm still proud that I'm doing a degree and it's thanks to Ada I even considered it.

'What do you hope to do with it when you've finished? I suppose you'll want to move on from care work?'

'I haven't decided yet. It's a long way off, and I'm happy here with Ada for now.' There's no way I'm telling him about my plans. The last thing I need them to know is that I want to be a spy – it'd be sure to shoot me to the top of their list of suspects.

'I'm sure you are.' He smiles, turning towards his boss. Does this mean they're finished?

'I think that's all we need to ask for now,' she says, looking at her notebook. 'Oh, one last question. Can you tell us about Mrs Rosewood's health?'

'Her health? What's her health got to do with anything?'

'Just answer the question, please, Scarlet. Is Mrs Rosewood in good health?'

'Well, of course not, or she wouldn't need me, would she? She suffers from rheumatoid arthritis so she needs me to help with getting around, dressing, anything involving moving, really. She's not got diabetes or dementia or anything like that.'

'Does she take any medication?'

'She takes anti-inflammatories and she's careful with what she eats. Do you want a list?'

'Yes, but we'll need Ada's consent. Shall we come up and ask?'

'What, now? She's asleep, and I'd have to copy them all down from the bottles. Some of them have rather long names, and Ada's always grumpy when she wakes up.' I know I'm sounding cheeky, but it's true – if they want everything written down correctly, it's what I'll have to do, and Ada wouldn't take kindly to being asked for her permission now.

'No, we need to be getting on. We'll come back in the next day or two and pick it up from you then. What about the rest of the family? Does anyone else use any medication? Painkillers, for example?'

'Not that I know of – you'd have to ask them. Theo sometimes takes stuff when he has a rugby injury, but no one's on anything like that on a regular basis as far as I know.'

'Thank you, that's helpful, Scarlet.' She gives me a tight smile, getting up as she does so, and Sergeant Carter is quick to follow suit. I go downstairs with them and see them out politely, closing the front door carefully in an effort to stop my hand shaking. I know what 'one last question' means. That's the real reason they were here. They've found the morphine.

TEN

I like Fridays. At least I do when I'm not expecting to be arrested for murder. Ada doesn't have anything on so we choose something different to do every week. We take turns but we both seem to suggest outings the other likes too, and I think we've been surprised by this at times. Sometimes it's just a mooch round the shops, especially when Christmas is coming, and if she's had a busy week we might stay at home or potter in the garden. Neither of us wants to stay in the house today, though, not when there's a risk of the police coming back, and I pick Bempton Cliffs. They have walkways which you can take the wheelchair round and a little café for lunch. We've been before and I know Ada likes it. It's a bit of a drive but the roads aren't busy and we'll enjoy the breeze and the sunshine. Ada reminds me to hunt out her binoculars for bird-spotting and she suggests Polly might like to come too.

'It'll do her good to get out a bit before she goes back to London,' she says. We have a leisurely coffee while Polly goes for her swim and set off in time to arrive for lunch in the café. It's a beautiful afternoon and the site isn't busy so we take our time, soaking up the sunshine and watching the gannets whirling above the cliffs. Ada spends most of the time telling us about when she was a girl and went camping with the Girl Guides in Dorset. There are cliffs there too, but she says these ones are better for birdwatching. She doesn't talk much about her childhood; I reckon she likes us to think she was born clever and a judge and everything. Today's different, and if Polly and I weren't both preoccupied by other matters, we'd have enjoyed it, maybe even teased her a little. As it is, I can't stop thinking about the morphine and whether the police think it has anything to do with me, and Polly's head is no doubt full of her boyfriend. Could he be connected to Max? This question is enough to set me off on a whole new train of thought and Ada tells me off more than once for daydreaming. It's a relief when she says it's time to go home; I can't help but feel that time away from the house is time wasted. We drive home in silence; Polly's got her earphones in and Ada's drowsy after a day in the fresh air. By the time we get home, Emma and Theo are pulling into the drive and it's gone five o'clock.

'You look like you've seen the sun,' says Emma, and I put my hand up to feel the warmth in my cheeks. Polly's pink too, but not Ada, who never goes out without her hat.

'Yes, we went to Bempton so we've had the wind as well,' says Ada. 'It's been a lovely afternoon, hasn't it, Polly? We've certainly blown the cobwebs away.' Ada likes her old-fashioned phrases, and this, together with her reminiscing, gives the disconcerting impression of her being a normal old lady. Reminding myself that nothing could be further from the truth, I pull Ada's chair out of the boot and help her into it while Polly collects our bags from the back seat.

'Have you had a good week, Theo?' Ada asks. Theo's not a grunt and shrug sort of teenager, but he seems preoccupied now.

'What? Oh, yeah, fine. I'm going out tonight, Mum. Can I grab something to eat before I go?'

'Oh, Theo.' Emma's unlocking the front door while Theo jiggles impatiently from one foot to the other, waiting to get in the house. 'I wish you'd told me earlier. I've defrosted a whole salmon for tonight. I was relying on you to eat at least half of it. There'll be way too much for your father and me, and you know Polly won't have any.'

'Sorry, I thought I'd said last night. Won't it keep for another time?'

'No, you didn't, and no, it won't.' Emma doesn't like last-minute changes of plan at the best of times, but she sounds crosser than usual today. I suppose it is Friday – she's probably tired at the end of the week.

'Why don't you ask Gran and Scarlet to come down for dinner?' says Polly. 'It might be nice for Scarlet not to have to cook after driving us around all day.' She gives me a grin, and it's nice to think she's thinking about me in this way, even though I know Ada would have been happy to get us a takeaway.

'What about it, Ada? Scarlet? You're welcome to join us if you like.' Emma knows Ada doesn't like to impose. She's always been extremely clear on what she calls 'family boundaries' and 'private space'. I know she likes to be asked, though, and she's quick to agree.

'That would be lovely, Emma, thank you. We'll have a cup of tea and freshen up. Shall we come down at six? I'm sure Scarlet won't mind giving you a hand.'

'Sure,' says Emma. 'And maybe bring a bottle with you? It is Friday night after all, I think we can afford to enjoy ourselves a little.'

'There, Theo. See what you're missing? A Friday night family rave-up.' Polly punches him on the arm as they go through to their bedrooms. Theo, unsurprisingly, doesn't look too disappointed to be missing out on salmon with his granny, and I reckon I know where he's going. To meet that girl.

* * *

Ada holds tight to her bottle of Chablis as I wheel her into the lift. She's asked me to help her put on her favourite blouse, and I suppose it's as close to an occasion as we're going to get – a family evening without a meeting. I know she can be obstinate and frustrating, and she's driving me nuts with her secrecy right now, but Ada's got a heart where it counts, and she loves her family unconditionally. She always jumps at it when they ask her to join them like this, even if it is just to eat up the fish.

When we get down, we find Emma's decided to make an occasion of it too, with sparkly cut glasses and candles on the table. Polly's hulling strawberries, and there are spoons on the table as well as knives and forks, so it looks like we're having dessert as well.

'Doesn't it all look festive!' Ada says. 'Here, Emma, put this in the fridge. It's been cooling since we got home so it should be all right.'

'Ooh, that looks lovely.' Emma wipes her hands on her apron and slams the oven door closed on a tray of dauphinois potatoes. 'We'll save it for the meal. Daniel's due home any minute now – would you like a gin and tonic while we wait?'

'Why not? As you say, it's Friday. I'll take that as an excuse,' says Ada. Polly pours her drink and hands me a Coke. It's in a fancy glass with ice and lemon, so even I can feel a sense of occasion. It's nice the way she never asks if I want something stronger. I went to a party once with some of the girls at the care home and I ended up wishing I hadn't. They wouldn't let up, pushing me to have something alcoholic and teasing me, saying I was a baby for not drinking. I'd like to see them try living with an alkie for a mother without vowing never to look at a drink again. But it's not going to happen, so I give parties a miss these days. I've just pushed Ada into her favourite spot by the window when we hear the front door opening downstairs.

'Good,' says Emma. 'He'll have time for a quick shower if he wants one before dinner.' It takes a moment or two before we realise Daniel's not alone. He's already talking as he comes into the house, and not in the raised voice he'd use if he wanted to be heard upstairs. And there's another voice too. A woman. Is it the police again? Surely even DI Twist has gone home by now. But no, it only takes a few seconds to confirm it's not her. This voice is higher-pitched, with an American accent, and whoever it belongs to is stressed, and that's not a word I could ever imagine using in connection with Ronnie Twist. We can't hear what they're saying yet, but I can tell from Daniel's tone that he's having to calm whoever it is down. It's the same one he uses when he's talking to Emma after Theo's hurt himself on the rugby pitch. There's not time for more than a quick exchange of puzzled looks between us before Daniel emerges onto the landing, closely followed by a tall blonde woman. He's talking as he comes round the spiral, assuming it's only Emma in the room.

'We've got a visitor, darling. She wants to ask...' He breaks off as he sees the table, set with its glasses and candles and place mats for five people instead of four, and quickly realises there are more of us here than he'd realised.

'Oh, hello, Mother. Scarlet. Are you joining us for dinner?' He goes over to Ada and gives her a kiss on the cheek, leaving the woman standing by the stairs.

'Daniel?' Emma doesn't need to say more than his name to convey her feelings, although he's already half way to her side to give her a peck of her own before returning to the woman.

'This is Hayley. She was a friend of Max Silento. Hayley, this is my wife, Emma, my daughter, Polly, my mother, Ada, and Scarlet.' He leaves Hayley to either work out or wonder who I might be and he doesn't seem to notice Theo's missing, so distracted is he by this woman. There's a pause while we wait for him to tell us what's going on and it takes him a moment to remember we don't know why she's here.

'Umm... Hayley's very upset about Mr Silento's death and wanted to talk to us about it. Is that right?' He turns uncertainly to the woman for confirmation, and she nods silently. She had plenty to say on her way upstairs but she seems lost for words now, perhaps taken aback, as so many people are, by the room itself as well as the number of people in it.

'Now?' Emma's tone is not inviting. 'Couldn't you come back tomorrow? We're about to eat, as you can see.' She indicates the table, at the same time managing to communicate a clear message that she's not issuing an invitation to join us.

The woman gathers herself, seeming to grow in height as she does so. She's only been standing there for a minute, but it's long enough for me to assess her wardrobe and I have to admit I'm impressed. Emma always looks well-groomed and I'd give anything to have her clothes, but this woman's on another level. She's got that glossy look you see on actresses in American TV shows. Her linen jacket has a beautifully stitched edging and I can't see so much as a hint of a crease. The dress underneath looks like a cross between silk and cotton, and it skims her body perfectly, showing off her figure at the same time. Her heels are not quite high enough to give her problems on the stairs and her hair and makeup are flawless. She's wearing chunky gold jewellery which I'm sure is real, and even Polly must be able to spot the designer handbag.

'I could come back, but I'm here now and I won't keep you long. I'll only take a few minutes of your time.' She takes herself to the sofa and sits down with the air of someone who's accustomed to getting her own way. Even so, I can hear a tension in her voice which suggests she's nervous. Or scared.

'No problem.' Daniel's clearly captivated, and if Emma doesn't act quickly he'll be offering her a drink and dinner. Fortunately, Ada takes over before Emma can tell us what she's really thinking.

'I'm sure we can spare a few minutes,' she says, politely but with an edge of steel this Hayley woman would do well to pay attention to. 'Don't you agree, Emma?'

'Fine.' Emma whisks herself away from the kitchen, turning the oven down before coming to sit in an armchair. She brings her drink with her, and I reckon she's making a point about her evening being interrupted. She'll be furious at the idea that her delicious dinner might be spoiled, never mind the intrusion of this woman and her questions. I have some sympathy with her, although I'm intrigued to know what it's all about.

'I'm sorry to interrupt like this,' says Hayley, although she doesn't sound it. 'I've only arrived in Beverley today. I was staying at Tickton Grange, but it looks like I'll be here a while longer than I'd planned, and I've moved to the Beverley Arms. To be closer to Max. I mean... closer to where he... Oh dear, can you give me a moment, please?'

Despite her haughty looks she's got tears in her eyes, and I wonder if they're real. She picks up her handbag to take out a handkerchief, and as she does so it turns round in her hand and I can see the logo in the bottom corner. A shiny gold 'HH'. Of course – I thought she looked familiar. She's Hayley Harper of Harper's Handbags. I read an article about her a few months ago. But what's her connection to Max Silento? I'm sure the others are wondering the same thing, and Ada doesn't waste time in getting to the point. As soon as Hayley's found her hanky, she's on the case.

'I'm sorry for your loss, Hayley, we all are, but why are you here?'

'Because I'm… was… his fiancée. We were going to be married.' Hayley can't keep the tears at bay now, and it's either time to feel sorry for her or to admire her skills as an actress. Polly can't help a gasp escaping, but she covers it with a cough, and no one speaks for a minute. I can feel a tension in Emma that's about more than an interrupted dinner, but it doesn't show in her face, which is focussed on Hayley. I turn towards Daniel, hoping he'll say something. I guess it would look unfeeling to hurry her up now, but my stomach is getting ready to rumble with hunger.

'I'm so sorry. It must be a difficult time for you.' Trust Daniel to know what to say – living with Emma's given him plenty of practice in calming people down over the years. 'But why are you here? Why do you think we can help you? Wasn't that what you said on the doorstep? That you wanted some help?'

'Yes, I did say that. It was to make you let me in.' Hayley blows her nose silently and without damaging her makeup. It's very clever, and I wonder how she manages it.

'So what was the real reason?' Emma's hard voice is in stark contrast to Daniel's calming tone, and Hayley seems to decide playing the helpless female isn't her best option after all. She sits up straight again and dabs the tears gently from her cheeks.

'To talk to Polly.' Everyone looks at Polly; we can't help it. She turns pale and sticks her nose in the air defiantly.

'Why?' She can't help a wobble in her voice, and Daniel,

apparently having cast himself in the role of referee, jumps to her rescue.

'I expect you know Polly was due to perform with Mr Silento at the festival, but she didn't actually meet him. They were due to meet at the reception on Friday evening and then rehearse the next day. So there's nothing she can tell you. I'm sorry. I understand you wanting to talk to people who knew him or who worked with him here, but I'm afraid Polly's not one of them.' I can see Polly relax a little as Daniel explains the situation. He sounds so sensible and calm, and Emma's quick to bring the conversation to a close.

'There we are, I hope that settles the matter for you, Hayley. As Ada said, we're sorry for your loss, but I don't think we can be of any further help to you.' Emma gets up as she finishes speaking, clearly expecting Hayley to take the hint and do likewise, but she doesn't.

'It doesn't settle anything, I'm afraid. It's Polly's connection to Max in London I want to ask about.'

'In London? Polly?' Ada can't keep the surprise out of her voice, annoyed, I'm sure, that there's something going on she didn't already know about. Or maybe because something she *does* know about is about to be revealed. I steal a quick glance at Polly. I know what's coming next, and so does she, and I feel sorry for her, knowing this was something she would rather not have to discuss. She's not about to provide the information herself, though, and I suppose she's hoping Hayley's merely guessing rather than acting on prior knowledge.

'The police gave me Max's things today,' says Hayley. 'I was going through them and I found a programme for the festival. I was looking through, trying to distract myself from everything, and I started reading the biographies at the back. You know, where they tell you about the performers.'

'Yes, I think we all know what a biography is,' says Ada, impatiently. 'What's your point?'

'I was reading Polly's, and it says you study at the London Music Conservatoire. Is that true?' Hayley's starting to sound more like a police sergeant than a grieving fiancée, and I wonder if she's picked it up from DI Twist. She must have spoken to the police at some point – perhaps she has something to hide too.

'Yes,' says Polly cautiously. She must know where this is going now, but she's not going to help Hayley, that much is obvious.

'Max taught there. But I expect you knew that already?'

'I didn't, as it happens. I suppose he might have mentioned it if we'd met, but I'm a string player, not a pianist, and I don't know who teaches in the other departments. There are a lot of people teaching there, you know. I doubt any of the students know who they all are.' Interesting. It looks like Polly's gambling on the police not having told Hayley about her interview on Tuesday, and I think it's probably a risk worth taking. Why would they tell Hayley everything, especially if she's under suspicion herself?

'Hmm.' Hayley doesn't look convinced, but she can't say much more without getting into a pointless argument. She's not finished, though.

'Are there any other students at the college from around here?'

Polly's thrown by the abrupt change of tack, and answers readily enough. 'From Beverley? No, not that I'm aware of.'

'I doubt it,' says Daniel. 'I'm sure we'd know if there were. It's a huge achievement to get in; they made a big fuss of Polly when she was offered her place. There was an article in the local paper about it, and on the school website. I'm sure we'd have seen if anyone else got in as well. And Polly was heavily involved in the youth music scene; she'd have certainly heard of anyone else, wouldn't you, Poll?' Polly nods, grateful for Daniel's support. I note that no one's mentioned Max's visits to Beverley and guess everyone has their reasons for keeping this to themselves, even though I don't know what they are yet.

'That's as may be, but Max came to Beverley a month ago, and I want to know why.'

'Didn't he tell you?' Ada asks. 'I'd have thought you would know, as his fiancée.'

'No. He didn't. I only found out about it today, when I looked through his things. There was a return ticket to Beverley in his pocket. He must have come up for the day without telling me.'

'Perhaps it was to make arrangements for the festival?' Ada suggests. 'That would make sense, don't you think?'

'No, it wasn't that. I've already asked the organisers and they said it was all arranged through his agent. There wouldn't have been any need for him to come beforehand, anyway; he just turns up and plays. I was surprised he was coming here, to be honest. He usually prefers to perform at much bigger venues.' That's put us in our place, hasn't it? It's a good point, though. What was a famous pianist like Max Silento doing at a tiny festival like this one?

'Well, it wasn't anything to do with me,' says Polly. There's an unexpectedly decisive tone to her voice, and Emma and Daniel look first surprised and then impressed.

'Are you sure?' This woman's persistent, I'll give her that. 'I have reason to suppose Max had a particular reason for coming to Beverley. A personal reason. A personal reason which you,' and here she directs a steely gaze at Polly, 'might know about.' A hushed silence hangs in the air before Polly pulls herself out of her chair, mustering as much dignity as she can manage.

'Are you suggesting I was... involved with Max Silento?'

'Well, were you?'

'No, I was not. I've never met him, and why you think I'd have anything to do with a man old enough to be my father, I can't imagine. It's a ridiculous suggestion.'

'I'm sorry you think so, but I have to ask. Since the police don't seem to be.'

'What the police might or might not be asking is beside the point,' Emma cuts in. 'As we said before, we're sorry for your loss, Miss Harper, but I think it's time you left, before you say something you may live to regret.' Emma's shaking with anger, and I guess this is what mother tigers look like when they're defending their young. Daniel shoots her an admiring glance, and he takes the stunned silence as an opportunity to bring the conversation to a close.

'I don't think there's anything more to be said,' he says kindly but firmly as he gets up from the sofa. 'I hope you'll understand if we ask you to leave us to our evening now? My mother's quite elderly, as you can see, and it doesn't suit her to eat too late.' This is a total lie and we all know it, but it's a good ploy and Ada lets it go, allowing herself to adopt a suitably vulnerable expression.

'I think there's a lot more to be said, but I'll go; I know when I'm not wanted.' Hayley retrieves her bag and stands up at last. 'I'll be back, though. There's more going on here than you're letting on. I can always tell when there's a lie in the room. You don't get as far as I have in business without learning to tell when someone's hiding the truth, and I won't leave town until I've found out what happened to Max. If it weren't for me, they'd never have done a post-mortem in the first place, and if the police can't do their job properly, I'll find out what's going on for myself.' The tears have vanished, and we can see she means every word. Daniel starts to speak but she cuts him off.

'No, please don't give me any more of your platitudes; there's really no point. Goodbye. I'll see myself out; I don't want to keep you from your meal any longer than necessary.' She sweeps herself out of the room and down the stairs before anyone can reply, leaving a stunned silence behind her as she slams the front door.

ELEVEN

Dinner wasn't a festive occasion after all. It was a shame, as the food was delicious and they all seemed to like Ada's wine, but even Daniel couldn't get anyone to cheer up, and no one seemed to know whether we should be discussing Hayley or not. Once he'd come out of his trance, Daniel was keen to speculate on matters such as why she wasn't staying with Max in the first place, and why it had taken her so long to read the festival programme. I thought he had a point and I would have expected Ada to join in, but she was quick to pick up on Emma's attempt to change the subject, leading me to suspect she knows more about Hayley than she'd like to let on. My brain was spinning, wondering if she might be the missing link, but why would she come to the house if there was a connection? Wouldn't she want to hide it? Or maybe she came to threaten someone, but couldn't because we were all there? It was all too much for me to think about and I only made the briefest of notes in my book before falling asleep.

Ada's not got anything planned for today and she sleeps in late. It's hardly surprising after all the excitement yesterday. We spend a quiet morning with the newspaper, and after lunch she tells me she'd like a lie-down and I can have the afternoon off. It's a lovely day so she suggests I might like a walk. Emma and Polly are both around if she needs anything, and she seems keen for me to go out, so I do. I head into town rather than the Westwood. I'm not a fan of healthy walks, despite what Ada would like to think. I could do with getting some work done and decide to head for the library for a couple of hours. I've not got my laptop with me but I can access tasks through the university portal instead.

I walk slowly into town, thinking about where I've got to with the case, and I wonder how DI Twist is getting on. She's found the morphine and the connection between Polly and Max, although that's only through Jessie so I'm not sure how important it is. She must have spoken to Hayley, but she won't know Hayley's been to see the family. So that's a small advantage to me, as well as my finding Emma's phone. I can't afford to be complacent, though. I don't know who that man on the bench is, and the police have got far more resources at their disposal than me. I'll have to work hard if I'm to find out what Max's connection was to the Rosewoods before they do.

I decide I have to speak to Hayley. She could have nothing to do with Max's murder or the family. In which case she only came last night because she thinks there was something going on between Polly and Max. She wouldn't be far off the truth there, and if she's nothing more than a grieving fiancée, she'll want to know what's going on as much as I do and she could be a useful ally in digging up more information.

On the other hand, she might be more involved than she let on. Maybe Hayley has a connection to someone in the family herself. Maybe she was there to warn someone. There was a definite hint of menace in her tone when she left. Was it a veiled threat for someone that she couldn't say outright because we were all there? Whether she has anything to do with it or not, she seems to suspect someone in the house of having something to do with Max's murder. She's right, of course, and I need to talk to her before she gets too far ahead of herself. I've been so absorbed in my thoughts I've walked past half a dozen shops without thinking to look in the windows, and I'm only a few yards away from the Beverley Arms. Maybe that work isn't so important after all. And why shouldn't I treat myself to a cool drink on a hot day?

I know it's a long shot, expecting to bump into Hayley, but the hotel is as good a place to start as any and there's a table coming free in the courtyard so I treat myself to a lemonade and a bag of crisps. I can't see the front entrance but she might come in or out this way, especially if her room is at the back of the hotel. And there's always a chance I might see Theo's girlfriend. I doubt she's got anything to do with things, but it would be fun to have another look at her.

I spend half an hour spinning out my drink by scrolling through the news on my phone and googling Max Silento at Polly's music college. She could easily have been telling the truth when she said she didn't know he taught there, even though I know she wasn't. There are dozens of people teaching all sorts of subjects like conducting and accompaniment. It's all very interesting, although completely irrelevant to the murder, and I have to admit defeat at last. I've not seen Hayley or Theo's girl and I can't afford another drink here. I know Ada won't be expecting me for ages and the library will be closing in an hour's time; it hardly seems worth going there now. I wonder what I'm going to do with myself; I've not got much money now until my next payment from Ada, and I've never been one for window shopping.

Hesitating in the covered archway which leads back out onto the pavement, my eyes come to rest on the church opposite. It's St Mary's, where Polly's concert was held. I'd not been inside before and it was really nice in there. Daniel told me there's a carving of the rabbit from *Alice in Wonderland* somewhere near the back, hidden away so you have to know where to look. We didn't have time to locate it last week, and I think I might go in and see if I can find it. As I cross the road, I notice a bench near the church gate. The rabbit can wait. I'll have a good view of the hotel entrance from the bench, and I'll only wonder what I might have seen if I don't take the opportunity to sit on it now.

It's lucky the bench is a bit shaded as it means I can still read my phone. I charged it overnight so there's still lots of battery left, and I check out the fashion pages on Instagram, looking up every few seconds at the hotel opposite. It's getting close to four o'clock, and even though Ada won't need me yet, I'm getting bored and decide to have a look for the rabbit before I go back. As I get up, I see Hayley coming out of the hotel. She's striding out in a sundress and heels, her handbag on her arm and designer sunglasses perched on top of her perfect hair. She looks like a woman on a mission rather than one who's about to browse the shops, but maybe people who own multi-million-dollar businesses always walk that way. I've had plenty of time sitting with my drink and on the bench to work out the best way to approach her, and I jog along the pavement so as to 'accidentally' bump into her when she crosses from the other side.

'Oh, sorry!' I try to sound breathless and immature as I collide with her. 'Oh! It's Hayley, isn't it?'

'Yes, but I'm in a hurry, I'm afraid.' She must think I'm a fan, maybe an Instagram follower. Well, I am, but it's not why I'm accosting her. I want to put my hand on her arm to stop her, but I don't think that would go down well, so I walk beside her, matching my stride to hers.

'I was hoping to bump into you, actually. It's Scarlet. We met last night. At the Rosewood's.' This brings her up short. She stops and turns towards me, squinting in the afternoon sun.

'Oh, yes, sorry. I didn't recognise you.'

'It's OK, people always look different in new places, don't they? I was wondering, Miss Harper, if you've got a moment? It's about what you were saying last night. I think I might be able to help.' Her eyes narrow a little and I can almost hear the cogs whirring in her brain. Yes, she's definitely got something to hide, or she wouldn't have to think like that. It's over in a flash and she's quick to slip back into what I'm sure is her normally cool persona.

'I suppose I have got a moment... Scarlet... is that right?' I nod as she pulls on her sunglasses and looks around furtively. 'Do you know somewhere quiet we could go to talk? I'd rather not go back to the hotel; I've been cooped up there all day and I don't want to be recognised if I can help it. It's good publicity, of course, but a nuisance when you want some privacy.'

I think she's got a lot to learn if she thinks the people of Beverley will be falling over themselves to take a selfie with her, but I say I know somewhere we can be private and take her to the tapas place. Cafés will be shutting soon and I don't know what the pubs are like, but there's a big sign outside advertising tea and coffee as well as cocktails, so it should do. We ask for a table near the back and it's a little booth, where Hayley can sit with her back to the door and not be spotted by even the most diligent of admirers.

'Perfect,' she says as she removes her sunglasses and tucks them into her bag. There's the inevitable faff around ordering – coffee for me and a herbal tea for Hayley – and we make small talk until the drinks are in front of us. Once it's safe to assume we won't be disturbed, Hayley wastes no time in getting to the point.

'So, what's this all about? And I'm sorry to have to ask, but who exactly are you? I mean, I know your name – it's Scarlet, right? – but are you Polly's sister?' Interesting. She can't be very well informed about the family if she has to ask, unless it's to mask the fact she knows more than she wants to let on.

'No,' I say, with a little laugh, although I like the idea the family dynamics might have made her think it. 'I'm Ada's carer. She has rheumatoid arthritis and needs a lot of help. She used to have daily carers coming in but she asked me to live in for a month when the family were away a couple of years ago. And it worked out well, so I stayed on.'

'Oh, I see.' She doesn't seem too interested in the detail, which is fine with me. She takes a sip of her tea before continuing. 'You're not actually one of the family, then, are you?' I don't like the way she says this, but it will help me if she thinks I'm impartial, so I let it go.

'No, I'm not, and I think there's something weird going on. That's why I wanted to talk to you.'

'Really? How so?'

'Well, to start with it was little things.' I've had plenty of time to plan what to say and how to say it, and I keep my voice low and confidential, leaning in towards her and waiting for her to do the same. 'Look, Hayley, can I call you that?' She nods and puts her cup down. 'Before I go on, you've got to promise you won't repeat any of this to anyone. I think there's something going on, but I could lose my job if the family find out I've been talking to you, and I can't afford for that to happen.'

'Yes, I understand.' She's looking serious now and I can sense a change in the air, as if she's starting to trust me. 'I'd prefer our conversation to be confidential too. I want to find out what happened to Max but I don't want to see myself splashed all over the newspapers. Our engagement was very recent and very private. Max wanted to keep it a secret until we were actually married. I'm not sure why, but it was for the best in the end, and at least it's kept me safe from reporters. I gather they've been pestering the staff at the Beverley Arms and I've been lucky to escape. They seem to have backed off for the time being, thank goodness; I suppose they've got new stories to follow now.' Hayley sounds like she knows a lot about reporters, and I suppose she would in her line of work. I guess we've been lucky not to have attracted attention ourselves, although I don't suppose DI Twist has been telling the whole world about every detail of her investigation.

'I suppose they have,' I say. 'And yes, this will be strictly between the two of us. That's a promise.'

'So, what were these little things?' Hayley relaxes a little now she's reassured of my discretion and pours some more tea.

'It's hard to know where to start.' I speak slowly as it will help me to make sure I don't give away more than I mean to. 'Looking back, I think Emma's been tense for a while, and when I think about it, I reckon it started around the time Polly called to say she was coming home to play in the festival.'

'Why would that be? Don't they get along?'

'No, they get along fine. And she was pleased at first, you know, asking when she was coming, how long she'd be staying, stuff like that. Then Daniel got on the phone and he asked why it was such short notice, the programme must have been arranged long ago and was she stepping in for someone who was ill. Polly said no, it was a last-minute addition, Max Silento was coming to play, and he'd requested a particular piece to play with the string quartet who were already booked to perform, and it was a sextet, so they needed another viola player and someone suggested her. And while she was explaining it all, Emma went very quiet and then said it would be lovely to see her and they'd talk soon but she had to go out now. Then Daniel carried on talking to Polly, although I don't know where Emma went.'

'You seem to have been able to hear a lot of this conversation,' says Hayley. 'Were you in the same room?'

'Yes, Ada and I spend a lot of time with the family.' I'm safe to say this – she's no way of finding out it's not true, and we were both down there last night, after all. No need to tell her about how well you can hear people in the family room if you sit near the top of the spiral while Ada's asleep.

'OK, so Emma's been tense and you think it's to do with Max coming to the festival,' says Hayley. 'What else?'

'Well, there's Polly, of course.'

'Of course. What about her?'

'She's been acting... I don't know... secretively?' I'm not going to dump Polly in it by telling Hayley about Jessie, but if I bring her into it Hayley's more likely to tell me what she knows. And I'm sure she knows something.

'In what way?'

'Maybe strangely is a better way of putting it. She usually stays home for the whole of the holidays, but she's planning on going back to London early. To go to the Proms, she says, but she's never been interested in going before. And I've seen her on her phone when she doesn't know I'm looking. She had a funny expression on her face – sort of pleased and guilty at the same time. I wondered if she has a boyfriend in London she's not telling us about. But maybe that doesn't have anything to do with Max.'

'Maybe not, but we can't ignore the fact she attended the college where he taught. She might have a friend who knew him, even if she's not made the link herself.' She's not stupid. I must be careful how much I say to her if she's this good at making connections. 'Any other "little things"? Or maybe "big things"?' Hayley asks.

'Well, Ada seems to want me out of the house more than usual – like today, for example, she told me to go out. And Emma and Daniel have been arguing, which isn't like them.' No need to say it was about a false alibi.

'Hmm.' Hayley's looking thoughtful and this encourages me to carry on.

'And Emma said she was ill on Thursday and she took a day off work, but I'm sure she wasn't ill at all – she normally drags herself in, even if she's got a temperature. And then, and this might sound silly, but Theo's got a girlfriend he's not told anyone about. I saw them together in town this week. I know teenagers don't tell their parents everything, but Theo's not normally the secretive type.'

'Theo? Who's Theo?'

'He's Polly's brother. He was out last night so you didn't see him. He didn't say where but I reckon it was to meet this girl. I think she works at the Beverley Arms, so she might have been there the night Max died.' If that isn't enough to get her hooked, I don't know what will be. And I've given away all I'm prepared to risk for now. It's her turn now. Hayley lets out a big breath that I hadn't noticed she was holding and signals for the waitress.

'I need another drink. Something stronger. I'll have a large glass of dry white wine. Scarlet? My treat – choose whatever you want.'

'I'll have a Coke, please. With ice and lemon.' Hayley looks surprised but she's got more on her mind than my choice of beverage.

'That's a lot of "little things", isn't it? The question is, what do they all add up to?' Hayley pauses while the waitress puts our drinks down and takes a sip of her wine.

'That's what I was hoping you might help me with,' I say, putting on my best not-very-clever expression. 'It's such a relief to be able to talk to you, Hayley. You know, to someone who wants to find out what's going on as much as I do. I've not been sure what to think. I like the Rosewoods, of course I do, but something feels wrong at the moment, and I don't like it.'

'Have you thought about going to the police?' I thought she might ask this, and I'm ready for her.

'I did think of it. They've been to the house, you know.'

'Have they indeed? Why?'

'Promise me you won't tell anyone I've told you?'

'Yes, of course. Go on, why?'

'They found out Max was in Beverley before the festival. From his phone. It had an app which recorded his movements and it showed him being near our house. I'm surprised they didn't tell you about it.'

'Well, they didn't.' Hayley's face hardens. I can imagine how she looks at a board meeting with underperforming staff, and I'm glad I'm not one of them. 'What did the Rosewoods have to say about it?'

'They all denied any knowledge of him or why he would be there, of course. But I'm sure at least one of them is lying. I just don't know which one it is. I've been trying to find out more but I don't want to go to the police before I'm sure. Before I've got some real evidence. Or they might go back to the family and I'll lose my job. Can you see why it's so difficult?'

'Yes, Scarlet, I can.' Hayley leans back in her seat and takes another sip, deep in thought. I let her process what I've told her, waiting for what I hope will be the reaction I've been aiming to provoke.

'Scarlet.'

'Yes?'

'I've got a proposition for you.'

'Yes?' She's clearly the sort of person who likes to be in charge, so I'll let her spell it out for me.

'I want to find out what happened to Max. And you want to find out what the Rosewoods have to do with it.'

'Well, yes, I do. Or, rather, if they have anything to do with it at all. I'd much rather they didn't, but if they do, I want to know what it is. Does that make sense?'

'Absolute sense. I'd feel the same in your position.' I doubt Hayley Harper has ever found herself in anything like my position, but I let it go.

'So,' she continues, 'I think we should work together. To find out what happened to Max. Between us we know more than the police do, and I don't trust them anyway, not after they've kept the information from Max's phone from me. Who knows what else they haven't told me? No, if they can work it out, that's fine, but I'd rather not leave it all up to them.' I have to work hard to stop myself smiling; she sounds like something straight out of Agatha Christie. I guess she's bored, stuck up here in Yorkshire away from her glamorous lifestyle, and a bit of sleuthing will keep her occupied. And it's exactly what I'd hoped she would say.

'Oh. Gosh. Yes, that's a great idea… Yes, let's do that. If we're both finding out stuff we'll get much further, won't we?'

'Of course we will.' She smiles at me, and I know I've got her.

'Can I ask you a question, Hayley?'

'Sure.'

'I hope you don't mind, but Daniel was talking about you last night, and wondering about you, and if we're going to work together, we can't keep secrets about all this from each other, can we?'

'No,' she says slowly. 'All right, what do you want to know?'

'Well… why were you staying in a different hotel from Max? And why did it take so long for you to find out about Polly, you know, from reading the programme?'

'Oh, there's no mystery there.' She relaxes back in her seat again. 'I told you, Max wanted to keep the engagement secret, and it would hardly have helped if I'd stayed in the hotel with him, would it? And as for the programme, well, classical music's not my thing. I didn't see a programme for the festival until after Max died. It was amongst his possessions when they returned them to me a couple of days ago. I was looking through it when I came across Polly's bio and the reference to the college. I knew it was where Max taught and started to put two and two together.'

'Oh, yes, I see.' The bit about different hotels makes sense, but not the rest. 'Sorry, what do you mean? Two and two together about what?' Hayley's not told me anything I don't know or couldn't have worked out for myself yet, and maybe this is the hint I've been looking for. She's looking at me as if I'm a puzzle waiting to be solved and I decide the time's come to pile on the pressure.

'Two and two about what, Hayley? What haven't you told me? We can't work together if you don't tell me everything you know.' There's still no response, and I start to feel impatient. I can't hang around here all day; Ada will be expecting me back by six at the latest and it's already coming up for half past five.

'Look, Hayley, if you don't trust me enough yet, let's leave it for now. I'll go away and we can meet again when you're able to tell me everything. I'll carry on by myself and so can you, and when you decide you're ready to work together you can let me know. Here, I'll give you my mobile number.' I start to look in my bag for a piece of paper and a pen, but she reaches across the table and grabs my hand.

'No. It's now or never. You're right, I haven't told you everything. It's hard for me to trust someone I've never met before. I've had stalkers and all sorts in the past, it goes with the territory in my job, but it's left me nervous of getting close to new people. I'm sure you understand.' I nod, not wanting to interrupt her now she's got started, gently removing her hand from my arm and putting the pen back in my bag.

'But this is different. If I want to find out what happened to Max I have to forget all that and focus on the facts. I'm not sure why you want to expose the people you work for, but I guess it's about wanting to know the truth, and I'm with you on that.' I nod again – this interpretation of my motives suits me well enough.

'So…' She sighs heavily and glances around the restaurant to check no one's near enough to overhear her. 'I'll be honest with you,

Scarlet. There was another reason for my staying at a different hotel to Max. Apart from his wanting to be private. It's the reason I gave the police, but the truth is Max didn't know I was in Yorkshire at all.' She pauses for a swig of her wine and I hope she's not going to think better of her decision to open up to me.

'Go on.' I try to sound encouraging and take care to mirror her movements by taking a sip of my own drink.

'I came up on the day he died, but I didn't arrive until late and I'd planned to go see him after the concert was over. I knew there wasn't any point in talking to him before then, he'd be too full of nerves.'

'What did you want to talk to him about?' Hayley takes a deep breath, but I know it's for show – it's clear she's decided she's going to tell me.

'I was going to break off the engagement.' She pauses, waiting for a reaction. I suppose she's used to people hanging on her every word and exclaiming every time she says something she thinks is interesting.

'Oh! Why? Oh, sorry, it just popped out. I'm sure it's not relevant; you don't have to tell me if you'd rather not.' But she's on a roll now – I'm probably the first person she's spoken to about it, and the floodgates are opening, as they say.

'I'd found out he was having an affair.'

'No! How awful for you!'

'Yes, it was. I can't begin to tell you how angry I was, Scarlet. I was this close, this close,' she holds up her index finger and thumb less than a centimetre apart, 'to getting hitched to a cheat. I can't believe I was so stupid. My friends always said Max was after my money, and I'm starting to think they were right after all.'

'But wasn't he famous? Didn't he have enough money of his own?'

'Not as much as he wanted. And it was peanuts compared to my salary. He was well known in musical circles, but you don't earn anything like as much from playing the piano as you do from running a designer handbag company. I guess he might have made more after moving to New York. He had a job lined up in a music school, and there are so many more opportunities in the States.' Hayley can't help a note of superiority creeping into her voice, and I'm beginning to see why Max might have wanted to spend time with an admiring younger woman.

'How did you find out?' I don't need to ask if she wants to tell me this time, she's barely waiting to draw breath.

'I arrived back from the States on... when was it? ...I've lost track of the days. Anyway, the day before I came up here. I went to my apartment, which Max was quite happy to share with me before we got married – it's much nicer than his poky place – and found I'd just missed him. I didn't know where he was, only that he was away from London. He didn't always tell me where his concerts were, we're both away – *were* both away – so often, it wasn't worth going into detail. Anyway, the next morning I was putting on my makeup and I knocked a jar off the dresser and it fell into the trash can. I reached in to get it out and I saw some scraps of paper in there. It always annoys me when Max forgets to recycle. I'm committed to saving the planet, you know, and even the tiniest bit of paper makes a difference.' I'm not sure this is strictly true, but now's not the time to point it out.

'What were they?' I've a pretty good idea I can guess, but Hayley won't thank me for depriving her of a major revelation.

'Hotel receipts. For a place in London. Why would he need to stay in a hotel in London? And he always keeps receipts anyway, for his tax return. He's very particular about claiming his expenses.' She pauses, and I see her eyes are shining. 'Oh dear, I mean he *was* very particular. You know, Scarlet, even though I'm furious with him, I've not stopped loving him. Who knows, I might have forgiven him; he could be extremely persuasive.' She's got her handkerchief out now and it looks like her tears might be for real.

'Oh, Hayley, how awful for you. I don't know what to say.' I give her a moment, but I need to get home now or Ada will send out a search party. 'Um, Hayley, look, I'm sorry, but I have to get home. Ada's expecting me back before six and it's nearly that now.'

'Oh, goodness, so it is. I'm sorry, Scarlet, I hadn't noticed the time.'

'Shall we arrange to meet again? After I've had a chance to find out more about the family? And maybe you'll be able to find out more about what was going on with Max?'

'Yes. Smart thinking.' Hayley's quick to recover her composure and she manages to put her hanky away, cover her reddening eyes with her sunglasses and signal for the bill all at the same time. I have to admit it's impressive. She pulls out the latest iPhone and consults what I assume is an online calendar.

'Shall we say Tuesday? At three o'clock? I've got virtual meetings set up between now and then. I hadn't expected to be here for so long, and the business won't run itself.'

'Yes, I should be able to manage an hour. Ada will be at her U3A meeting so I have some free time and she won't know I'm meeting you.' I can see Hayley has no interest in my domestic arrangements so I get up, ready to leave. 'Thank you, Hayley. I feel so much better knowing I've got your support.'

'You're welcome, Scarlet. I'll see you Tuesday.' It's clearly a dismissal, and I take the hint. She's busy with the waitress and her credit card as I walk away, so she can't see my smile as I walk out of the door. She's fallen for it. Hook, line and sinker.

TWELVE

'Are you happy here, Scarlet? In the house?'

'Yes.' I was surprised. Ada hadn't asked me any personal questions for a while. Not since I moved into her spare bedroom. She used to, when I was on the rota. She was a real nosy old woman back then, always wanting to know about where I lived, where I went to school, what happened to my mum. I didn't like it at first but she was a good listener; she sounded like she really cared about me, and I told her a lot in the end. I guess she got plenty of practice asking questions back when she was a judge.

'What about the rest of the family? How do you get on with them?'

'They're nice. It was good to get to know them a bit before they went away.'

'Yes, I'm glad you came for that extra week before they left. I think Daniel's a lot happier knowing he's shown you how the burglar alarm works.'

'And the washing machine.' Daniel loves his gadgets, and it was a good job he'd had a week to show me how the house worked before they left for Scotland. He'd left me his mobile number, but I'd been determined not to need to bother him with stupid questions about how to turn the lights off.

'They like you, Scarlet. I knew they would, and I'm glad you've been here while they're away.'

'I've enjoyed it.' I didn't dare tell her how much. The best thing about that week had been being part of a family. They'd invited me to join them for Sunday lunch and it was just like I imagined a perfect family would be – everyone sitting around the table, teasing each other and watching TV on the big squashy sofas afterwards. I was already trying to work up my courage to suggest to Ada that I stay on after they got back. There were all sorts of ways I could make myself useful, I was sure.

'I'm pleased to hear that, because I'd like you stay on.'

'Stay on? Here, d'you mean? For how long?'

'Permanently. I'd like you to live here. With me. My health's not getting any worse, but it's not getting any better either. I'm going to need help for the rest of my life, and I'd like it to be you who looks after me. How would you feel about that?' I couldn't speak. I hadn't dared to hope, and yet I'd not been able to rid myself of the thought that maybe, just maybe, I might be allowed to live there forever.

'You'd have time off,' Ada continued, preoccupied with the practical arrangements. 'Emma would step in twice a week, she's happy to do that. And Daniel would pay you directly instead of through the agency. You'd have the use of a car to help get me around, and you'd have time to carry on with your studies, I'd make sure of that.'

'But I can't drive.' It was a stupid thing to say, but it was all I could think of.

'Daniel will arrange lessons for you, that's the easy part. Have a think about it; I don't expect you to make a decision straight away. If you'd rather go back to coming in each day, that's fine, I'll look for someone else to live in later on. I'll understand if you'd rather go back to your old housemates. Or maybe you were thinking of living with your mother one day?'

'No.' That was one question I could answer without hesitation. 'No, I won't be doing that.'

'Scarlet?' She was looking at me, and I couldn't quite fathom her expression. There was the kindness in her eyes that I'd sometimes seen *before, but something else too. A watchfulness that felt calculating, although I couldn't think why. I guessed it was the fact that I suited her well and it would be hard to find someone else who did.*

'I've already decided, Ada. I'll do it.'

'Good,' she said, a small smile on her lips. 'I'd hoped you'd say that. I've come to rely on you, Scarlet. I wouldn't want anyone else to look after me now. I can count on you, can't I? To help me? Always?'

'Of course you can.' I returned the smile as I got out of my chair. 'Now, how about a cup of tea?'

Ada's words felt strange at the time, but I was too excited to dwell on them. At last, a real family of my own. I knew Ada would die one day, but that was way ahead. In the meantime, I'd get to live in this gorgeous house, doing a job I enjoyed and working towards a new qualification and a new career someday. Who would turn down a chance like that?

* * *

The next six months were the happiest of my life. I didn't have a care in the world. I liked looking after Ada. She was clever, funny when she wanted to be and never took any nonsense. She always said what she meant. If I got anything wrong, she would tell me soon enough, but she never held a grudge. I knew a lot of people thought she was difficult, but I reckoned she just liked to get her own way. Who doesn't? The difference with Ada was that she wasn't afraid to let you know. I felt safe, knowing I could stay. It made me relax and enjoy life in a way I hadn't allowed myself to before. It seemed that Ada felt the same, and that was when we started to do more together. I'd been used to spending the evenings in my room, watching telly or reading articles on my phone, but she suggested I join her in the sitting room one evening and she introduced me to programmes I'd not seen before. I usually watched shows about houses and reality TV, but Ada loved programmes about detectives and spies – real ones and fiction, she didn't care which. She said the true-life ones taught you most of what you'd need to be a real spy or a detective, and that sort of thing was useful for anyone to know about. And she liked the made-up ones as light relief; she said they made her laugh. I'd never watched that sort of thing before and I was hooked. I loved the secrecy of it; I reckoned I could do most of that spy stuff easily enough, and Ada agreed with me. She helped me to look up MI6 on her laptop – that was before she bought me one of my own – and find out how to apply. There was an online test you could do to find out if you'd be any good at it, and I did very well. Ada said I should apply once I'd finished my course; she said I was a natural.

Ada made sure the whole arrangement was done properly, making me sign a contract and getting Daniel to set up a pension for me. I was surprised by that, but he said it was a legal requirement, and Ada told me that was right.

'It wouldn't look good, a retired judge evading her employment responsibilities, would it? No one's above the law, after all,' she said, all business-like but with a twinkle in her eye, as if it was a joke. She helped me with tax and health insurance. And she made sure I had time to study every day. She said I'd made a good choice of subject, that computer programming and maths would give me excellent options for the future. I knew she was talking about when she'd died, so that I could stay on here and pay my own way. I felt like I was sorted for life. It was wonderful. And then I found out the real reason for it all.

THIRTEEN

I don't know what Ada was up to on Saturday afternoon but she wasn't in a good mood when I got back. She didn't want to tell me what she'd been doing while I was out and her probing of my activities lacked commitment, so I told her I'd had a good long walk and thanked her for the suggestion. Then I made lasagne, which I know is her favourite, and she cheered up a bit over a glass of wine and a film about the *Washington Post*. It was a good story but I spent most of the time thinking about Max moving to America and wondering if this was important. I needed to make a list of questions to ask Hayley on Tuesday and then memorise them. It wouldn't look good to sit down in front of her and produce a list like some rookie reporter.

It's obvious at lunch on Sunday that everyone's trying to be normal. It's a sunny day again, so Daniel and Theo decide a barbecue would be better than a roast and take charge of things, even going to the supermarket to get the food.

'You can freeze the joint, can't you?' Daniel says. 'Go on, Emma, put your feet up in the garden with the paper and let your men take over for once.' He's an expert at getting Emma to relax, and there's a smile in her voice as she says all right, that would be lovely. Ada goes down as soon as they're out of the house, saying she wants to talk to

Emma about some work which needs doing in the garden. She's got a cagey air about her, and I watch from the window as Emma wheels her round the garden. They stop beside a few bushes and trees, but it isn't long before they park themselves on the far terrace. It doesn't look as if they're talking about gardening to me, and I'm sure Ada wants Emma on her own without Daniel knowing or me hearing. They sit there for more than half an hour, frowns on their faces for most of it, until Emma brings Ada back for her coffee.

'It looks lovely outside,' I say. 'Would you like me to bring the coffee onto the balcony?'

'No, it's a nice thought, but there's a bit of a breeze and I don't want my newspaper flying around in it. We'll be outside for lunch and I don't want to get overheated. Can you bring it over here, please, Scarlet? I'd like to get started on the crossword before we go back down.' It's not hard to tell when Ada doesn't want to talk, and this is definitely one of those times. I bring my laptop out and decide the distraction of an hour's work before lunch will do me good.

When twelve o'clock comes Ada brings a bottle of red wine down which she says will go well with the meat, and Polly invites me to help her make the veggie burgers and salad. She doesn't seem to want to talk any more than Ada did. She's probably wishing she hadn't told me so much about Jessie, so I make small talk about Theo and Daniel and their dubious barbecuing skills to lighten the atmosphere. It seems to work, and by the time we take the food outside she's more like her old self. It's a lovely afternoon. No one mentions Max or Hayley, and I can almost persuade myself everything is getting back to normal. Ada seems to think so too when we finally get back to the top floor after an afternoon spent laughing at Theo and Polly arguing about whether it's more important to feed the planet or save it and why the two aren't necessarily the same thing. It feels like swimming through a verbal tidal wave when they get going but I enjoy it, even though I've no idea what to say when they ask me what I think.

I'm enjoying myself so much I don't have time to think about the murder, but as soon as I wheel Ada out of the lift and into her room for a rest I'm brought back down to earth. It's been no more than an interlude, and it takes all my willpower not to ask Ada what she was talking about with Emma this morning. I'll only antagonise her if I do, and I daren't risk upsetting her. I've done well to keep my investigations hidden from her so far, and she doesn't even know about the police interviewing me, or Polly, come to that. I wonder if I should tell her; I might be able to persuade her to tell me something if she knew the police are asking questions about morphine. No, best to keep it quiet. I need her to think I did it for as long as possible. At least until the papers are signed; once that's done I'll be safe.

* * *

I spend a long time writing up my notes and planning what to do next. Having set everything down on paper, I sleep well and get up with a spring in my step. Ada's in a good mood and I'm glad I didn't do anything to upset her last night. She says nothing to suggest she suspects I'm still 'investigating', and I'm happy because I've got her well and truly fooled into thinking this is the case. I spend the morning in the library, using the walk either way to think about Hayley. Her ignorance about the family seemed to be genuine yesterday and I can't believe she's got anything to do with the murder herself, but she's my best source of information about Max. I'm beginning to wonder if his connection to the Rosewoods might lie in his past, and I decide I need to ask if she knows anything about his earlier life. I steal some time from my studies to look him up on the internet but there's not much about his private life – it's all about winning competitions and who his teachers were. There's a mention of Polly's music college too, but he's not worked there for long and it doesn't say anything about who his students are.

I go back to the library for a bit while Ada's playing bridge. I've neglected my work recently with everything that's been going on and I need to put in some extra time if I'm going to meet Hayley tomorrow. I immerse myself in algorithms, producing what I think might be some clever ideas and hoping my tutor will think the same. Ada's in high spirits when I collect her, saying she and her partner beat their big rivals 'most convincingly'.

'I'm in the mood for a celebration, Scarlet,' she says as we trundle home in the late afternoon sunshine. 'Not only because of the bridge, I'm sure you know what I mean.' She turns in her chair to look at me, and I give her a smile.

'Yes, I know,' I say, confident she's more than capable of carrying on the conversation herself.

'I feel as if we're on the brink of a new start, don't you? I think it may be time to plan for the future. For you, I mean. You've only a year left to finish your course now. I think we should be looking ahead and thinking about what you'll do next. You're a talented girl, Scarlet – the sky's the limit, you know.'

'It's nice of you to say so,' I say. 'But I'm happy as things are. I wouldn't want to leave you, Ada, or the family. And doing something new might mean I had to.'

'Oh, I think we can cross that bridge when we come to it. Where there's a will there's a way, as they say.' I can't help smiling at her. Ada's always had a weakness for clichés when she's in a good mood, and I don't want to spoil her moment.

'I'm sure you're right,' I say, although I'm pleased to see we're nearly home and further discussion on these lines is prevented by the mechanics of getting into the house and up in the lift. Ada's good humour isn't fading in a hurry, and she decides she'll get pizzas for the whole family.

'They're not my thing, as you know,' she says. 'But I feel like treating the family. It did Emma good to have a break from the cooking yesterday and I'd like to see a smile on her face again. 'Will you send them all a message on that family group chat thing you use? If Theo's out at rugby practice or something it will keep for when he gets home.'

'I don't think they have rugby practice in July, Ada, but I'll let them know,' I say. 'And would you like me to order the pizzas?'

'Yes, that would be very helpful. I suppose they'll have something Polly can eat, will they? I can never remember what it is she will and won't have these days. And perhaps they'll have something civilised for me?'

'I'll sort it out, don't worry. Do you want a cup of tea now?'

'Yes, thank you, dear. And maybe a little rest too. It's turning into a busy day.' She almost sounds like a normal little old lady when she talks like this and I'm not entirely convinced it's an act. I know her too well not to have my suspicions but it's quite restful to go with the flow, and I help her into bed and make her an Earl Grey before messaging Emma and ordering the food.

* * *

'We seem to be joining you a lot these days,' Ada says as we emerge from the lift. 'I hope you don't think we're intruding, Emma, I just felt like celebrating my bridge win.'

'I'm not going to complain if it saves me cooking,' says Emma. 'It'll be a treat for us all – thank you, Ada.' She comes across and gives Ada a kiss on the cheek, not something she often does, but a look passes between them I've not seen before and I store it up in my mind to work out later. Daniel's home already and it seems Theo doesn't have sports practice for once. The strains of Polly's viola drift up the stairs from her room, only interrupted by a ring on the doorbell which we assume is the pizza delivery.

'Will you go down, Theo?' says Emma. 'I don't suppose for a minute that Polly will notice the bell. And maybe you can knock on her door on your way?'

'Sure.' Theo gallops down the stairs at a speed he saves for special occasions like pizza deliveries. We can hear him open the door but he doesn't shut it as quickly as I expect him to. And there's the sound of a longer conversation than a delivery would require. There's more than one voice too – a man and a woman by the sound of it, and it doesn't take a genius to work out who it must be.

We wait in silence as we hear them mount the stairs, first Theo and then, inevitably, the detectives. Theo has collected Polly on his way and she follows in their wake. One glance at the table laid for dinner, not to mention the time, tells them they're interrupting.

'Oh dear, you're about to eat,' says DI Twist, although she doesn't sound particularly sorry about it. 'I hope you don't mind our dropping in. We won't take up much of your time, but we thought this would be the best time of day to come so as to find you all in. I'm sure you'd prefer this to our asking you to come to the station.'

'Of course. Please, sit down.' Daniel indicates the sitting end of the room and we hear the doorbell ring again. DI Twist looks as if she's about to say something but Daniel's already steering her towards the sofa and the rest of us are gathering round in the positions we found ourselves the first time the police came to the house. She glances towards her sergeant and gives a little shrug as Theo goes back downstairs without being asked, although there's less of a spring in his step this time. We wait in silence while he brings up the boxes and Emma puts the food into the oven to keep warm, no one feeling up to making polite conversation. Sergeant Carter has his tablet at the ready to take notes and DI Twist sits calmly, gazing over towards the kitchen. It's worth admiring, I know; I couldn't stop staring at it myself the first time I saw it. It's modern, of course, but not stark like you often see in magazines. Emma told me once she'll go with modern but not with cold, so there's lots of cream rather than white, which I think looks great with the shiny black marble work surfaces. Our little kitchen upstairs is much homelier but I hope DI Twist won't be getting the chance to look at it any time soon.

Theo and Emma return to the sofa and DI Twist tears herself away from the culinary delights at the other end of the room, getting into her flow without any apparent need for mental adjustment.

'When I said we'd hoped to find you all in, I may have given you the impression we need to talk to you all. That's not the case.'

'Oh?' says Daniel. 'I'm sorry, what do you mean?'

'We only need to speak with Polly, Scarlet and Mrs Rosewood.

The younger Mrs Rosewood, that is.' It takes us a moment to work out she's talking about Emma rather than Ada and our hesitation allows her to continue without interruption. 'We're more than happy to move to another room with the three of you if you prefer? Or to speak to you individually rather than as a group.' There's a pause while she waits for a response. I don't think any of us want the whole family to hear whatever it is DI Twist has to say, but to admit as much would look suspicious so none of us says anything.

'It's all very mysterious,' says Daniel, breaking the awkward silence. 'But I'm sure there's no reason why anyone needs to disturb themselves. Why don't you tell us all what it's about and then we can eat sooner rather than later?' He's clearly got no idea there's anything to be worried about which is interesting in itself, and I find myself feeling a little sorry for him, even while my legs are going to jelly. Whatever's coming next isn't likely to be good, and I concentrate on making sure my face shows nothing more than innocent curiosity.

'Fine with me,' I say, since Polly and Emma aren't saying anything, and they nod mutely when DI Twist looks towards them.

'All right,' she says. 'We've been looking at CCTV footage from the hotel for the duration of Mr Silento's stay. It's enabled us to identify people with whom he came into contact in addition to those in his diary. There's one person we've been unable to identify, so we're interviewing anyone of a similar description who may have a connection to Mr Silento.'

'I thought we'd already established that no one here has any connection to Mr Silento,' Ada says. It bursts out of her like a gunshot, and we're all taken aback. I'm not surprised, though. She's taken care not to say anything to me about the case but I'm sure she was convinced the investigation was over and she'll find it hard to accept it's not. It's not like her to explode like this, and I can see the detectives taking note of her vehemence.

'On the contrary, Mrs Rosewood. A connection to Polly has already been made, and we have found no reason to dismiss the evidence from Mr Silento's phone concerning his proximity to this house on not one but two occasions.' DI Twist's voice has hardened, and I can see from Ada's expression that she realises it might be better to hold her tongue for now.

'The video footage from the night Mr Silento died shows a woman in the corridor outside his room. The video doesn't show a face and she's wearing a cap of some kind, so we can't see her hair colour or whether it's long or short, but there's enough to tell us it's a woman of medium build and height. We need to find this person as a matter of urgency.'

'What's it got to do with us?' Theo asks. I can hear an edge of anxiety in his voice and wonder why he's suddenly so bothered when all he's shown so far is a ghoulish interest in the case before remembering his girlfriend. She works at the Beverley Arms, doesn't she? Maybe she's the connection after all, although it seems unlikely.

'The woman in the video is of a similar and height to your sister, your mother and your… to Scarlet,' says DI Twist, looking at each of us in turn as she speaks.

'But there are lots of people who look like us!' Polly protests. 'It's not as if we're all especially tall, or short, or… built like weightlifters or something. There must be a thousand people in Beverley who it could have been.'

'I'm sure there are,' DI Twist agrees. 'But Mr Silento wasn't outside their houses just a few days earlier. We'll need the three of you to confirm for us again exactly where you were on the night of Max Silento's death, specifically between the hours of seven and midnight.' She looks round the room expectantly, as if wondering who'll volunteer to speak first. Emma hasn't said a word so far, and Polly and I both turn towards her. She's the oldest after all – let her go first. It's Sergeant Carter who clears his throat, pulling Emma's attention back into the room, and she almost jumps in her seat before paying attention.

'Well, I've nothing to add, Inspector. I was here all evening with Daniel. We watched some television and then I had an early night.

I'd had a busy week at work and wanted to be fresh for Polly's big weekend.' She smiles across at Polly, who busies herself with a loose thread on her jumper so as not to have to look at her mother.

'And you, Mr Rosewood? You were here as well?'

'Yes,' says Daniel. Maybe it's having to lie for Emma that's behind his exasperation, or perhaps he's hungry, but we're all taken aback by his tone. 'As I told you before, I was here with Emma all evening. Look, Inspector, we've given you our statements already – do we really need to go over it all again?' DI Twist ignores this outburst. I know what she's doing – she's checking to see if anyone changes their story, but she's hardly going to mention that to Daniel.

'What about you, Theo? Were you home that night?'

'I was out with friends,' says Theo, quickly enough to make me think it was probably one friend in particular. But they aren't interested in Theo's whereabouts and DI Twist turns her attention to Polly.

'I think you also stated you were at home on the night in question, Polly. Were you with your parents?'

'We ate dinner together and watched a bit of TV.' She's sounding deliberately vague, and I wonder if she said that the first time she was asked or if she's trying to help Emma out. 'But I didn't stay up here for long. I did some practice and then I went to bed early too. We had rehearsals scheduled for the whole of the next day and I wanted a good night's sleep.' The pair of them sound too good to be true, and I think the detectives have to be suspicious, even if they weren't before. But they don't take it any further; it's my turn now.

'And you, Scarlet? Were you at home for the whole evening?' She knows what I said before. She can't honestly think I'm going to suddenly say I was out, any more than Emma or Polly would have done. She's piling on the pressure – letting us know she's not letting go easily. But the other two didn't crack, and neither will I.

'Yes. I was here. With Ada. Like we always are on Saturday nights. I can't remember what we did exactly, but we usually play chess on a Saturday, don't we, Ada?'

'Yes,' she says, taking the hint. 'I can't remember who won, but that's hardly relevant, is it? I hope that covers it, Inspector? It seems a shame for you to have to waste your time chasing after people only to hear them tell you what you've heard them say before, but I daresay you have your methods.'

'Indeed we do,' says DI Twist. Her voice sounds calm and quiet, but there's a glint in her eye which makes me wonder if she was paying attention to more than our words. She nods towards the sergeant, who taps a few final times on his tablet and puts it away.

'I can't pretend your answers are satisfactory,' she says. 'None of you has an independent alibi; any one of you could have left the house without anyone being any the wiser. Now we have an idea of what the suspect looks like, we'll be investigating all possible angles. It's only a matter of time before we identify this woman.'

'Wait a minute,' says Daniel. 'Suspect? Suspect for what?'

'I thought I made it clear when we first came to see you, Mr Rosewood. This is a murder investigation. This woman is more than a person of interest. We don't simply want her to "help with our inquiries". She's our prime suspect for the murder of Max Silento.'

* * *

You don't expect Monday nights to be exciting at the best of times, but even Ada's pizzas can't give us a lift. We're all starting to get tired of our meals being interrupted by unwelcome visitors, and this one is consumed in near-silence. Even Theo manages to work out it isn't the time for questions, and Ada and I eat as quickly as we can before making a swift departure.

I can't keep quiet any longer; as soon as we get upstairs I explode. Quietly, of course. I know how easily sound travels up those stairs and I don't need the rest of them listening in.

'Ada, this can't go on. You have to tell me what Max Silento has to do with this family. The police are suspecting half of us already – who knows how long it will take for the rest of you to be dragged in even if they don't cart me off to jail first? This can't be what you wanted. You have to level with me. If you don't, I'll... I'll—'

'You'll what? Go to the police? I don't think you will, Scarlet, and you know it as well as I do.' She's whip-quick with her answer and I can see what it must have been like to be on the receiving end of her displeasure in court. She sees I'm taken aback with the strength of her reaction and deliberately softens her tone.

'I know it's hard for you, Scarlet, but hold your nerve and it will be fine. I promise you. We always knew there might be difficulties, but it will pass. They're scouting, putting on a show of investigating because that silly fiancée woman asked for an inquest. They'll let it go eventually and put it down to natural causes. As I always said they would.'

I open my mouth to speak and then close it again. I know what she's saying, and it should be true, but it isn't. It's not just a matter of holding my nerve. It would be if things had gone to plan, but they didn't. I'd love to tell her what really happened, but it will all be for nothing if I do. A bargain's a bargain and if Ada finds out I've not kept to my side so far, she's bound to question whether she can trust me in the future. And then what's to stop her from deciding the whole thing's off? Not that any of that will matter if I'm arrested. They know about the morphine, they've got me on CCTV outside Max's room. What will they find out next?

FOURTEEN

I don't know if I can stand this much longer. The uncertainty, the fear of what will happen next. It's harder than ever to behave normally with Ada but I manage it somehow. If I've learnt anything, it's that Ada's not going to tell me anything she doesn't want me to know. I suppose I should have known there'd be a limit to how much I could count on her. I find myself simmering with resentment, telling myself she's asking too much of me as I go about my morning duties, and although I do my best not to let it show, Ada must have picked up something. She keeps thanking me for doing things which would normally go unremarked, seemingly wanting to make amends. She's staring out of the big window when I bring our coffee through, gazing into the distance. She doesn't turn to me straight away but once I'm sitting opposite her with my own mug I see an expression cross her face which seems like someone making up their mind about a problem before she turns to face me. She's wiped all emotion away, but I know her too well – she's got a secret and she's about to tell me what it is.

'Scarlet.'

'Yes?'

'Will you get out my diary, please? I want to make an appointment.'

'Now?'

'Yes, not next week! It will be on the desk.'

'All right.' I go over to her old-fashioned bureau. It belonged to Ada's mother and it's always fascinated me, with the little sections inside the pull-down lid for envelopes and stamps and everything. There's no way it fits in with this modern building but Ada would never part with it and I can understand why. Her diary's inside, where it always is. Ada's one of those 'everything in its place' sort of people; she never loses anything.

'Thank you,' she says, pulling it open with the little ribbon inside. Ada was a dab hand with a mobile phone and computer before her hands seized up. She returned to a paper diary a few years ago, and she likes to have one that's not too small so there's room for her big loopy handwriting. It won't be long before she asks me to write in it for her, I'm sure, but she'll carry on doing it for herself for as long as she can. She's riffling slowly through the pages, one for each day, although there won't be much in it other than her usual activities.

'Hmm,' she says. 'I think Thursday would be best, or maybe tomorrow, if he can manage it.'

'If who can manage what?' If she's talking aloud, she can hardly blame me for asking what it's about.

'I need to make a phone call,' Ada says, sounding rather pleased with herself. 'Could you bring me the telephone, please, dear?' I could mention it would have been easier to get it whilst I was finding her diary, but I don't. She puts the handset with its oversized buttons to one side and turns to the back of her diary, where she keeps all her addresses and phone numbers. She doesn't often use it; her memory for numbers is amazing, but perhaps this is one she doesn't use very often. I've almost finished my coffee by this time, whilst Ada's is sitting undisturbed on the table by her side. Very little keeps Ada from her morning coffee – what's going on? She presses the buttons laboriously, checking carefully against the list of numbers, and only a few seconds pass before someone answers. I can't hear what they're saying; she doesn't need to press the speaker button when the phone's up close against her hearing aid.

'Yes, you can help me, thank you very much. This is Ada Rosewood speaking. I should like to make an appointment to see Mr Cartwright as soon as possible. Might he be available tomorrow?' She pauses while I assume the person on the other end is consulting a calendar.

'Yes, that would be convenient. I'll be there at eleven o'clock. Thank you. Goodbye.' Ada presses the off button and hands the phone back to me.

'There. All sorted. You can take me down there tomorrow before you go off for the afternoon.'

'Take you where?'

'Didn't I say?' Ada's feigning distraction while she laboriously writes in her diary. 'To see Mr Cartwright. His office is in the marketplace, so we shouldn't need to take the car.'

'But who's Mr Cartwright?' She's doing it on purpose, I'm sure, winding me up for her own amusement.

'He's my solicitor, Scarlet. I can't believe I've not mentioned him to you before. I talked with him some time ago about drawing up some important papers for me, and I've decided now's the time to sign them. And I want you to be there too. I think you might know why.' She's got a sparkle in her eye, and yes, I do know why.

* * *

There's no doubt I'm feeling better after this morning's conversation with Ada. I know she's on my side, even though there may be tough times ahead, and I feel bad for having doubted it. But it doesn't alter the facts. DI Twist is getting closer to the truth and nothing Ada does or says is going to stop her. With an hour to kill after dropping Ada off at her U3A meeting I walk around town for a bit, planning what I'm going to say to Hayley. The shop windows will be too much of a distraction so I avoid the town centre in favour of residential streets. The houses are so varied and interesting they're a diversion in themselves, but I find a field near Beverley Minster school and sit there for a bit. It's right next to the Westwood, which I make note of for future reference – it could be useful to know about if I end up trailing Emma and her mystery man again.

I can't spend long there but it's enough time to make a plan I'm happy with, and I set off back into town with a confidence I know I must take care to hide from the oh-so-famous Ms Harper. I can see her going into the café as I approach and I find myself looking sideways into a shop window to check my appearance. I'll never look as groomed as she does but there's no harm in doing my best. I can feel my heart rate increasing, and I stop outside a building society window, focussing on a poster about mortgages whilst going over everything in my head one last time. I've a sudden feeling that this meeting is going to be important, and I can't afford to mess it up.

When I walk into the café I see Hayley at her favourite table in the corner, scrutinising her phone. It's gloomy back there, but her glossy blonde hair makes her easy to spot. She's pushed her sunglasses on top of her head and I can see the corner of the drinks menu over her shoulder. She raises her head as I walk round to the opposite side of the table, saying hello, and I slide into the cushioned seat opposite. It's a booth rather than a table, so there's plenty of space for my bag next to me and I don't have to put it on the floor.

Hayley orders coffee for us both. I'd rather have a cold drink after sitting in the sun but I don't think it will help if I say so. I can't see Hayley's shoes but the top half of what looks like a dress is in evidence. It's pale blue like her eyes, with a faint, thin white stripe. It gives the dress a business-like air, and I imagine it looks very chic when teamed with the white linen jacket draped over the corner of her seat. She wouldn't want to put it beside her and risk creasing it, and I don't blame her. Hayley's not one for pleasantries where they're not needed and she gets straight to the point as soon as the coffee's on the table.

'So, Scarlet, what's new? Anything to report? Suspicious behaviour? Strange phone calls? Secret assignations?'

'It's only been three days since we last met, Hayley. There's a limit to how much can happen in that time.' Plenty has happened, of course, but too much of it is information I can't share with her. And she needs to feel she's in charge, so it's best to let her go first.

'If you've nothing to tell me, there's no point in us meeting, is there?' Hayley looks at her watch as if thinking she may as well leave. 'You've disappointed me, Scarlet. That Twist woman isn't telling me anything except to let her continue with her investigating. If she's even investigating at all. If you ask me, she's waiting for me to give up and go back to the States so she can say it was natural causes after all.'

'Maybe it was a heart attack,' I suggest. I have to try; if I can persuade her that this is the case perhaps she'll get off DI Twist's back and they'll call off their investigation.

'No way,' she says. 'Max was as fit and healthy as anyone I know. His agent insisted on a full medical every year before he went on tour and nothing about his heart ever came up in those. There's no way he died of a heart attack, but the police won't listen to me. I was pinning my hopes on you, Scarlet. There's no one else who can help me, but if you can't manage to find anything out either, we might as well call it quits.' She's getting her credit card out, ready to pay and leave without even touching her drink, and I know the time's come to stop her.

'The police haven't stopped investigating, Hayley.' She pauses, her hand half way out of her bag, clutching the card.

'Go on.' Eyes narrowing, she slowly returns the card to her bag.

'They came to the house again. Yesterday evening.'

'So why did you say nothing had happened? Weren't you going to tell me about it?'

'I wasn't sure, Hayley. I was frightened. They didn't exactly say we shouldn't tell anyone about it. Maybe the others have, I don't know, although I don't expect they will have done. I'm sorry, Hayley, I wanted to tell you but I thought I might get into trouble if I did. And I still might. If you let on I've told you.'

'I haven't and I won't.' Hayley leans back in her seat and scrutinises me. I try to look small and vulnerable, hunching into my jacket and wrapping my hands around my coffee cup while I look at her out of frightened eyes. Hayley rearranges her face into a sympathetic expression and picks up her own cup, as if to reassure me.

'Hey, Scarlet, I'm so grateful to you. You have no idea how difficult it's been for me, thinking no one cares about Max or how he died. Knowing you're here makes a real difference. You have my word, my solemn word, I'll never tell anyone we've even met, let alone talked about Max. Please. Tell me what the police came to see you about.' I let a pause hang in the air while I take time to make up my mind, hoping sincerely I'll get something in return.

'All right. They came to see us because they've got CCTV footage from the hotel on the night Max died. Someone visited his room late that evening and they don't know who it was. They can't see the face, but they can tell it was a woman. And whoever it was is the same height and build as us.'

'As who?'

'Me, Polly and Emma. We're all about the same height and size. And so are half the women in Beverley, I expect, but it's us they're interested in. Because of the phone.'

'Because of the...? Oh, yes. The phone.' Hayley takes a moment to let it sink in, but she's not stupid and it doesn't take long. 'So, they came to ask what? If any of you had been there? Surely they can't have expected anyone to put up their hand and say they visited Max that night?'

'No, I don't suppose they did. But they asked what we were doing again. We all had to go through our stories again, and of course we all said we were at home, but they didn't seem convinced.'

'And were you convinced, Scarlet? By Emma and Polly? Do you think there's a chance either of them could be lying? Could one of them have snuck out to see Max?' I know full well both of them could but I'm not about to admit as much to Hayley. I need to keep a few facts in reserve for the future and I think I've given her enough to be going on with. There's no harm in keeping her on the boil, though; I pretend to be thinking about it and sigh heavily.

'I don't know, Hayley, I really don't. They both seemed upset, but you'd expect them to, wouldn't you? And they only have each other and Daniel as alibis, so that's not exactly secure, is it? He'd be sure to lie for them if they asked him to.'

'And you were with Ada, weren't you? She'd lie for you, I expect.' Hayley looks up at me from under her eyebrows as she sips her coffee, challenging me to rise to the hint that she thinks I could be guilty of something.

'You don't know Ada very well if you think that. She's only interested in herself. And she's always going on about how important the truth is, even if it hurts other people. She used to be a High Court judge, you know.'

'Hmm. In my experience people in positions of that sort are as likely as anyone to think rules are for the rest of us, but I'll take your word for it. Did the detectives have any more information about the person on the video? If they could see it was a woman and guess her height and build, can't they see what she was wearing? Or her hair colour?'

'I don't know. Maybe they didn't say about the clothes because it would give away too much. And they said she was wearing a hat so they couldn't see her hair.'

'Yes, I guess so,' Hayley sighs. 'I didn't notice any particular likeness between the three of you when I saw you all last week, but I guess I was upset at the time. Hair colour does make a difference, doesn't it? Even if their faces are similar, Polly and Emma look different because of that. A blonde bob and long brown hair don't make for a strong family resemblance, do they?'

'I suppose not.' I don't like talk about family resemblance; it triggers memories I'd rather not think about. But Hayley's not thinking about me or my tone of voice and she ploughs on with her theories as if she were some great anthropologist.

'I've always been fascinated by genetics,' she says, signalling to the waitress to bring us more coffee. 'It determines so much about us, doesn't it? My business acumen, for example, which obviously came from my father. He was a merchant banker and he had a great head for figures, and strategy, just like me. You can't succeed in business without them.' I nod, sipping my coffee. I can't think of anything to say to all this. I'd like to stop her rabbiting on but I don't want to annoy her. I have to find a way to bring the conversation round to Max without her noticing.

'And there's our looks, of course.' Hayley's getting into her stride now and it seems there's no stopping her. 'All down to our genes. I've my mother to thank for my figure, but I always thought it most unfair I didn't inherit her hair. I'm not a natural blonde, but my mother was, and I started dyeing my hair as soon as I could. It always seemed to me that blondes really did have more fun, and it was strange to think it was related to what they call a recessive gene. Mine was a mousy colour before, like my father. Rather like yours, actually. Have you ever thought of colouring your hair?'

'No. I wouldn't want the bother of getting it done all the time.' I avoid hair salons if I can, with all their chattering on and wanting to know your business. A DIY trim of my fringe and split ends does me.

'I don't blame you. It takes forever and it costs a fortune. But it makes me sit down for a few hours every now and then, which must be good for me.' I smile politely but it's not necessary. Hayley's not a woman in need of encouragement from the likes of me.

'I've been thinking about a new style,' she says, twirling the ends of her hair and considering them thoughtfully. 'My stylist in New York, Alfredo, suggested I think about going for a dark brown colour and a layered look. Think "Duchess of Sussex", he said. Do you think it would suit me?' She tosses her sleek blonde tresses over her shoulder as she says this and looks at me as if she actually wants to hear my opinion. She must know people with more expertise on such matters than me, but maybe she doesn't have many real friends. At least not ones who'll tell her the truth. And although she'd probably never think it, this sort of thing is right up my street. I look at her carefully, trying to imagine her with dark hair.

'It might work. Your skin tone would suit a dark shade. But you'd have to think about your clothes. Some of them might not work so well with dark hair, but a colourist could help you there. What did Max think?' Hayley's been looking at me with a hint of surprised respect, but now her face crumples for a moment. She's quick to hide it and busies herself with the fresh coffee and the milk jug.

'I'm sorry, Hayley – I know he's not around now, but did you discuss it with him? It might help to make up your mind if you knew what he thought about it.'

'It's funny you should ask. I didn't ask him, but I know what he'd have said. The thing is…' She's upset again, I can tell. This could be my moment, if I play it cleverly enough. I wait, and she sits up straight again, squaring her shoulders as if preparing herself for a challenge.

'The thing is, Scarlet, I know he'd have liked it. Max preferred brunettes.'

'Oh?'

'Yes. He never said as much, but I knew.'

'How did you know?' I ask it quietly, hoping it will feel as if the question has come into her head of its own accord.

'Because I found a picture of his ex.'

'His ex?' A man like Max must have had loads of ex-girlfriends, but I let Hayley tell her own story.

'Yes. He'd had relationships before me, of course, but none lasting more than a few months. He told me about them all when we met, and I did the same. We'd both led such busy lives and spent so much time travelling that neither of us had managed to keep a relationship going long term. But when we met each other, we both said we'd change. Max took the job in New York and I appointed a vice-president for my company. We planned to take fewer trips once we were married and work from home more of the time. We had a gorgeous house lined up in New York, right by the park.' Her eyes are filling up again, and she's scrabbling in her handbag for a tissue.

'But then you found the hotel receipts.'

'Yes, and the more I think about it, the more certain I am I'd have forgiven him. I'm sure we could have worked something out. He was too good to lose.' She truly believes this, I can see, and I give her a moment to wipe her eyes.

'Tell me about the picture, Hayley.'

'Oh, yes. The picture. When I found the receipts I started to wonder what else he might have been hiding from me, so I started looking through his things. Properly, turning out everything I could find in his bureau, his drawers, his closets, everything. I knew he was away, so I had plenty of time. Even if he had come back I didn't care – I'd have confronted him with it all, I was so angry with him.'

'I don't blame you. I'd have felt the same.' A little bit of hero-worship won't hurt, and I make my eyes look wide and admiring, not that she needs any prompting.

'I found it in his closet. In a shoe box. Not an old one, that'd be a real cliché. No, it was in a newish one. He must have transferred everything so it would blend in. Maybe he knew someone would come looking one day. It didn't work, though, did it?' Hayley's smile is half rueful and half triumphant, and I wonder if she'd rather have not found anything at all. A little knowledge can be a dangerous thing, as Ada likes to tell me.

'I suppose it didn't,' I agree. 'What was in the box?'

'A photograph of a woman. A girl, really. In a park. It might have been Regent's Park, there was a bandstand in the background like the one there. I don't know why I noticed it, but I did.' Hayley frowns, as if in bemusement at herself, finally stopping for long enough to drink her coffee.

'Was that all? A photo?'

'Yes. It's strange, isn't it? Why hide such a small thing in such a big box? Maybe he thought it was better hidden there than in a drawer. And maybe it was the only thing he needed to hide.' If Max had only one thing to hide, I thought she could count herself lucky. But maybe it was a massive thing, and that wouldn't be so good.

'So who do you think she was? I assume you're guessing she was a girlfriend, but could she have been his mother? Or a sister, perhaps?'

'No. I've seen pictures of Max's family before. She wasn't one of the family. And they're all blonde, anyway – they have Danish ancestry, although you'd never think it from the name, and you can see it in their looks. No, this girl was dark-haired.' Hayley pauses, as if she's finally run out of steam.

'Was she pretty?'

'It was hard to tell. The photo was a bit blurred. But I could tell from her clothes it was taken a long time ago. In the nineties, I'd say. She had an outfit on which looked like something out of *Friends*.'

'So you think she's a girlfriend from long ago? When Max was much younger?'

'Yes. Who else could she be?'

'How old would Max have been at that time? In the nineties?'

'He'd have been in his early twenties, I guess, and just starting out as a soloist. He was taking part in a lot of competitions and studying in London, even though he'd finished at the college. He carried on working with his tutor from there for years.'

'So maybe she was one of his first girlfriends. You said he'd told you about his previous relationships. Do you think she might be one of them?'

'No. He always said he was what he called a slow starter with girls. He said his first one was when he was almost thirty. He said he was too busy studying before then for dating.'

'So who do you think she is, Hayley? You must have some ideas.' Hayley swirls the dregs of her coffee around and I reach for the cafetière to top her up.

'I'll tell you what I think, Scarlet,' she says, a catch in her voice. 'I think she was his first love. The love of his life. I think he couldn't bear to lose her completely so he kept her picture and hid it away where he wouldn't have to look at it and no one else would find it. I think it was because of her he never had a long-term relationship. And I think it was only when he met me that he realised it might be possible after all. And it's taken his dying to make me see it too.' She pauses, picking up the tissue again to dab her eyes.

'I was furious at first. We'd promised each other there'd be no secrets, and here he was, hiding not only an affair but his past too. But now he's gone, I can see it wasn't like that. I'm sure we'd have worked it out.' I can't share her certainty. In my opinion anyone who's having an affair when he's engaged comes into the dirty rat category, but saying so won't help, so I don't.

'So you think this picture shows he likes brunettes?' To be honest, it seems a bit flimsy to me.

'Yes. Looking back, in pictures I've seen of him with other women, there are more brunettes than blondes. And I know for a fact he didn't fall for me straight away. It took a while for us to fall in love. When he proposed, he said that was what made him sure I was the one for him. Knowing me first before falling in love with me.' It all sounds crazy to me, but never mind.

'Was that why you thought about changing your hair? To please Max?'

'It doesn't sound good, does it?' She smiles ruefully at me. 'A hot-shot business woman like me changing her hair colour to please a man. But it's true. I wanted him so badly I seriously considered doing it. I still am, although I don't know why. I just need to feel different. Maybe it's to do with having to make a new start. Without Max.'

'So you came up here to confront him? About the hotel receipts and the photo?'

'Yes. But there's more…'

'Yes?'

'I didn't come straight away. I don't like making decisions when I'm angry, and I knew I needed to prepare myself. And I needed some advice.'

'Advice?'

'Yes. This thing with Max was too big to throw away. I needed to know I wouldn't regret it if I did break up with him. I had to talk it through with someone first.'

'Who did you talk to?' Maybe she does have friends after all. Or one, at any rate.

'Paulo. He's my new vice-president. He's worked for me for years, and I'd trust him with my life. I called him, although God knows what time it was in New York, and told him everything.'

'What did he say?'

'He said he'd never liked Max but he knew I'd been happy with him and he wanted to help. If it were up to him, he'd break off the engagement immediately, but he knew I didn't want to, so he said I had to find out the truth about Max's past. Either I'd be able to handle it and then my mind would be at rest, or I wouldn't and I'd walk away, which would be great too as far as he – Paulo, I mean – was concerned.'

'That makes sense.'

'I know. He's been a good friend to me.'

'So what did you do?'

'I decided to find out more before confronting Max. He'd already left for the festival here, so I knew I had time to make some enquiries before he returned to London.'

'Where did you start?' This is even better than I'd hoped for. It seems she's about to hand me everything on a plate.

'I went to his agent. She's been managing his career for years and she knows him better than anyone.'

'Weren't you worried she'd tell him you'd been asking questions?' This seems a risky move to me, but I can tell Hayley's not the sort to conduct undercover operations; she's much more likely to march around asking whatever she wants and expecting answers as her right.

'Of course I was. But I decided it wouldn't matter if she did. It would give him a scare to know I was on to him and his secrets. He needed to know he couldn't hide anything from me, in the past or the present. I wanted it all out in the open, and I didn't mind how it got there. The more I knew, the better. And anyway, Belinda – his agent – knew we were engaged. She's no fool. She must have known I'd be in a position to influence him in the future and it would be sensible to stay on the right side of me, especially with him planning a move to the States.'

'I suppose so,' I say. 'What did she tell you?'

'Well, she admitted straight off that she knew Max was playing around with a younger woman. He'd bragged of it to her – can you believe it? I suppose he wanted to prove he was still attractive, even with his grey hairs. Belinda had told him not to be so stupid. She said he was lucky to have me and he shouldn't muck up his last chance at real happiness.'

'Good for her.'

'Yes, it was a surprise to find her so supportive. Although it might have had less to do with female solidarity and more to do with her being angry with him too.'

'What about?'

'She'd given him an ultimatum herself. She'd booked him in for a big tour of the States this month and he'd cancelled at the last minute. She was furious with him. She said it had cost her a fortune in compensation, although surely she's insured for that sort of thing? Anyway, she'd told him if he didn't want her to manage her career properly, he could do it for himself. If it happened again, she said she'd let him go. It's a big deal, an agent letting someone of Max's status go, although she'd have found out soon enough he was planning to do less touring and I don't suppose she'd have been happy about that either.'

'Why did he cancel? Weren't you in the States yourself then? Was he trying to avoid you or something?'

'No, I don't think so. Even if he had been there, and in the same city, I very much doubt we'd have had time to get together. I always have back-to-back meetings and he likes to rest or practise between performances.' There's a silence while she thinks about this, perhaps asking herself if this was really the case, or if her beloved fiancé was in fact spending time with other women. I don't voice the thought, it wouldn't help, and it's not long before she carries on with her story.

'Apparently he cancelled the American tour because he insisted on doing this festival in Beverley. Belinda had heard of it – she has other musicians on her books who've played here in the past, but they're not nearly as big as Max. She said he wanted some chamber music experience and fancied the company of other musicians, and this looked like the perfect opportunity. He only gave her a few weeks' notice, and the tour had been in the calendar for months. They had a big bust-up about it but he wouldn't back down, and he came up here. She still has no idea about why it was so important to him.'

'And do you?' I try not to let her see I'm holding my breath. I don't want her to stop now. Not when we're so close to what could be a crucial piece in the puzzle.

'No. But I've spent hours thinking about it and I can't ditch the feeling they're connected. The girl in the picture, the girl in the London hotel and the festival. It sounds crazy, I know, and the police aren't interested in my ideas but I have the strongest feeling about it. Do you understand that, Scarlet? Does it make any sort of sense to you?'

'I've read that when people look back on their gut feelings, they usually turn out to have been right. When we have the benefit of hindsight, we can see why we felt that way, even if there was no logical explanation at the time. I think you should trust your instincts, Hayley.' She gives me a little smile and pours the last drops out of the cafetière.

'Did Belinda know anything about either of the girls? Did you tell her about the hotel receipts? Or show her the picture?'

'Yes. I showed them both to her – what did I have to lose? She had no idea who the girl in the picture might be; she said it looked like it was taken before she met Max. And she couldn't say who he was seeing now, although she might not have been telling the truth about that. They go back a long way and she's very loyal, even if she is mad at him.'

'So, after you found all this out, you got on a train and came to Beverley? To confront him?'

'Yes. Only I was too late. And now someone's murdered him and I don't know why.'

'Do you think it could be one of them? The girl in the picture? Or the one in the hotel?'

'Now you put it like that, it doesn't seem likely, does it? Why would a girl he's only met a few times want to kill him? Or someone from so long ago who even his agent of thirty years doesn't recognise? Oh, Scarlet, I'm so tired of it all. My head's bursting with questions and there's no answer to any of them.' Hayley leans back in her seat, and I can see lines on her face for the first time since I've known her. I can see I won't get any more out of her, and it's nearly time for me to pick Ada up anyway.

'I know. It does seem like an impossible muddle, but I'm sure we can work it out between us. I think your instincts are right. Who's to say it wasn't one of them visiting him in the hotel? Keep digging, Hayley. Ask anyone who knows Max now, and especially anyone who knew him in the past, what they know about these women, and I'll see if I can find out more about his reasons for coming to the festival. If we know why it was so important to him, we might be a step closer to finding out who at least one of these mystery women is. Does that sound like a plan to you?' Hayley's clearly surprised by my taking charge so suddenly but she nods in a positive fashion, seemingly too exhausted by her revelations to say anything more.

'I've got to go now and collect Ada. I'll text you when I find something out, and you can do the same. There's no point in meeting again if we've nothing to tell each other, is there?' She nods again, and I can see her signalling for yet more coffee as I leave. I won't be texting her, and I don't expect we'll meet again. She's already given me everything I need.

* * *

It's not until Ada's in bed and I have some time to myself that I can process everything Hayley's told me, and putting everything down in my book helps me to get it all straight in my mind. There's a lot to write about, and by the time I've finished, I've identified three leads to pursue. Max's mystery girlfriend is the first on the list. There's no reason to dismiss Polly's friend Jessie yet, and I need to find out what she looks like. If she's a brunette, that will go some way to confirming it, and I can't deny she would provide a connection to Beverley – and to the family – through her friendship with Polly. The police's interest in her is important, I think, and I can't help wondering if she would look like Polly or me on a CCTV camera in a hotel corridor.

The girl in the photo is a promising find. Maybe the answer to who killed Max lies in his past, in which case the photo is a big clue. I'm sure Hayley's not given the original to the police; I wonder if it's in her room? No, it would be stupid to risk going in there; she said she doesn't like to leave her room in case she's mobbed by adoring fans.

But the biggest question of all, lodged in my brain as I reach over to turn out my bedside light, isn't about the girl in the photo and it isn't about the mystery girlfriend. It's about Max. What – or who – was important enough to make him ditch a lucrative tour and risk losing his agent in order to come to Beverley?

FIFTEEN

I don't sleep well. There are too many ideas and questions buzzing around in my brain and I can't shake the feeling I've missed something important. Hayley said something yesterday which I instinctively knew was significant. I didn't have time to think it through in the café, and then I forgot about it. She was telling me so many new things it was as much as I could do to remember the facts, never mind what they meant. I only fall asleep properly as the birds are starting to sing, and my alarm wakes me from a deep and unsatisfyingly brief sleep.

Ada doesn't appear to have had any such difficulties. She's sprightly and cheerful, looking forward to her outing to the solicitor and then a visit she's got planned with Emma to a sculpture park in the afternoon. There isn't time for our morning coffee before we set off into town but she promises me one in a café after our appointment.

'We'll go to the one by the jeweller's. They have delicious scones there, and I might treat us to one.'

'Lovely,' I say, since a reaction seems to be expected. And I have to admit, I'm excited too. I've a good idea what this visit's about, and even though my head's full of the murder it will be good to get everything settled with the lawyer.

It takes much less time than I'd expected. I thought we might be ordering an early lunch rather than coffee, but Mr Cartwright has everything ready for us and we're out in the marketplace again after only twenty minutes. We go straight to the coffee shop as planned and find a table in a corner. Ada prefers privacy to a view of the world going by, and I think she and Hayley might have something in common there.

'There, all sorted,' she says with satisfaction, once the coffee and scones are on the table. 'I hope you're happy now, Scarlet?'

'Of course I am,' I say, pouring the coffee. 'You've been very kind, Ada. I think Mr Cartwright was surprised by your generosity.'

'I'm sure he was, but it's no more than you deserve and you know it.' Ada watches to check I'm preparing her scone the right way. Ada has firm views on scones; she likes the jam on first before the cream, with no butter under any circumstances. 'I always knew you were clever and resourceful, and you've proved me right. You've done more for me – and for the whole family – than anyone could imagine. And I know I can rely on you to keep to our agreement in the future.'

'You can, Ada, I promise,' I say as I pass her plate back to her. 'But don't let's talk about it now; it makes me sad to think of a time when you're not around. And it's a long way off, I'm sure.'

'I'd hope so.' Ada takes a bite of scone, and we sit in silence for a moment. Ada never talks with her mouth full, and she'd tell me off straight away if I did.

'But it's best to expect the unexpected, don't you agree?' I know what she means, so I nod and sip my coffee.

'I know I'm in the best possible place, and you look after me beautifully, but at my age anything can happen and I don't want to leave any loose ends when my time comes, whenever it may be. It's as well to make your plans when times are good. I don't want this family to be in any doubt as to what my wishes are after I'm gone. And now they won't be.' Ada returns to her scone, not seeming to require a response, so I keep quiet. There's nothing to say, anyway. We've made our plans and I know Ada will stick to them for as long as she believes she can trust me. The problem is, if the police find out who murdered Max before I do, she might stop believing it, and I can't let that happen.

One thing about Ada, she doesn't make unnecessary conversation. Once she's dealt with her legal affairs her mind is quick to move on to other subjects and she asks me how my studies are going. This is easy. Ada's not a specialist in computer programming, but she's clever and she loves to learn new things, so I tell her all about my latest project, finding as always that explaining it to her helps me to understand it better myself. It's a welcome distraction from the murder and the knots in my stomach subside a little. I hadn't realised until now how badly the stress of worrying she'll find out what I've done – or not done – was affecting me, and I decide to give myself an afternoon off from investigating. It might help my mind to sort out some of the answers on its own. And maybe that comment of Hayley's will come back to me if I'm not trying to remember it.

Ada and Emma go out as soon as we get back, planning to have lunch on their way to the park. Polly's practising in her room, so I make myself a sandwich and spend the afternoon working. I'm in the middle of a unit on cyber-crime and it's fascinating. I'm so immersed that it comes as a shock to hear the whirr of the lift and Ada and Emma's voices as the door slides open. It's five o'clock already, and I've not even got up to make myself a drink since lunchtime.

'Hello, Scarlet. Hard at work, I see,' Ada says as Emma wheels her in. 'No, don't let me disturb you; Emma can take me through for a lie-down before dinner.'

'It's all right, I need a cup of tea anyway,' I say. 'Shall I bring you one?'

'That would be lovely. Thank you, dear.' She's looking tired as Emma takes her through and I wouldn't be surprised if she's asleep by the time I bring her tea. Emma comes back out as the kettle's boiling but she doesn't go straight down as she normally would.

'I hope you don't mind, Scarlet,' she says quietly, coming into the kitchen as I'm getting out the tea bags, 'but we can't have a family meal tonight. I have to be at work for an open evening and Daniel's got a deadline tomorrow so he'll be working late in the studio. I've told Polly and Theo to get a takeaway. Are you happy to do the same?'

'Of course. It might be best for Ada to have a quiet evening just the two of us. She's had a busy few days.'

'Yes, I suppose she has. You take such good care of her, Scarlet. We're all very grateful, you know that, don't you? I know it's your job, but you've always gone the extra mile for Ada. You've given her a quality of life she'd never have had otherwise.'

'It's not just a job; I like Ada. And I like living here. With all of you.' I don't know what else to say, and the truth seems the best option for once. I turn to her as I speak and notice the lines around her eyes and mouth. They definitely weren't there a month ago. She's got to know more than she's letting on, but I don't suppose she's about to tell me what it is.

'Well, that's good...' It feels as if she's about to say more, and I wait, teaspoon in hand. Then her mouth closes and she suddenly seems awkward, as if puzzled she's said anything at all. I decide I might as well put her out of her misery.

'I'll take Ada her tea,' I say, giving her a smile and edging past her and out of the doorway, mug in hand. 'Have a good evening.' Ada's fast asleep, sitting up in her bed. I put a pillow behind her head and leave the tea on the bedside table. By the time I leave the room Emma's gone.

* * *

I would never have expected a visit to a sculpture park to be an exhausting enterprise, but perhaps Ada's mental exertions have been as tiring as her physical ones. She sleeps for over an hour and I have to rouse her, knowing if I don't she'll be wakeful in the night. She looks relieved to hear we'll be eating on our own, and even the need to make a decision as to which takeaway to choose seems beyond her. I make an omelette instead, and we eat in front of an episode of *Miss*

Marple. Ada strongly disapproves of eating in front of the television as a rule and her choice of detective tells me all I need to know about her state of fatigue. I don't ask if she'd like an early night but turn off the TV once the programme is over and run her bath, even though it's only half past eight.

There's still plenty of light in the sky when Ada's tucked up in bed, and I open my laptop at the dining table again, thinking I may as well put in another hour or two before going to bed. It's done me good to focus on work instead of murder today, and a good night's sleep will set me up nicely for a fresh start tomorrow. I can hear the TV burbling up from below, Polly and Theo watching a movie with their pizza, I suppose. It goes quiet soon enough, and Polly calls up the stairs to let me know they're going into town to meet some friends. The house is silent for less than a quarter of an hour before I hear the front door slam and Emma and Daniel coming in. I listen as they open Polly and Theo's doors and find them out, and then make their way up the stairs to the first floor.

I've learnt to recognise every sound that drifts up the spiral stairs, and I'm expecting the rustle of the paper bags and cartons which Emma's favourite Chinese takeaway uses, but I hear the fridge opening and a cork popping first. It's not like either of them to drink midweek and I wonder what's up. I creep on bare feet to the top of the stairs and wait. Their voices are quiet, they're careful not to shout, but I've got good hearing. They start talking immediately, as if they've been arguing for a while before coming into the house.

'So tell me about Thursday,' Daniel says, his voice tight with anger. There's the flat thud of two glasses being placed none too gently on the kitchen table.

'What do you want to know?' Emma's voice sounds weary and I can hear a chair scrape back on the wooden floor and the slosh of wine in a glass.

'Why you pretended to be ill would be a good start.'

'I... there was an emergency. Something I had to deal with.'

'So why didn't you tell me?'

'You'd gone to work.'

'You have a phone, Emma, a pair of legs! You could have called. Or come to the studio.'

'I know, I wasn't thinking. I'm sorry, all right?'

'It'll be all right when you tell me what this mysterious emergency was.'

'It doesn't matter now, it's not an emergency any more. Can't you accept that and trust me, Daniel? Look, it wasn't such a big a deal in the end anyway. I probably overreacted. It's really not worth bothering you with now. How did you find out, anyway?'

'I called the school to check what time your open evening finished. Amy on reception asked if you were OK after your tummy bug last week. She said she thought you were still looking peaky and maybe you should have taken more time off.' I can hear Emma sighing, but she's not coming up with any answers. She must be racking her brains for something to say that doesn't involve meeting strange older men on benches.

'She's right, you know,' Daniel continues. 'You aren't looking good. You're always saying you're tired or going to bed early. You've barely spoken to me outside meal times for ages. I can't remember the last time we had a laugh together.' He pauses, and I can imagine the expression on his kind face as he looks at Emma.

'It's this murder thing, isn't it?' he says. 'You mustn't let it get to you, Emma. I know it's stressful with the police coming here and that awful woman… what was her name?'

'Hayley,' says Emma, without any apparent need to think about it.

'Yes, that's it. It'll soon blow over – anyone can see none of us had anything to do with it and they'll either work out who it was or put it down to a heart attack.'

'Will they?'

'Of course they will. That's what Mother says, and she knows her stuff. Anyway, what was so important on Thursday that you had to pull a sickie? I can't handle secrets between us. Please, Emma – talk to me.'

'I can't, Daniel. Please, leave it.' There's a break in Emma's voice. I know she's close to tears, but it's not working.

'I can't leave it, Emma. What's going on?'

'Please, Daniel. I've been working all day, I've had nothing to eat and my head's splitting. And the children will be home soon. I don't want them walking in on an argument.'

'Neither do I, but we can't leave things like this. Go outside; it's still warm and the fresh air will do you good. I'll find something in the fridge and bring it out. We'll eat together and talk over whatever it is properly. Hiding it isn't helping anything. I promise you'll feel better once you've told me what's going on.' He's not going to let go, I can tell, and the note of resignation in Emma's voice suggests she's thinking the same.

'All right.' The sliding doors open and I can visualise Emma stepping onto the terrace while Daniel rummages in the fridge. I tiptoe to the window and stand to the side of it. Emma's crossing the lawn in the direction of the summerhouse. I suppose she doesn't want to risk being overheard through our open windows. The garden faces west, with tall hedges providing privacy from the adjoining properties. There's a beautiful sunset, and I wonder how much longer it will be before Polly and Theo come home. Emma's in no state to notice the sky, though. She's facing away from the sun, staring with vacant eyes at the empty wrought-iron chair opposite her, probably busy coming up with a story Daniel will believe. It's not long before he joins her, carrying a tray with bread, cheese and grapes, together with the wine bottle and a carafe of water; he knows how to do these things properly. I stay in the shadows, watching and straining for any snatches of conversation. If I'm lucky they'll forget how easily sound travels on a quiet summer night and not bother to keep their voices low.

I'm not lucky. They eat first, both hungry at the end of a long day, but it's not long before the conversation starts up again, quietly at first and then with increasing agitation. Their bodies are tense and their voices raised, but I can't hear their words, only murmured anger from Daniel and defensiveness from Emma. After a while Daniel gets up and whirls away from the table, walking over to a nearby bush and leaving Emma with her head in her hands. They stay like that for a long time and I can feel the tension between them even though I'm so far away. Eventually Daniel squares his shoulders and returns to the table. He puts the plates and glasses onto the tray with careful precision and carries it back inside, leaving Emma alone in the gloom.

I want to carry on watching but I need the bathroom and I can't hang on any longer and Emma's gone when I get back. I tiptoe over to the stairs but there's not a sound from below until Theo and Polly return shortly after eleven. I hear them call goodnight to each other and the slam of their bedroom doors, and I know I'll hear nothing more tonight. I'd hoped for a good night's sleep but I'm not going to get it now. What has she told him? And was it the truth?

SIXTEEN

It was a Monday afternoon. Bridge club was cancelled; one of the old ladies had a cold and none of them like to risk catching one, and it was too late to find a replacement at short notice. Ada decided to fill the time by teaching me to play bridge, and although I'd planned on working at the library I thought it might be interesting, so I got out the little card table from under the stairs and a notebook, guessing it might be complicated. We were sitting opposite each other, next to the window with the view over the Westwood. She had the cards in her hand ready to deal but she put them down and leant back in her chair instead.

'Scarlet.' I looked at her. She had a funny expression on her face. *Careful, as if she were working something out.*

'Yes?'

'Can I trust you? Absolutely?'

'Of course.' *What sort of question was that?*

'Think about it, Scarlet. It's not as simple as it sounds.'

'You mean, can you trust me to keep a secret? I'm good at that. I've kept enough in the past. Until I told you about them.' *I'd told Ada things I'd never told anyone else. She's that sort of person.*

'Yes, I know you can keep a secret. It's more than that. I need something doing for me. Something I can't do myself. I want you to do it for me.'

'What is it?'

'I'll tell you once you promise you'll do it.'

'Why are you asking me? Why not Daniel? Or Emma?'

'You'll understand why when I tell you.'

'So tell me.' I had no idea. I just thought she was being weird. I never gave a thought to why she was acting so strangely. She paused, looking hard at me.

'The thing is, Scarlet, it's not strictly legal.'

'The thing you want me to do?'

'Yes.'

'Oh.' I looked back at her, but there was no clue in her face. 'Let me get this straight. There's something you want doing that you can't do yourself. You can't ask Daniel or Emma to do it because it's not legal. So you want me to do it and keep it secret. I'd hardly go telling people about it if it's not legal, would I?'

'I need you to keep it secret before you do it, not just afterwards.'

'I don't understand,' I sighed. I wasn't worried, just annoyed. And a little bit intrigued as well, I have to admit.

'You'll understand when I tell you what it is. The important thing is that I need to know I can trust you to do it and not to tell anyone I've asked you to.'

'But if it's illegal I'll get into trouble for it. Maybe go to prison. Won't I?'

'No. I've got a plan. I've worked it all out. No one will know you've done it.'

'Really? How does that work?'

'I've got a foolproof way to do it; you won't get found out... and I'll make it worth your while, Scarlet.' She watched me closely as she said it, looking for a reaction.

'How?' My mind was running on overdrive. I'd already worked out that I could be in trouble if I didn't agree to whatever it was she wanted me to do. Maybe she'd decide she didn't need me living here after all. Maybe my lovely new home and family would be nothing but a memory if I said no.

'I'll put in my will that you're to live here as long as you want after I've died. Rent-free. This whole top floor will be yours for as long as you *want it. And if Daniel wants to sell, you'll get a portion of the proceeds to buy your own place. And I'll leave you a lump sum: to get you started before you find a job. You'll be financially secure for the rest of your life, Scarlet.' I didn't know what to say. The single worry in my mind – what will happen to me when Ada dies? – gone, at a stroke. A home and a family. Guaranteed.*

'Would that be OK with Daniel and Emma?'

'Of course it would. And if it's in my will they won't be able to argue, will they? I paid for this house, after all. I can do what I want with it, and they know it. They like you anyway – you're one of the family now, Scarlet. Surely you know that.' My insides melt when she says that, I can't help it.

'All right. What is it?' I can't imagine what it might be, but it will be worth it, whatever it is.

'I want you to kill me, Scarlet. When the time comes. I couldn't bear to lose my marbles, so if I get dementia and it gets bad, I want you to kill me.'

SEVENTEEN

Ada has plans for the silver screen again today. She says it's some silly film about people in a balloon, but she knows her friend Maureen has no one else to go with.

'She has rather frivolous tastes where film is concerned,' she tells me as I coax a final wave out of her hair before applying the spray. 'But she sits through my choices, so I must put up with hers. And she has impeccable taste when it comes to food, so I can't complain.' I can't help smiling. Ada will happily watch almost anything other than horror, and she knows it. She's a closet film buff, and she always gets the obscure movie questions right on *University Challenge*. But she doesn't think it befits a person of her standing to admit to enjoying the lighter side of cinema. I once asked what her favourite movie of all time was, but she wouldn't tell me, ticking me off for using American language.

'It's film, Scarlet, film. Movie is a horrible Americanism, and I won't have it in my house.' She puts up with Theo saying it, though. Polly too, come to that. Maybe I'll try it again sometime and see what happens. I've a sneaking suspicion it's *The Day of the Jackal*, and she has a secret crush on Edward Fox.

I drop Ada at the cinema at the appointed time and take myself off to the library for a couple of hours' work. It's too lovely a day to stay inside for long, and when one o'clock comes I take my packed lunch onto the Westwood. Ada and Maureen are going to a posh restaurant and Ada said they'll take their time so not to pick her up until three o'clock. It won't be worth going back to the library, and I decide to treat myself to a snooze and a sunbathe instead. It's not a long walk from the library, and I take the little path up beside the field I found before, next to the school.

The children are out in the playground and I look at them through the railings. They seem happy enough but I know they won't all be. My eyes scan the outer edges and yes, there he is. The outsider. There's always one, standing on their own in a forgotten corner. This one's looking at a bench as if trying to make up his mind about something. I see him straighten his back and march over to it, almost defiantly. Straight away, a girl comes over to him, a bit older than he is. She leads him to a group of children and they let him join their game. I look back at the now-empty bench and see there are words painted onto it in bright colours. Squinting, I can make them out – Friendship Bench, it says. I wish they'd had one of those at my school.

Thinking about my school isn't going to put me in a good mood so I direct my mind to other topics as I pass through the kissing gate and onto the Westwood, wondering where the best place is to sit if I don't want the cows to eat my lunch. I decide on one of the benches by the path, where Emma met her man last week. I can walk up towards the mill afterwards and find a quiet spot to sunbathe. I'm checking the traffic before crossing one of the roads which cut the pastures into sections and looking to see if one of the benches is free when I spot him. It's that man. Emma's man. He's walking through the kissing gate and heading for the benches. Surely he's not going to meet Emma again? I can't believe she'd risk it after last night. My mind is racing and my first instinct is to hide myself in case Emma appears too. But I've every right to be here with my lunch – why should I hide? No, I must. It's a wonderful opportunity to find out what he's up to and maybe even who he is, and I can't waste it. If

I choose my spot carefully I should be able to keep an eye on him without being seen by Emma if she joins him.

Watching the man out of the corner of my eye, I cross the road, heading up the hill towards the mill instead of down towards the path, and then over to the trees. There's a big group of women with babies having a picnic and I hope they'll draw attention away from me if it's needed. I spread out my jacket and sit down to eat. I've a book in my bag from the library, and I hide my face behind it, novel in one hand and sandwich in the other. I've taken my eye off the man for a moment while I organise myself, and when I look up I almost think I've lost him, but no, he's on the bench, reading a newspaper. He doesn't look very absorbed; he keeps peering over the top of it in a nervous fashion, and I think he could do with some lessons in how to blend in.

Fortunately for him he doesn't have to spend too long looking shifty. After only five minutes a look of recognition crosses his face and he starts to fold up the newspaper. He's been looking along the path towards town, which isn't the direction Emma came from last time, but I suppose she could have driven over from work and parked nearby; she was hardly likely to pretend to be ill again. I scan the path but I can't see her. I've been so certain it will be Emma I almost choke on my sandwich when I see who's approaching the bench. No wonder they were both so upset last night. Emma must have told the truth about her affair after all. Why else would Daniel be coming to meet this man?

Daniel's carrying a paper bag, and he opens it as he sits down beside the stranger. He takes out two bottles of water and two parcels wrapped in smaller paper bags. I don't have much experience of such matters, but I'm pretty sure it's not normal behaviour for a husband to offer lunch to his wife's lover, and that's what Daniel appears to be doing. They're not exactly smiling at each other, but body language is one of my talents, and I'd bet a lot on their not being about to have a fight, or even an argument.

I watch from behind my book as Daniel hands the man a drink and a sandwich. They both put them down on the bench beside them, their movements identical, along with their slumped shoulders, even though they've not got much else in common, with Daniel's tall frame and fair hair and the shorter stranger's dark grey cut. I can see now he's even older than I thought, definitely too old for Emma. Old enough, I realise, to be her father. But Emma's father lives in Australia so it can't be him. I've not met her parents yet, only heard about them. They meet up with the family every year in Scotland, where they've got a house. Emma doesn't have a Scottish accent, but I suppose she's lived in England for a long time, and maybe Australia before then.

So if it's not Emma's lover, and it's not her father, who is he? As I watch, they start talking, Daniel first. He's agitated now and the older man seems shocked, but it's not long before he puts his hand on Daniel's knee to stop him. It's his turn now, and he talks for a long time. He's calm, but his face is sad, and he keeps looking at Daniel to see how he's reacting. Daniel's got a fixed expression on his face. He's looking at his shoes and he keeps nodding as he listens. The older man stops talking at last and waits. They both sit still for a long time and then Daniel eventually looks up from his feet, his shoulders dropping as if with a sigh. He gestures to his lunch and they both start unwrapping their sandwiches.

They eat for a while, watching the mothers and babies in silence. Then Daniel asks a question and they're off again. They're both animated now, as if discussing a problem and not agreeing on its solution. Daniel's looking cross and frustrated, and the other man's face is apologetic and defensive in turn. They've obviously got a lot to talk about and I wish I'd found a closer spot where there might have been a chance of overhearing them. They've been at it for nearly an hour when Daniel looks at his watch and scrunches up his sandwich wrapper. He must have come out during his lunch hour. He doesn't usually leave the studio when there's a deadline approaching, and he won't be able to stay for long. The other man pats him on the back as if encouraging him. If I didn't already know Ada's a widow, I'd be tempted to think he was Daniel's father. Maybe he's an uncle? But why would Emma be sneaking about meeting Daniel's uncle?

Lost in thought, I watch Daniel make his way along the path and then turn down Westwood Road towards town. The other man opens his paper again and reads for a few minutes before doing the same. They clearly want to avoid being seen together but I'm struggling to think why. I've only got an hour before meeting Ada but there's no reason why I shouldn't follow the man again. Last time I saw him, he was wheeling a suitcase towards the station, suggesting he doesn't live locally. If he's staying in a hotel I might be able to figure out a way. I get up when he does and keep my distance as he walks into town, but he doesn't stop at any of the hotels. He walks straight to the railway station again, crosses the bridge and stands on the platform waiting for the Hull train. I go into the main entrance and look up at the departures board. There's a train due in five minutes. I check the timetable and realise that if I follow him to Hull I won't have time to see what he does next and get back here before picking Ada up.

Sighing with frustration I leave the station, telling myself to calm down. Even if I did see him get on a train to London or Manchester or wherever, how would I know how far he was going? If I were to stand any real chance of finding out who he is I'd have to follow him all the way home, and I can't do that. I do have some information, though. He had an overnight case before but he didn't today, and he was meeting Daniel at lunchtime and Emma in the morning. Which suggests he lives far enough away for an overnight stay to be preferable, but not so far he can't manage a day trip if there's an emergency. And I reckon this *was* an emergency. He met Daniel soon after one o'clock, so where could he have come from? I don't know enough about journey times; I've never gone further than York and that's always been on the bus. My phone's too small to look at the train booking websites properly. It will have to wait for this evening and my laptop.

* * *

Ada's had what she describes as a 'highly satisfactory repast', and thanks to my having read at least some of the classics on her 'must-read' list, I know what she means. I tell her I'm glad to hear it and ask was the film satisfactory too?

'It was entertaining enough. Although why anyone would plan a journey to three thousand feet and fail to take a hat, I don't know. I don't mind them taking liberties with the facts in these historical dramas, but even the Victorians had common sense, I'm sure.'

'I'm sure they did.' I can't help myself from sounding absent-minded as I push the wheelchair towards the car park. My brain's full of the day's events, and I've still got a nagging feeling I've missed something. It's to do with Hayley and what she said to me the other day. It's starting to annoy me, although I'm sure the answer will come to me if I can only stop myself from worrying about it.

'Are you all right, Scarlet? You seem rather distracted. And you're looking a bit pink, I must say. Have you been sitting in the sun?'

'Yes, I have. I took my sandwich onto the Westwood and it was so nice I stayed there for a while. I must have overdone the sunbathing.'

'You'd better take a hat next time,' Ada says. 'We can't have you getting sunstroke, can we? Who'd look after me if that happened?'

'Who indeed?' I say, opening the car door and positioning the wheelchair beside it. 'Shall we let the air flow a bit before you get in? Never mind sunstroke, we don't want you roasting either.'

'Thank you, Scarlet, that's thoughtful of you. And when we get home let's both have a lie-down. You look as if you need it as much as I do.'

* * *

Ada was right. I do need a rest, but not for the reasons she thinks. I help Ada into her bed and open the window wide, pulling the curtains across it to darken the room. Back in my own room I do the same for myself and set my alarm for five o'clock. I'm tempted to get out my book and write down my observations of Daniel and the stranger or look up train times on my laptop, but that can wait. I'm too tired to do it properly and I want to give my brain a chance of remembering what Hayley said without the risk of falling properly asleep. I lie on the bed, close my eyes and make myself remember my relaxation techniques. I haven't needed to use them for a long time, not since coming to live here, but I find it's like riding a bicycle, once learnt never forgotten. Not that I ever learnt to ride a bicycle. I relax each and every muscle in turn and listen to my slow and steady breathing. My eyes shut of their own accord and I pull a picture of Hayley and me in the café into my mind.

My visual memory has always been more reliable than my auditory one. It's why I write down everything people say as soon as I can. I can see every detail of Hayley's clothes, hair, makeup and jewellery as if she were sitting in front of me now, but it's harder to recall the conversation. I know I could get out my book now, but I'm certain whatever it is I'm searching for isn't there. I make myself think slowly and carefully, trying to focus on my responses rather than Hayley's words. I read somewhere that we remember things best when they stimulate emotion, and I'm sure the elusive detail I'm after will be revealed if I can summon up my feelings that day.

I remember how nervous I was as I stepped into the café and I can feel my heart rate increasing immediately. I'm excited, my head full of plans to get Hayley to tell me everything she knows. I'm making sure I appear weak, ineffective. I know she likes to be in control and I'm doing my best to flatter her. I'm thinking quickly. I need her to talk, but it seems as if I'll have to reveal something first. I'm terrified that she'll walk away as soon as I tell her about the CCTV footage, and I'm heaving an internal sigh of relief as she starts to talk about the photograph. I try to keep a neutral expression as she talks about her vice-president and Max's agent, mentally recording her revelations about Max cancelling his tour and insisting on coming to Beverley at short notice. I'm doing my best not to start thinking about what it all means, forcing myself to wait until later for fear of missing any details now. I'm wishing I could have written it all down as she was talking and wondering why I didn't think to press the record button on my phone before I sat down.

There's nothing new there, no details I'd forgotten before. I've missed something – what is it? A feeling I've surprised Hayley, and in a way which makes me smile. There's a point at which she gives me an unexpectedly admiring glance. What are we talking about? I let the feeling of satisfaction flood my brain and visualise Hayley while I do so. She's tossing her hair over her shoulder in a way that's reminiscent of a teenager rather than a middle-aged business woman. Her hair. It was when we were discussing her hair. I was telling her she'd have to reconsider her wardrobe if she changed her hair colour and how a colourist could help her. She clearly didn't have me down as someone likely to have an opinion on such matters, and I experienced a rush of triumphant satisfaction at the expression on her face.

I sit up in bed, no longer in need of rest or breathing techniques. I've got it. The snag in my brain. At first glance, it has nothing to do with the murder, but I'm convinced it's significant. I didn't allow myself to consider the implications of anything Hayley was telling me at the time, knowing I needed to hold onto the facts until I could transfer them into my book. This didn't look like an important fact so I didn't record it, but my brain knew I needed to consider it. Hayley talking about her hair colour is important, but why?

I decide a cup of tea will help. I don't need to wake Ada just yet so I take my mug into the living area and open the French windows onto the balcony in the hope that the fresh air will help me to think better. I go back over what I can remember of our talk about hair, frustrated by the knowledge I would have more to go on if I'd thought to write it down at the time. Relax, Scarlet, being cross won't help you to think. Why was Hayley thinking of becoming a brunette in the first place? Even though she's getting on a bit, the blonde suits her. Why were we talking about hair anyway, in the middle of a discussion about murder?

Of course! It was for Max. Hayley thinks Max preferred girls with dark hair, so she was going to change hers to suit him. I played along with her at the time to keep her happy even though I can't imagine anything more ridiculous. But there's more to this than

Hayley's personal appearance; maybe Max's girlfriend had brown hair. I wonder what Jessie looks like – I'll have to ask Polly. Come to that, Polly's got brown hair. Maybe she was the one having a relationship with Max and Jessie's a red herring. It seems unlikely, but not unlikely enough to stop Hayley suggesting it when she first came to see us. If Polly were Max's girlfriend it would explain his coming here, but wouldn't she have been more upset about his death? And my theory about her having a boyfriend in London would be wrong. Or maybe not – she could have dumped Max and then got a new boyfriend. And Max could have come to Beverley to try to win her back. She could have gone to the hotel to tell him to leave her alone and then killed him. It's a possibility, but I'm not convinced there's sufficient motive.

I sigh to myself. It's not a great theory but it's the only one I've got right now. It's coming up to five o'clock. I'll have to wake Ada soon and there's no time to do anything more now, but I know what I need to do next – I have to talk to Polly.

EIGHTEEN

It's Ada's turn to choose our Friday outing but she says she'd like a quiet morning in the garden. We can go somewhere after lunch, she says, perhaps to Burton Agnes to look round the gardens, but she's not feeling up to a whole day out. She doesn't seem like herself and I can't help but feel a twinge of anxiety as we go about our morning routines. Ada's never denied the pain she's in with her condition but she's not let it stop her from doing what she wants to. Her mind has always been as sharp as a knife, and despite her fears, she's shown no sign of deteriorating mentally in the time I've known her. This need for a restful time, coming as it does after her long sleep yesterday afternoon, makes me wonder. Is she starting to slow down after all? And might it be a sign of something more sinister? I try not to let it show but I can't be doing a very good job of it, and Ada's always been an expert at reading people's minds.

'Don't worry, Scarlet, I'm a little tired, that's all. It's been a busy couple of weeks, not to mention the worry all this silly police investigation is causing us. Even though I know there's no need to worry, it's been a strain. And if a person of my age can't take a morning off from the busy social whirl, there's something wrong with the world, don't you think?'

'I suppose so,' I say, and she certainly sounds like her old self now, even if she doesn't quite look it. 'Do you want to go outside for a while? It's a beautiful day.' I'm hoping she'll decide to sit in the garden with her crossword so I can talk to Polly, but Ada has plans of her own in that department.

'Yes, that would be lovely. Perhaps you could wheel me down to the terrace? And would you ask Polly to join me when she gets back from her swim? There's something I want to talk to her about.'

'Of course,' I say, hiding my frustration. It looks as if I'll have to take my turn in asking Polly questions, but at least Ada hasn't decided to go to the other end of the garden. If they stay on the terrace I should be able to hear what they say.

Ada's still only half way through her coffee when Polly comes back, and I pop down and ask her to join her grandmother.

'Oh dear, it sounds rather like a royal summons, don't you think?' she says. 'Any idea what she might be about to tell me off for?'

'Don't be daft, she probably wants to teach you how to do cryptic crosswords,' I say as I turn back up the stairs. 'Do you want to have lunch with us? I'm making a salad and there'll be plenty of it.'

'Thanks, Scarlet, that would be great. I'll come and give you a hand when I've finished with Gran.' She heads out onto the terrace, while I go up to the kitchen and stand by the open window overlooking the garden. By the time I get there Polly's found herself a cold drink from the fridge and is flopping down in a chair opposite Ada.

'Aren't you hot out here, Gran? I'm baking.' She takes a long drink from the can and sticks her legs out in front of her to get the most out of the sun.

'No, dear, I'm in the shade, in case you hadn't noticed.' Ada puts her newspaper and reading glasses on the table and turns her chair to face Polly. 'Did you have a nice swim?'

'Yes, it was great. I love it when the pool's not busy; it's why I go early in the morning, before the school groups start coming in.'

'I daresay it will be different next week, when they break up for the summer holidays,' says Ada. 'But you won't mind that, will you?

You'll be back in London by then.' Polly's silent for a moment, and Ada's quick to pick up on it.

'Polly? You're going back to London on Monday, aren't you? Isn't that what you said? So you can go to the Proms?'

'Actually, there's been a change of plan,' says Polly, her voice suddenly flat. 'I'll be staying a bit longer after all.' There's a pause. I reckon Ada's waiting for Polly to say more, but she takes another swig from her can and stares out across the garden.

'Polly…' There's an uncharacteristic softness in Ada's voice, but Polly doesn't want sympathy.

'What was it you wanted to talk about, Gran?' Her voice sounds impatient and there's something about it which suggests she's fighting off tears. I can only see the tops of their heads, but I can see that Polly's is turned determinedly away from Ada.

'You've not been yourself recently and I want to know why.' You could never accuse Ada of beating about the bush, and I smile to myself at her directness.

'It's hardly surprising, with the police hounding us about that man being murdered,' Polly snaps. 'I don't suppose any of us are ourselves right now. Especially me and Mum and Scarlet. You try being a murder suspect and see how it makes you feel.'

'I hope that won't be necessary,' says Ada, not without a hint of humour in her voice. 'And I do understand the difficulty of the situation for you all. But I sense there's more to it, Polly. Why this sudden change of plan? Don't you want to go to the Proms after all? Or is it to do with money? I'm sure it's not cheap going to concerts these days, even if you are standing up when you get there. I'd be happy to help with the cost of the tickets if it would support your studies.'

'It's sweet of you, Gran,' says Polly, turning towards Ada at last. 'But it's not that. I… I think it would be better for… better for Mum if I stayed. She's not coping well with all the fuss about Max Silento. You heard how disappointed she was when I told her I was going back. I thought it might help if I stayed.'

'I'm sure it would help her, but it's not the real reason, is it?'

'What do you mean? What other reason could there be?'

'A boyfriend reason, perhaps?'

'A… what boyfriend?' Polly's voice is genuinely surprised, but there's an edge to it that tells me it's because Ada's guessed rather than because she hasn't got one.

'I have a better understanding of such things than you might think. Being old doesn't mean I've never been in love. Or unhappy. It simply means I've got more experience of these matters, and I'm able to recognise them in others. Like you.' Polly doesn't reply and she turns away from Ada again, pulling her feet up onto the chair and curling into a ball.

'Well? Am I right?'

'I don't want to discuss it,' Polly says, barely audible from where I'm standing. I hope she uncurls soon and talks to Ada rather than her knees.

'Well, that's a pity, because we are going to discuss it. At least we are if you don't want me talking to your parents about it.'

'Why would you? It's none of their business. And none of yours,' says Polly, straightening up and looking at Ada. I can't see her face but I can imagine it. I know what Polly looks like when she's cross, and I also know Ada's more than up to dealing with it.

'Because it's making you unhappy, and problems shared are often problems halved.'

'Oh, Gran, you and your clichés.' Polly can't keep the smile out of her voice, and I suspect Ada's used this one on purpose.

'It's just a saying, and in my experience it happens to be true,' says Ada. 'Come on, Polly, tell me what's up and I promise you'll feel better for it.'

Polly drains her can and sighs. 'All right. I do have a boyfriend.'

'And?'

'And what?'

'Does he have a name? An occupation?'

'Yes. He's called Sam. He's a student, a viola player like me. We met in the orchestra. That's all there is to it.'

'So he's the reason you wanted to go back to London?'

'Yes.'

'So why the change of plan?' Ada's using her kind voice, and I know it's because she thinks Polly's been dumped.

'Does it matter now?' Polly demands. 'I'm staying for Mum and I'll go back in September. Why does it matter so much?' Even Ada seems sufficiently taken aback by this outburst to stop her questioning.

'I'm sorry, Polly, I don't want to upset you, but are you still seeing this young man? Is he still your boyfriend? Or has it maybe... finished?' There's a long silence. Polly's turned towards the garden again, and there's something in the air which feels as if she's making up her mind about something.

'Yes,' she says at last, a note of resignation in her voice. 'It's over now. That's why I'm not going back next week.' I can hear the distant chime of St Mary's church bells in the hush that follows. It's twelve o'clock. Ada will be wanting her lunch soon. I'll have to be super-quick with the salad, but I daren't leave the window yet in case I miss something important.

'Polly.' Ada's voice is firm but gentle. 'I need to ask you something. Don't get cross at me – it's only to set my mind at rest. And to give you the opportunity to tell the truth. I'll keep anything you tell me secret, I promise.'

'What do you mean? I've already told you the truth. What else do you need to ask?' Polly sounds exhausted. There's no doubt she's stressed to the eyeballs about something, but I'm no more convinced than Ada that we've heard the full story.

'I believe you've had a boyfriend, but I can't think of any reason why you'd hide a viola-playing student from your family. What was your real reason for keeping it secret?'

'There wasn't a reason – I just didn't think it worth mentioning, that's all. And now I know why: it was to stop everyone poking their noses in, like you're doing now. What does it matter, anyway? I told you – it's over now.'

'Yes, so you said, and I'm sorry it hasn't worked out. But I can't

175

help wondering why you didn't mention this… Sam, did you say? I wonder if you were ashamed of him for some reason?' Ada's keeping her voice calm but it's not working.

'Ashamed?' Polly sounds incredulous and exasperated. 'Why should I feel ashamed…' She pauses, her whole body stiffening. 'I see. I know what you're suggesting. And it's disgusting. How could you even think such a thing?'

'Think what?' Ada asks. It sounds an innocent question, and I can't tell if her tone is genuine or not without seeing her face.

'You think Max Silento was my boyfriend. Don't deny it, Gran, it's obvious. Why would you care so much? Why else would you prod and pry like this?' Ada seems lost for words for once, which is fortunate as Polly's on a roll.

'Let me make it nice and clear for you. Max Silento wasn't my boyfriend. Have you got that? And unless you want me to change my mind and go back to London after all you'd better stop talking about him. Hasn't that man caused this family enough problems without you making it worse?' Polly stands up and marches inside. I think it's safe to assume she's forgotten about lunch, and it's just as well. I don't know what excuse I'd have made to explain why I've not even started on the salad.

* * *

It's obvious Polly won't be joining us. Ada eats her salad quietly and then decides Burton Agnes is too far after all and she wants an afternoon reading her book in the garden.

'I've decided that I don't sit out there enough. Here we are in the middle of a glorious summer with a beautiful garden of our own. There's no need to go chasing around the county when we've got this on our doorstep. I'll sit in the shade outside the summerhouse and read my book about Russia, the one Theo gave me for my birthday. He went to a lot of trouble to get it, and the least I can do is read it. It will give us something to argue about over dinner.'

'I'm sure he'll love that,' I say. 'Do you want me to come with you? In case you need anything?'

'No, you take some time for yourself, Scarlet. Haven't you got a deadline coming up? I'm sure the extra time will be useful for your coursework. I'll take my bell and ring it if I need anything. I'm sure you'll hear me if you keep the window open.'

'All right, thanks, Ada, that'll be great,' I say. Although I won't be spending all afternoon working. Not if Polly's still in the house.

Once Ada's settled on the shady summerhouse terrace with her coffee, book and a bottle of water, I head inside and wash up before setting up my laptop on the table. Just in case. Then I go down and stand outside Polly's door. She's normally practising at this time of day but there's silence. I cross my fingers behind my back and knock. There's no answer so I take a deep breath, knock again and open the door a crack.

'Are you OK, Polly?' She's lying on her bed, staring at the ceiling. I thought there might be signs of tears on her face, but it's pale rather than damp and she looks calm enough.

'Oh, Scarlet, it's you.' Polly sits up and swings her legs over the bed, pushing straggles of hair off her face.

'You didn't come up for lunch and Ada told me not to get you. I wondered if you weren't feeling well. Have you eaten? There's some salad left if you'd like it. Ada's out in the garden with her book so she won't need me for a while.'

'D'you know, I think I might like something to eat,' says Polly. 'I'm sorry I didn't come up. Gran and I... we...'

'Had a bit of an argument?' I give her a grin, and she nods ruefully. 'She has her moments, doesn't she?' I say. 'Come on, I'll bring the salad down to the kitchen and we can have a chat if you like. Or not. I don't want to intrude.'

'You're not intruding. And thank you. A chat would be good.'

Polly wolfs down the food as if she's not eaten for a week; I suppose her morning swim must have made her hungry. I make us a cup of green tea when she's finished and we sit on the sofa, gazing out over the garden. Ada's immersed in her book and I remind myself to keep an eye on her. I don't want her knowing about this conversation.

'You don't have to tell me what the matter is, Polly. But it might help. I won't tell Ada anything if you'd rather I didn't.' I keep facing forwards, knowing it's easier to tell a secret if you're not looking at your audience. I take a sip of tea and wait for Polly to make up her mind. It doesn't take long.

'You know what that Hayley woman said the other day?' Polly plunges straight in as if she's been waiting for the chance to unburden herself and I'm taken aback, my thoughts racing to try and remember what Hayley said to us all as opposed to just me.

'From what I can remember, she said a lot of things,' I say, trying to keep my voice light. 'Which thing were you thinking of?'

'About me being Max Silento's girlfriend.'

'Oh. Yes, I remember that thing. But don't the police think it was your friend Jessie?'

'Yes, but Gran's got it into her head that it was me who was Max's girlfriend. She started asking why I'm not going back to London next week and was it because of a boyfriend. I told her yes it was and then she started asking if it was Max. I couldn't believe she'd think such a thing, and I got cross at her. More than cross. I lost it completely and stormed off.'

'Gosh.' I do my best impression of someone who doesn't know what to say. I know Ada didn't actually suggest Max was Polly's boyfriend, but I'm not about to question her version of events. I wait a suitable time before carrying on, as if needing time to digest this news. 'Is it true, then? About you having a boyfriend, I mean? And I didn't know you weren't going back to London. Is that true too?'

'Yes and no.' Polly sighs deeply, as if she's got the weight of the world on her shoulders. It all seems a bit out of proportion if her only problem is a boyfriend, and I wonder if Ada was right about her and Max after all.

'What do you mean, yes and no?'

'Well, I do have a boyfriend. I hadn't told anyone because I wasn't sure I wanted to carry on seeing him. While I was up here I decided I didn't, so I was going back early to break it off with him. I didn't want to do it by text – it wouldn't be fair. And that's why I didn't tell anyone about him. There wasn't any point if we were splitting up.' This sounds a lot more likely than Max being her boyfriend, but there's still a hooded look to her eyes that suggests she's not telling me the whole story.

'So why have you changed your mind?'

'It's complicated, Scarlet. And it's not really my secret to tell.'

'All right. As long as you're OK, that's what matters. But if it helps to talk, you know I can keep a secret.' I keep my voice calm. She's not going to tell me anything if she feels under pressure, but I'm sure she's on the verge of it. And as before, it's all she needs to hear to keep the floodgates open.

'It was for Jessie. That's why I stayed. And it's causing me so much stress. I need to get back to finish it with Sam. He keeps calling and texting and asking if he can come up here to see me, and I feel terrible putting him off all the time. I just need it to be over.'

'I'm sure you do, it sounds awful.' I pause for a moment. 'But what's it got to do with Jessie?'

'The police were right; it was her Max was seeing. I didn't know before he was… before he died. She called me soon after – it was the day we had coffee in the library, do you remember I had to leave to take a phone call? It was Jessie. She was in a complete mess about Max and she didn't want the police finding out. She hadn't told her parents about him and she knew they'd give her all kinds of grief if they found out she'd been dating an older man. She went off travelling round Scotland to get away and think things over but she was gutted when she heard Max had died. She really loved him. He'd promised to marry her – can you believe it? And can you believe that she believed him?'

'No, but people do strange things when they're in love,' I say. Like decide to change their hair colour. I wish I could ask her what colour Jessie's hair is but it would sound strange so I don't.

'I suppose they do,' Polly says. 'Anyway, Jessie was desperate to know what had happened to Max but she couldn't ask for herself so she asked me to stay here and find out for her. She keeps texting me about it but I haven't found out anything. I'm not a detective, how am I supposed to work out what's happened? I keep telling her it was natural causes but she won't believe it. I don't know what to do, Scarlet, it's driving me mad. All I want is for my life to be simple again.' Polly's worked herself up into a state now, and I go to the kitchen and pull off a piece of kitchen roll for her to blow her nose with.

'Thanks, Scarlet,' she sniffs. 'You're right, it does feel better to have told you. Even if it doesn't look it.' She half laughs and blows her nose again before turning towards me.

'I don't suppose you could help, could you?'

'Me?' I know exactly what she means but it won't do to let it show.

'Yes. You watch detective and spy shows on TV all the time with Gran, don't you? Would you know how to find out what happened to Max? If Hayley's right and the police aren't trying properly, perhaps you could find out something.'

'I don't know, Polly. What if there isn't anything to find out? What if it really was natural causes?'

'It wouldn't matter.' Polly's sounding more decisive now, and she pulls herself up straight on the sofa. 'If you did some snooping, you could tell me what you do and what you find out – or don't find out – and I could tell Jessie. It wouldn't solve the Sam problem, but at least it would keep Jess off my back. It would be such a help, Scarlet, please say you'll do it.'

'All right,' I say slowly. 'It might be fun to try. But don't tell Ada, I don't think she'd like it, do you?'

'No way! And who knows, maybe you'll even crack the case, as they say, and then it will all be over and I can go back to London and sort Sam out too.'

'Who knows, maybe I will.' I smile at her, knowing that after this conversation I'm a step closer to doing exactly that.

***

Ada enjoys a long afternoon with her book and I use the time to tie up some loose ends. A search on Facebook confirms Jessie is indeed a brunette. I record this and my conclusions regarding Polly in my book. I'm convinced she's still hiding something but it can't be about Max, or why would she have asked me to find out what happened to him? I decide to remove her from my personal list of suspects, which will save me some time. Unlike the police, who I'm sure won't have eliminated her yet. But it will only be a matter of time before they run Jessie to ground, and then they'll be focussing on other leads too. Like Emma. She's the only one left. She has to have something to do with Max Silento and his death, and it's time for me to work out what it is. If it weren't for her blonde hair, I'd have had her down as a possible candidate for Max's mystery lover, but Jessie has taken on that role in any case.

I spend some time on rail travel websites and find it would be hard to make a day trip to Beverley from anywhere further than Manchester or London. There aren't many direct trains to Hull, where you have to change to get here. Places like Birmingham and Liverpool involve too many different trains and Edinburgh's too far. It doesn't take me long to realise that this isn't going to help me to work out who the man on the bench might be. But there was something about Emma and Daniel's body language when they were with him which suggested they both know him well. Perhaps he's an old family friend or a distant relative. I'm sure he's connected to the murder in some way or other – why else would they both be sneaking around meeting him secretly? Perhaps Polly or Theo could tell me about him. I think I've quizzed Polly enough for one day. I'll have to ask Theo.

Talking to Theo is easier said than done. He's out a lot even when he's not at school, either with friends or playing sport. Or with his girlfriend, I suppose. She had dark hair too, and she works at the Beverley Arms. Have I missed something there? Could she have killed

Max Silento? She's a brunette and young, and if Jessie's anything to go by he seemed to like younger women. Maybe he made a pass at her and it all got out of hand and she killed him accidentally. I spend more time than I should considering the possibility before realising I'm letting my imagination run away with me and the whole idea's ridiculous. There are so many ways in which it wouldn't add up it's not true. I've spent all this time working methodically and finding new leads; I can't allow myself to be distracted by a whim now.

I can't think of any obvious opportunities to get Theo on his own before Sunday lunchtime at the earliest. This feels like a long time away, and I can't help but envy DI Twist, who can march into people's houses and ask questions any time she likes. She can work so much faster than me in this respect, although I suppose I've got the advantage of being able to eavesdrop on people's private conversations. I check the time and decide that whether she's ringing her bell or not, Ada would welcome a cup of tea. Sighing, I tell myself I'll have to be patient and get up to fill the kettle.

NINETEEN

I don't have to wait long after all. Ada and I are finishing our evening meal when we hear footsteps on the stairs. I pride myself on being able to recognise everyone in the family by their tread but it takes me longer than usual to work out who it is this time as Theo has modified his usual heavy thump in the interests of politeness.

'Hello, Theodore,' Ada says with a smile. 'To what do we owe the pleasure? And would you like some dessert? We were about to have some strawberries. There'll be enough for Theo, won't there, Scarlet?'

'Hi, Gran. No thanks, I'm eating later,' says Theo, and he perches on the arm of the sofa.

'You're looking very smart,' I say, as I take our plates into the kitchen. 'Are you going out tonight?' There's a pause while I pick up the glass bowls filled with strawberries and place them on the table.

'Um, well, yes and no,' Theo says, reminding me of Polly and her prevarications earlier this afternoon.

'What's that supposed to mean?' asks Ada.

'Well, I am supposed to be going out. It's Josh's birthday and he's having a barbecue but I'm stuck for a ride. Mum just called – there's been an accident on the A164 and she's stuck in traffic, and Dad's working late on his deadline. Everyone else has already left and I can't get a lift now, so I was wondering…' He trails off, looking at me from under his eyebrows.

'If Scarlet could give you a lift,' Ada finishes for him. 'Just spit it out and ask, Theo. There's no need to beat about the bush.'

'I don't know,' I say, looking towards Ada. 'How far is it? I'll need to be back for Ada's bath and so on.'

'It's a little way past Driffield. About half an hour each way, I suppose, maybe a bit more,' says Theo. 'Would it be too far? I don't want to mess up your evening, Gran. It doesn't matter if I don't go, it's only a barbecue.' He's trying his best but it's obvious he wants to go to this party and I wonder if his girlfriend will be there.

'I'll be all right on my own for an hour,' says Ada. 'I'm quite happy to carry on with my book and I'm sure Scarlet won't be back too late. Although you can't start using her as a taxi service, Theo, as I'm sure you know.'

'I won't,' says Theo, a wide grin on his face. 'I've got my test booked in six weeks' time anyway, so I'll never need to ask again.'

'If you pass,' Ada reminds him.

'Of course I'll pass, Gran. Then it'll be me chauffeuring you around instead.'

'We'll see about that,' says Ada. She loves a bit of banter with Theo and I know she'd let him drive her any day.

'Give me ten minutes and I'll be down,' I say. 'I'll load the dishwasher before we go and get your gran settled for the evening.'

'Thanks, Scarlet. Thanks, Gran,' says Theo, already half way to the stairs. 'You're the business.'

'That's kind of you, dear,' says Ada as I clear the dishes. 'It's not your job to chauffeur Theo around, and I'll make sure he doesn't take advantage of your kindness. There's no guarantee he'll pass his test and we don't want him assuming you'll help him out whenever he wants.'

'It's fine,' I say. 'I'm happy to help any time, as long as you don't mind.' And especially when I've been racking my brains for a way to get Theo on his own.

* * *

When I first came to live in this house I couldn't believe the number of vehicles on the drive. I've never been interested in cars. Kids at school would talk about different models and what they wanted when they grew up but I can only describe them in terms of size and colour, and I've never seen the need to know any more about them than that. I haven't lived anywhere with a drive before. Lena and Oskar had a car; it was a little white one, usually dirty, and they kept it on the road. Oskar used it for work and he was always complaining he could never find a space for it. He often ended up leaving it two or three streets away and then rushing out to move it as soon as a place came free outside the house.

The Rosewoods don't have that problem. They have a huge drive with plenty of space for a big blue car for when they all go out together, a small white one with a soft top which Emma likes to drive to work in the summer and a middle-sized grey one for the winter, with enough room for Theo's sports bags. Then there's a little black one for Theo while he's learning to drive. They didn't trust him with any of the others, although I reckon he's hoping to have a go in Emma's convertible at some point. Even though they have four cars Daniel hardly ever drives any of them except when they go on holiday or one of the children needs a lift. He cycles to work, which seems mad to me with all those motors at his disposal.

When I came to live here Ada said I'd have to learn to drive so we could go places together. She paid for me to do an intensive course and I learnt quickly. I passed my test after only three months, and I got full marks in the theory test. I was proud of that. I especially liked the bit where you have to spot the hazards. I've got exceptionally sharp eyes, Ada says, and it's true. It comes in useful for snooping, and it'll be an important skill in the future. She bought us a medium-sized red car with a big boot for her wheelchair. It's automatic, which I like. I don't see the point in changing gears if you don't have to.

185

Theo's waiting on the bench by the front door when I come down, car keys in hand. He bounds out of the door, thanking me profusely as we go.

'Thanks for this, Scarlet. I promise I won't ask again, I know Gran doesn't like me taking advantage.'

'It's all right, you're not. When have you ever asked me for a lift before? And it's nice to get out of the house anyway, I've been cooped up indoors all day.'

'Cool – I'm glad to be of service, as Gran would say,' Theo says as he buckles his seatbelt. 'Shall I put the address in the satnav?'

'Sure. It's near Driffield, isn't it? You can put it in while we're driving, I know which road to start on.' Theo consults his phone and taps around on the satnav while I get us onto the Driffield road. He carries on looking at his phone for a while and then taps some more on the car display to connect it to the media system. It's not long before his choice of music is filling our ears, and I have to admit it makes a change from Classic FM, which is Ada's choice of entertainment.

'That's better,' he says, pushing the seat back to make room for his long legs. 'Doesn't Gran's classical stuff drive you crazy?'

'I've got used to it. It's not so bad. It's the adverts I can't stand. They're always on about insurance or equity release, whatever that is.' I need to steer the conversation onto a track where I can ask him about the man on the bench. I've not had as much time as I'd expected to plan for this and I've been racking my brains for a way in ever since Theo asked for his lift. It's not easy; I can hardly ask him if there are any old men in the family who Emma and Daniel might be meeting in secret. I decide I'd better keep the conversation going while I'm thinking. It won't help me if he resorts to his phone for company.

'You must be looking forward to the end of term. What will you be doing with your time? Sailing? Tennis?'

'Yeah, if I can get lifts to the coast.' He turns to me with a grin. 'Only joking. I'll sail with Dad and play tennis in town.'

'And there's your trip to Scotland. I guess that's coming up soon.'

'Yeah, it'll be cool seeing Grannie and Gramps. And the sailing's great up there, even if the weather's terrible half the time.'

'Don't your grandparents ever come to stay here?' It seems odd to me, only seeing grandparents once a year, but what do I know about grandparents anyway?

'No, they've got a farm with lots of animals so they can't go on holiday too often, and they love Scotland so we all go there.' Theo doesn't seem bothered by this arrangement and I suppose it's what he's always been used to, so he wouldn't. And he's got his other grandparent living with him so he's hardly deprived of family.

'Have you ever been out to visit them in Australia?' This is going well, and I can feel the conversation moving securely in the direction I want it to.

'No, Mum doesn't like flying. We Skype them sometimes so we've seen a bit of the farm. It's not very different from here, to be honest. I'd love to go one day but Mum and Dad don't seem keen on the idea. They say it's better to explore places that are more different from home, like South America or Africa. Maybe they're right – what do you reckon?'

'I don't know. I've never thought much about it. What does Polly say?'

'Oh, she's not into travel. Unless it's to do with music. She's not even bothered learning to drive or she could have given me a lift tonight. I suppose it didn't help with her boarding in Manchester and then moving to London. There's no point in having a car in London, is there?'

'I suppose not,' I say. The satnav's telling me to prepare to turn right and we pause to let it repeat the instruction twice before we're on the new road.

'Do you have any other relatives? In Scotland, perhaps? Or London? That's where Ada used to live, isn't it?' I don't think the question's unreasonable, coming as it does after Theo's talk of his summer holiday.

'No.' There's no hint of surprise or suspicion in his voice. Good.

'You've got a small family, haven't you? Not like some you see, with aunts and uncles and cousins all over the place.'

'I suppose we have.' He doesn't sound at all interested, which I suppose is a good thing.

'I've only got a small one too. It was just my mum and me until she died. And now there's only me.'

'Oh.' Theo's surprised, and why shouldn't he be? I don't make a habit of talking about my family. 'I'm sorry about your mum,' he says after an awkward pause. 'That must have been hard.'

'Yes it was, but it's OK, it happened a long time ago.' I don't want to talk about it, but it suits my purpose so I keep going, making it up as I go along. 'I lived with my gran but she died a few years back. It was looking after her that made me want to work with the elderly.'

'Oh, right, cool.' Theo's showing no sign of being interested, but I don't care.

'I've got a godmother, but she was a lot older than my mum and we fell out of touch. It's a shame – it's good to have older people in the family, don't you think?'

'I suppose so,' says Theo. 'I wouldn't know, there's only my grandparents in ours. The only other old people I know are teachers. And the coaches at the cricket club. I never know what to say to old people anyway, except for Gran, of course, she's different.' There we are. There's no need to pursue the conversation any further, and I'm about to change the subject to a topic he might find more interesting when Theo drops his bombshell.

'I don't suppose godparents are the sort of thing people have when their parents aren't married. Were yours? Married?'

'Umm… well, no, they weren't. My mum wanted me christened though, so I suppose that's why I had one.'

'What about your dad?' Theo's phone beeps and he starts tapping a text, paying minimal attention to my answer.

'I didn't know him. It was just Mum and me. She didn't like to talk about him.' At least this bit is true, and it's good to feel back on more solid ground.

'Oh, right. Like Polly,' Theo says absent-mindedly, still tapping, his matter-of-fact tone at jarring odds with the implications of his words.

'What do you mean, like Polly?'

'Well, she doesn't know who her dad is either.'

'Sorry, Theo, you're losing me. Isn't Daniel Polly's dad?'

'No.' Theo laughs, looking up again now his message has been sent. 'Of course not. He looks nothing like her for a start, does he?'

'Well, no, but I thought maybe she took after your mum's side of the family.'

'She probably does, but we're only half siblings, Polly and me. I can't believe you didn't know – weird.' We're interrupted at this point by the satnav, and I can see from the display that there's not far to go.

'I don't suppose there's been a reason for anyone to mention it,' I say once the mechanical voice is quiet again. 'I guess it's not really my business, is it?' I turn and give Theo a brief smile, to show I've not taken any offence, but it doesn't seem to have occurred to him that I might, and he ploughs straight on, filling me in on the family history.

'Mum met Dad when Polly was small – about one, I think. They got together and Dad adopted Polly; it's why she's called Rosewood even though she used to be called Stevens. And Mum and Dad aren't married, even though Mum changed her name too. She doesn't believe in marriage, but she liked the idea of everyone having the same name. She says she didn't want to feel left out. Crazy, huh? My mate Ben's parents are married but his mum kept her old name, and my mum's the opposite. Oh, look, we're here.' The satnav confirms we have reached our destination and Theo hops out, managing to wave to his friends and shout a thank you and goodbye to me all at the same time. He goes into the house without a backward glance, leaving me parked on the road with my mouth open and my brain frozen in shock. I'm still sitting there when he comes rushing out of the house and opens the passenger door.

'Oh, great, you're still here – is the satnav playing up or something?' he says, reaching down into the footwell. 'I forgot my bag – tell Mum I'll be staying over. I'll get a lift home in the morning.'

'Sure,' I say. I don't know how I manage to make my voice sound normal, but I do. I reach forward to programme the satnav to hide my face, which I've not had time to rearrange, and he's gone, his mind already on the party. I watch him as he returns to the house, a tow-headed boy, as the poets might say, without a care in the world. I'm still preoccupied with hair colour, I can't help it. As I drive slowly home, not wanting my distracted brain to risk an accident, I ponder this. Theo's as blond as his parents, and I don't know why I didn't question Polly's brown hair earlier. There's no way Dan and Emma could have produced a child with her hair. It must have come from her father, and I wonder who he might have been. A one-night stand, perhaps, or a ditched boyfriend. It's hardly likely to matter now.

TWENTY

What is it about the police and Saturdays? I know they don't have weekends off like other people, I've seen enough detective dramas on TV to have learnt they have to keep going when there's a big investigation on, but I didn't think we'd qualify for another weekend visit. Nonetheless, when I hear the doorbell ringing repeatedly late on Saturday afternoon, I feel a sense of déjà vu as I run down the stairs. Ada's in the garden with the rest of the family, playing croquet before setting up the barbecue, and I've been doing some coursework while it's quiet. I tell myself not to be silly, it's probably one of Theo's friends or yet another delivery for Emma, but when I open the door I see my instincts were correct. There they are, DI Twist and her faithful companion, Sergeant Carter.

'I'm sorry to disturb your afternoon,' she says, although she doesn't sound sorry in the least. There's no point in pretending she isn't so I don't waste time on pleasantries.

'Who do you want to see this time?' I must sound abrupt, and I know it won't help. 'Sorry, I didn't mean to sound rude. It's just that I was—'

'Expecting someone else?' asks DI Twist.

'Not exactly. It was a surprise, that's all. Do you want to come in? Everyone's outside, but I can round them up for you if you like.' Now

I sound like a sheepdog. It must be nerves; I don't usually say stupid things like this. I tell myself to pull myself together and try to calm myself down by imagining myself in DI Twist's shoes. She's dressed for work but with a subtle weekend twist. She's got a T-shirt underneath her jacket rather than a buttoned shirt, and loafers rather than heels are peeping out from her linen trousers. No open toes, despite the hot day – I don't suppose they'd be suitable for chasing criminals.

'That would be helpful, thank you. We'll wait here while you get them,' she says, coming inside and sitting on the bench in the hall. She immediately fixes her gaze on the painting on the opposite wall. It's a seascape, chosen by Emma, who says she likes to look at it when she comes out of her bedroom each morning. DI Twist seems to like it too, although her sergeant's more interested in whatever app he's got open on his phone.

There's no apparent need for further conversation at this point so I call the others in and we all troop upstairs. I suppose the terrace isn't the best place for a police interview, even if the nearest neighbours are half a mile away behind a thick hedge. Once we're sitting down, DI Twist repeats her apology.

'Please don't worry, we're happy to help if it means your investigation is nearing its completion,' says Ada. 'We've not enjoyed being involved in a murder inquiry, and the sooner it's over, the better. But perhaps you've come to tell us you've brought matters to a conclusion?'

'No, we haven't. It's far from over, I'm afraid,' says DI Twist, and I can feel a tension in the air that wasn't there before. I'm part of it, I know; I hadn't realised how desperately I wanted her to tell us they'd decided Max died from natural causes after all.

'We've uncovered new information that requires further investigation and we have some questions for you all.' I'd have expected a reaction to this, perhaps from Daniel, with his usual bewilderment at why they're here in the first place, but there's a silence. Even Theo doesn't seem to have the energy to ask what's going on. Maybe it's the heat.

'Sergeant Carter has been leading this area of the investigation,' says DI Twist, 'so I'll hand over to him for the time being.' She nods in his direction, and I see she already has her neat little electronic tablet out ready for her turn at note-taking. It's one of the latest models and I'm sure the police service won't have provided it for her. She must be a bit of a tech junkie like me.

'Yes.' The sergeant leans forward slightly, glancing at his notebook to remind himself of what it is he wants to ask. 'I believe it's the... er, the older members of the family that our questions will be most relevant to. There's no particular need for the younger people to stay, is there, boss?' DI Twist shakes her head, although she's looking with more than a hint of challenge at Polly.

'No, but we may need them later, so it would be wiser to stay put for now.'

'Very well,' says the sergeant. 'And we'll try not to take up more of your Saturday than is necessary.' He smiles at Ada, maybe thinking he'll win her over with his boyish charm. I could tell him not to waste his time, but it's more fun to watch him trying. She stares back at him stonily, leaving him with no option but to plough on with his questions.

'We've reason to believe Mr Silento was married,' he begins. He doesn't appear to have finished his sentence, but he's stopped in his tracks by Polly.

'Married? No, that can't be right. He was engaged, not married. To that woman – Hayley, wasn't it?' She looks round the room as if for confirmation.

'It's true that Mr Silento was engaged to Miss Harper,' says Sergeant Carter. 'But if he had gone on to marry her he would have been committing bigamy.'

'I don't understand,' says Polly. 'What are you talking about?'

'Stop interrupting and let the sergeant explain, Polly,' says Emma, irritation in her voice. There's something else there too, but I can't pin it down. I'll have to work it out later.

'Mr Silento married over twenty years ago, not long after he graduated from his music college. To a young woman named Phoebe

Johnson. A marriage certificate was found amongst a dossier of papers which he'd left in the hands of his solicitor. They've only recently come to light, and we are keen to know what became of this woman. The solicitor is concerned as well, of course, as she may have some claim on his estate.'

'And you think she might have had something to do with his death,' says Theo, proud of himself for having put two and two together for once.

'We can't say at present, but we are exploring all leads,' says the sergeant, resorting to classic police speak, and I'm on the verge of a hysterical giggle at the well-worn phrases, which I didn't suspect real detectives ever used.

'So how can we help you with this one? There must be other people better placed than us who can help you. Mr Silento's friends and relations and so forth?' Ada's tone suggests she can't imagine how we could possibly be of any assistance, but I know her too well not to be able to detect a hint of uncertainty in her voice. This isn't good, and I wonder if anyone else has picked up on it.

'I can assure you, we have pursued more obvious avenues already,' DI Twist interjects sharply. 'However, none of Mr Silento's acquaintances can tell us anything about her, and we're having difficulty in tracking down her family. This leaves us with limited options, as I'm sure you'll understand.'

'I suppose Johnson is a rather common name,' Theo says, apparently forgetting there are two detectives sitting in the room questioning his family.

'Quite,' says DI Twist. I wonder if her sergeant's going to be relegated to note-taking duties again, but she looks over at him and he takes this as a signal to continue.

'We're asking everyone who came into contact with Mr Silento while he was in Beverley if they have any knowledge of Phoebe Johnson,' he says. 'We believe she may have been a music student at the same college as Mr Silento, but none of the colleges in London have records going back that far. The marriage took place in a register office in London, and her occupation was given as student. We're looking through old birth certificates to try to find her, but it's a long job, as I'm sure you can imagine.' He smiles apologetically round the room, perhaps hoping for a little sympathy for his herculean task, but none's forthcoming, and we all look at him blankly.

'Does the name mean anything to any of you?' he asks. There's a muffled chorus of noes, shaking heads and puzzled expressions, and the sergeant looks over at his boss.

'Please think very carefully,' says DI Twist, looking at Emma, Daniel and Ada in turn. 'We are asking you to think back over twenty years, and we don't necessarily expect you to remember events from that time immediately.' She's speaking calmly and quietly, but there's a hint of steel in her voice, just to let us know she's on the case. There's an uneasy silence, during which no one seems able to meet her eye.

'I appreciate that one of you may have information you'd prefer to keep private. If that's the case, please contact me soon. It won't look good if anyone here later turns out to know something they haven't told us.' She lets the half-threat hang in the air, and it seems everyone in the room is trying to avoid her eyes. Except for Theo, who's looking enthralled by the whole thing.

'But what if she's dead?' he asks, apparently unable to contain himself. 'She might be, mightn't she? How could it matter then what anyone has or hasn't told you?'

'Everything's important in a murder investigation,' DI Twist says firmly. 'Everything. Even a brief acquaintance or a single word can be significant in ways you can't begin to imagine. We've not found any reason to dismiss the significance of Mr Silento's presence near your house in the days leading up to his murder. And our investigations regarding the CCTV footage are still very much underway. In the light of this situation, we must ask you all to stay in the area. I hope you've not got any immediate holiday plans? It's important you all remain available for the time being.'

'We always go to Scotland in the summer, but we're not due to go for another three weeks,' says Daniel. 'But Polly was planning to return to London on Monday.'

'I daresay we could allow that,' says DI Twist, turning towards Polly. 'We're already liaising with the Met, and they could send someone to talk to you if we need to ask you any further questions.'

'It's all right,' says Polly. 'I can stay here a bit longer. It's not important.' I'm careful not to meet her eye, but I know she'll be relieved to have a reason to stay put without having to think up an excuse of her own. Emma permits herself a smile when she hears this, but DI Twist's next words soon wipe it from her face.

'Please don't underestimate the importance of honesty in this matter. I would urge you all most strongly to tell me anything that could be of relevance to the case. If there's something you'd rather share confidentially, please contact me at the station. I'll leave my details with you now.' She gets up, taking a sheaf of little cards out of her pocket, and goes round the room, handing one to each of us. We're all sitting there staring at them as she heads towards the stairs, sergeant in tow, saying they'll see themselves out, thank you.

* * *

The stunned silence which follows is broken by Theo's long whistle.

'Wow!' he says. 'It's like being in a movie, isn't it? Or one of those TV shows you like to watch, Gran. I think I'll keep this as a souvenir – I've never had access to a detective's private line before.'

'You'll do no such thing,' Ada says sharply. 'If you want my advice, Theo, you'll put it in the bin. I've a good mind to find out who that young woman's boss is and lodge a complaint about harassment.'

'Don't be ridiculous,' Daniel says, and we all look up in surprise at the anger in his voice. 'They're asking lots of people the same questions, not just us; you of all people should know better than to stir things up. You'd only draw attention to us, which is the last thing we need, as you well know.' He stares meaningfully at his mother, who merely holds up her card, waiting for someone to relieve her of it. I jump up and take it from between her fingers, noting Emma's avoidance of Daniel's gaze and the look of astonishment on Theo and Polly's faces.

'Dad? What's going on?' Polly's voice is wobbly, and I expect she's wondering whether it's time to come clean to the police about Jessie's involvement with Max.

'Nothing's going on,' says Emma firmly, getting up and collecting cards from the rest of the family. 'But we're all fed up with this constant questioning. It's getting on everyone's nerves, and who can blame us? We mustn't let it get to us, must we, Ada? Families need to stick together at times like this, don't they?' They exchange a glance, but I can't tell if it's conspiratorial or the opposite.

'Let's go back outside,' says Daniel, keen to change the subject. 'I think it's time to light the barbecue, don't you?'

'But Dad!' Theo says. 'You can't just pretend none of this happened! Why do the police keep coming back here? What's this murder got to do with us? Don't you want to know why they won't leave us alone?'

'We know why they won't leave us alone. It's because of me,' Polly blurts out. 'If it weren't for him teaching at the college and my playing in the festival, they'd never have bothered themselves with us. That stupid phone app – he must have gone to all sorts of places around town. There must be hundreds of people he could have been visiting. And thousands of people who look like the woman on the CCTV. If it weren't for me they'd never have come here in the first place. It's all my fault, and now I don't know what to do about it.' She bursts into tears and rushes from the room, closely followed by Emma.

'Now look what you've done,' says Ada. 'Leave it alone, Theo, can't you see you're upsetting everyone with your ghoulish interest in this unfortunate man's death? It's only a matter of time before they tell us it was natural causes and our lives can all go back to normal.' She glares at Theo, who has the grace to look abashed.

'Sorry, Gran. I didn't mean to upset Polly. Shall I go and say sorry to her?'

'No, leave her alone. Your mother's with her and she'll calm her down. Give her a hug when she comes out and don't mention this horrible business again. Do you think you can manage that?' Her voice has softened now; she's never able to stay cross with Theo for long.

'Come on, Mother,' says Daniel. 'We'll go and deal with the barbecue. Scarlet, would you mind giving Theo a hand with the drinks? I think we could all do with something cool.' Always the expert at defusing an awkward situation, Daniel guides Ada's wheelchair towards the lift, and Theo opens the fridge in search of cold drinks.

'It's past twelve o'clock so I guess it's beer for Dad and white wine for Mum and Ada,' he says. 'Coke for you and me – do you think Polly will be OK with sparkling water?'

'I'm sure that'll be fine,' I say, getting glasses from the cupboard. 'You pour, I'll get the ice.' The conversation's stilted, which I guess is to be expected, and I cast around for a less contentious topic.

'Are you planning to sail this—' I'm interrupted by a beep from my phone. Only a very small number of people have my number and most of them are in this house. I have a good idea who the message might be from but if I'm right it won't do to let Theo know.

'Do you want to get that?' Theo asks.

'No, it can wait. It won't be anything important. Like I was saying, are you planning to go sailing this weekend?'

'Yeah, hopefully. If Dad's not too tired. He was working till all hours last night. He wasn't even up when I got back this morning. I think he only woke up about an hour ago.'

'Of course!' I say, picking up a tray. 'How was the party?' We carry on in this vein until we join Daniel and Ada on the patio. Emma and Polly join us soon after, Theo gives Polly her a hug, and we all do an excellent job of pretending everything's fine.

* * *

My time's my own on Saturday afternoons, so Ada doesn't comment when I leave the garden, saying I've got some shopping to do. I checked my phone in the toilet half way through lunch, and, as I suspected, there was a message from Hayley. I suggested meeting her at the café at three o'clock, and this gives me time to practise using the record function on my phone and to check it still works when the phone's in my bag. When I get to the café I find Hayley standing outside, looking annoyed.

'It's full,' she says, her voice tight with irritation. 'I don't suppose anywhere else will be any better. I'd forgotten how busy it would be on a Saturday. We'll have to go back to my room, although it seems a shame on a sunny day like this.'

'We could go on the Westwood,' I suggest. 'It's a nice place for a walk – have you been up there yet?'

'No, and I'm not about to in these shoes.' I don't suppose she was planning on country walks when she packed to come up here, and her high-heeled sandals wouldn't be happy on grass even when it's bone-dry like today.

'Oh, yes, sorry. OK, I guess we'd best go to the hotel.' There's no point arguing with her and we backtrack through the shoppers to the Beverley Arms. As we walk through the courtyard, Hayley stops a waiter and asks for coffee to be sent to the room. It's a nice big one, with a sofa and chairs set around a low table.

'I asked for a room with a terrace, but the only one free was the room Max slept in, and I couldn't stay there,' Hayley says with a shudder. 'I don't like first-floor rooms anyway. I'm sure the locks on those outside doors aren't as secure as the electronic ones inside.'

'I'm sure you're right,' I say, and I put my bag on the floor, as close to Hayley's chair as I dare. Not that I need worry – she's far too busy with her own belongings, hanging up her jacket in the wardrobe and checking her phone before putting it on the dressing table. There's a knock on the door and she opens it to let in a waiter with a tray of coffee. We wait in silence as he puts it on the table, neither of us having much to say we want to be overheard.

'The police came to see me this morning,' Hayley says. 'Do pour, Scarlet, I expect it's ready now.' I push the plunger down carefully and pour coffee into the classy modern white cups. They'd look nice in Ada's kitchen, but she says plain white is common and she prefers mugs now her fingers are stiff. I know Hayley's waiting for a reaction but I make her wait while I add milk and sugar, stirring mine slowly before sitting back in my chair.

'Yes, they came to see us too. Just before lunch. They seem to have had a busy morning.'

'It's not funny, Scarlet.' I hadn't meant it to sound like a joke, but I suppose it did come out that way.

'No, sorry. Of course it isn't. It's interesting, though, isn't it?'

'Interesting? It's scandalous! After all the time I spent trying to convince them that the photo I found is important, they turn up and say it could be significant after all. And not because she's an old girlfriend. Oh no, she's his wife! His wife! How *dare* he?' Having held it together till now, Hayley's finally surrendered her cool composure.

'I—' But she doesn't need any encouragement. I'm clearly here to be an audience, not a participant.

'Paulo was right all along. It was my money he was after. How could it be anything else, when he was keeping so much from me?'

'I know, it's unbelievable.' I sip my coffee and wait for her to calm down so I can find out if she's got anything useful to tell me.

'And that attorney of his! Do you know, we actually sat in his office, drawing up our wills? And all the time, he knew – the attorney knew – that Max was married! What a rat!' I've never heard anyone say 'attorney' in real life before; now I really feel like I'm in a TV show.

'I suppose he might not have known. He may not have seen the documents themselves. If they were in an envelope, I mean.' I suggest meekly. 'Did you sign the wills?'

'What?' The change of topic gives Hayley pause for thought, and she reaches for her cup at last. 'No, we didn't. We were only discussing them. He – Mr Morris, the lawyer – was going to write something down for us to look at the next time we saw him. And Max said he might have a final detail to add. Mr Morris wasn't too happy about that; he said it would have to be done as a codicil. I didn't know what the fuss was about; we wouldn't have needed them for long, anyway. We were planning to get new ones drawn up once we'd settled in New York.'

'So Max might have had another will?' I ask. 'Do you think it might be important? If this... this wife is still alive?'

'I can't imagine, and I don't want to,' Hayley says, a new air of certainty in her voice. She drains her cup and reaches for the cafetière. The caffeine seems to be doing her good, and she sits up straighter once she's added more milk to her cup. 'Do you know, Scarlet, I'm beginning to think I had a lucky escape. If Max hadn't got himself murdered, I could have ended up committing bigamy, with this woman lurking in the background waiting to cause trouble. People do that, you know, stay hidden for years and then turn up when they fancy it. She could have seen Max marrying me and then sold her story to the papers. Can you imagine?' It all seems rather unlikely to me, but I don't say so, and she doesn't give me a chance to anyway. 'There might even be a child – who knows? Someone who'd crawl out of the woodwork claiming to be Max's abandoned son or daughter. It doesn't bear thinking about.' She finally pauses to sip her coffee, giving me time to ask a question.

'What will you do now, Hayley?'

'I think I may go back to London. Even if they do find out who killed Max, I'm not sure I care now. Why should I? A secret wife, another girl on the side, maybe a child lurking in the background, lies left, right and centre. I thought I wanted to know what happened to him, but I don't. He was a rat, and I'm well shot of him. I should have listened to my friends all along.'

'And I suppose it will save you having to change your hair,' I say with a smile.

'True – although I still like the idea of a change. A new me. One who doesn't fall for lying toads.' Hayley puts down her cup decisively. 'I'm sorry, Scarlet. I feel as if I'm letting you down. We agreed to work together on this and I won't be able to do that now. I hope you won't mind too much.'

'No, it's all right,' I say, trying to look understanding rather than relieved. I don't want anything more to do with this woman, and I was starting to wonder why she was telling me so much anyway. Doesn't she have any friends to talk to? Maybe they're all in America and still asleep. At any rate, I'm glad not to have to think of a way to stop seeing her. There's nothing more she's going to be able to help me with, and the last thing I need is her telling the police I've been spying on my own family.

'You've been great, Scarlet,' she says as she gets up. 'Thanks for your help.'

'You're welcome,' I say, wondering if I'm picking up her American speech. 'It will probably turn out to have been a heart attack anyway.'

'Probably,' she agrees, apparently as keen to get rid of me now as I am to leave. 'Goodbye, Scarlet.' I notice there's no suggestion about keeping in touch. I don't suppose Hayley's the type to make hollow gestures, and she'll be relieved I haven't mentioned it either. Although I wouldn't have minded having one of her handbags.

I walk home slowly, checking the recording on my phone and finding out it's worked perfectly. Not that there's much use for it – Hayley didn't tell me anything new. When I get home, Ada's sitting by the window doing her crossword and I make us a cup of tea. While I'm waiting for the kettle to boil I put my hand into my back pocket and find something inside. It's DI Twist's card. I'd slipped it in there absent-mindedly when I was helping Theo with the drinks. I look at it – DI Sharon Twist. Ah, that explains it. I'd wondered the first time she said it how she came to have a name like Ronnie. I don't blame her. Sharon sounds like something out of *EastEnders*; no one's called Sharon nowadays. I wonder how she came by the shortened version and when. I've never had a nickname, and you can't shorten Scarlet to much except Scar, and that's a horrible name. I flick the card against my fingers a couple of times before putting it back in my pocket, and as I pour the boiling water onto the tea bags I wonder if anyone else has kept hold of theirs, and if she gave one to Hayley too.

I'm relieved not to have to see Hayley again. She was becoming far too ready to share her intimate details with me. I'd never expected someone so successful to be so emotionally needy, and I can see why she might not have anyone else to talk to, even allowing for the timezone issue. I bet the only people who really listen to her are on her payroll. It's strange to think of her with a musician. I'd have thought a rich lawyer would be more her type. Although she wasn't very impressed with the one who drew up her will. Wait a minute – Hayley *did* tell me something new. I was so busy being annoyed by her that I didn't notice it at the time. Max wanted to add something to his will. I don't know much about wills, but I'm willing to bet he was going to add in a new beneficiary. And that it was someone in this house.

TWENTY-ONE

Ada didn't lose her marbles, as she liked to put it. She told me her foolproof plan, and to be fair, it sounded like it could work. I knew about air bubbles already. And I knew about morphine, of course. I just hadn't connected the two in that context before. And I definitely understood Ada not wanting to lose her mind. I've looked after enough people with dementia to know how awful it is. She said I'd be doing the whole family a favour, not just her, and I had to agree. She had plenty of morphine from when her husband had died of cancer and she showed me a big syringe for the air and where to put it between her toes, where no one would think to look. And she showed me her will, ready to be signed, where it said I could stay in the house for ever. She said I'd know when the time came. It would be the day when she didn't know who I was. Then we got on with our lives.

I almost went back to being as happy as before she asked me. It felt weird, knowing I could end up killing someone. But I told myself I'd have to get used to that if I wanted to be a spy. I didn't have a choice anyway, unless I wanted to go back to a dingy rented room with no family and no future. And with Ada staying as sharp as she did, I let myself believe she'd die of something else and I wouldn't have to do it after all. I passed my AS levels in record time and Ada helped me apply for an online degree course. I couldn't believe how much easier it was to learn than when I was at school, and Ada said it must be because I was happy. I'd forgotten how much I enjoyed maths, and computing changes so quickly, everyone's in the same position whether they've had four years out of school or not. It suited me not to have to go to a 'proper' university; it was a relief not to have other students around wanting to go clubbing and poking their noses into my business. Ada encouraged me to use the library, she said it was good for me to have a change of scene, but she bought me a laptop of my own so I could work at home too. It felt like my life was sorted at last. Then everything changed.

It was the week before the festival. Polly was home, stressy and practising all the time, and Emma was acting weirdly too, all uptight. I assumed it was because of Polly. They get on all right most of the time, but when Polly's stressed, Emma is too — they've always been like that. I didn't say anything to Ada about it, but she wasn't her usual self either, and poor Theo got his head bitten off every time he made a joke about Polly's scales. It was getting to the point when I couldn't wait for the festival to be over and life to get back to normal when Ada paused in the middle of doing her crossword one morning and looked at me, as if sizing me up.

'Scarlet.'

'Yes?'

'There's something I need you to do for me.' This sounded bad. The last time she needed me to do something for her was the day she asked me to kill her. I put my book down and waited.

'It's about our arrangement. You know the one I mean.'

'Yes, I know.' We only had one arrangement, and it wasn't one I was likely to forget about. 'It's not time, is it? There's no way you're...'

'Dotty?' She smiled. 'No, Scarlet. It's not time, as you put it, but I need to alter it — add to it, in fact.'

'Add to it?' I had no idea what she could mean.

'Yes.' She paused, as if searching for the right way to put something. 'I suppose you could say we're going to need a practice run.'

'A practice run? But how—'

'Stop repeating everything I say and let me finish, Scarlet. How can I explain if you keep interrupting?'

'I'm sorry, Ada. Go on.'

'I want you to kill someone else first.'

'What?' It was all I could think of to say; my brain wouldn't work properly.

'I need you to kill someone else first, with the same method. It's for the sake of the family, the whole family. A man is threatening us, and if we don't get rid of him he'll destroy everything we have here. There'll be no Rosewood family, no house, no future here for you, or for anyone else for that matter. I'd do it myself, but I'm stuck in this chair, so I'm asking you to do it for me. For the family. For all of us.' Ada stopped at last but I couldn't speak; my mind was frozen with shock.

'And it will be good practice for when the time comes for me,' she added. For a moment, I thought she had gone dotty after all, but she'd filled in half the crossword already so she couldn't have done. She was serious; she wanted me to kill someone. I was still having difficulty finding the words, but I knew what to say to her last comment.

'Don't be ridiculous, I don't need practice! You've always said it's a foolproof method, so don't pretend it's for my benefit. If you want me to kill someone just say so.' I couldn't help myself. I'd never spoken to Ada in this way before, but I couldn't believe she was asking me to commit murder for her. 'Who is it anyway? And what can he do to us that's so bad you want him dead?'

'I can't tell you that, Scarlet. It's best if you know as little as possible. The important thing is for you to trust me to know what's best for all of us. If there was another way, I wouldn't ask you, you know that. But if you want to keep everything I've given you – your home, your family, your future – you'll do it. And I really do think it will be good preparation for when you join MI6.' She smiled determinedly as she said this, and I couldn't help but smile nervously back. I couldn't afford to upset her, I knew that much, even then.

'It is foolproof, remember,' she continued. 'And I've worked out how you can get to him. It'll be a chance for you to try out some of the tactics we've talked about. No one will think it's anything but natural causes; you'll be completely safe.'

206

'What we've planned is nothing like killing a perfect stranger and you know it. Whoever it is won't drink a shot of morphine for me and then lie down nicely ready to be injected with air. And where will he be? How would I get there? And how do you know the police wouldn't work out it was murder? I could end up in prison.'

'Yes, I know that. It's very unlikely, but a risk, nonetheless. Look, Scarlet, I know I've no right to ask so much of you but I don't know what else to do. If you can't help me, I'll have no alternative but to start making plans for a very different future. And I'd have to give you notice, of course. If he's not put out of action, this family will come under the very worst sort of attack within a matter of days.'

'Days? How is that even possible? What's it about, Ada? Can't you tell me, and maybe I can help you think of another solution? What about Daniel? Or Emma? Can't they help?'

'No! No one else must know. They don't know anything about it, and even if they did, there wouldn't be anything they could do. This has to stay between you and me. If you try telling anyone else, I'll deny it, and who do you think they'll believe?'

I opened my mouth but the words wouldn't come. She was right. I had no option. If I didn't do what she said, I'd lose everything. She was looking at me. Waiting.

'All right, Ada. Tell me who it is.'

TWENTY-TWO

Everything feels wrong on Sunday. We're not having lunch together because Daniel's booked a restaurant for this evening. It was in aid of Polly going back to London, and even though she's not going now, he said we should keep the booking and that it will do us all good to get out of the house and enjoy a nice meal. I suppose he's right, but it leaves Ada and me at a bit of a loose end. She likes her routines and it doesn't feel right to be eating a salad on our own for Sunday lunch. We muddle through somehow and spend the afternoon in the garden with our books. I'm reading a spy novel Ada recommended while she's immersed in her book about Russia. Theo joins us for a bit and they get into an argument about socialism and capitalism which they both seem to enjoy. I'm not paying much attention to my book, even though I keep turning the pages to stop Ada from asking questions, and it's a relief when she dozes off and I can think properly.

I spent a long time writing down my latest findings last night and considering what to do next. I wrote each person's name at the top of a clean page and listed the evidence for and against them like old-fashioned detectives do in books. I've always thought it sounded a waste of time but it turned out to be very helpful. It was easy to dismiss Theo as a suspect, and even though Daniel met the man on the bench, I can't see him as a serious contender. Which leaves Emma and Polly.

Polly's link to Max through Jessie is undeniable, and the more I think about it, the harder I find it to believe it's a coincidence. She's been keen to agree that Jessie was his girlfriend, but could it be a smokescreen for her own relationship with him? Is Sam a figment of her imagination? But if it was her, why did she ask me to find out about the murder? Was it a bluff? Is she in league with Ada? Was that whole argument for my benefit? If it is Polly she's an amazing actress, but perhaps that's not so far-fetched – she's managed to keep plenty from her parents so far.

I turn my thoughts to Emma. She's been tense for ages – since before the murder. She met that strange man, she doesn't have an alibi for the night of the murder, and – most importantly – I'm convinced there's something going on between her and Ada. Maybe the 'threat' was to do with a secret from Emma's past that only Ada knows about; that would explain their talk in the garden, which I've thought all along had nothing to do with flowers. If it is her, there must be a clue somewhere in this house. I need to search again; in places I've not looked before. I scold myself for not having spent more time looking for evidence; following people is more exciting, and I've probably done more of it than was strictly necessary, although with five other people living in the house it's seldom empty, and I don't want to be caught rummaging through other people's belongings.

'Scarlet? What are you thinking about? You look as if you're miles away.' Ada's woken up and caught me at it.

'Oh, I was thinking about my book. It's complicated, isn't it? I need a bit of time to think it all through.'

'I suppose it is complicated, but not for a clever girl like you. You were frowning, dear. I hope you're not worrying about those detectives and their questions? It isn't only us they're talking to; remember that. If they were going to find out anything I'm sure they'd have done so by now.'

'I know. I've got a bit of a headache, that's all. Maybe I've been in the sun too long. I think I might go in and have a lie-down if that's all right.'

'Of course it's all right. And have a good long drink of water – you may be dehydrated. We don't want you feeling unwell for our meal out tonight.'

'Thanks, Ada.' I pick up my book and go inside. I make sure to draw my curtains in case she's looking and lie down on the bed. In the cool darkness I go through the house room by room in my mind, planning where I'll look when I have the place to myself. Because this headache isn't going to go away. It's going to turn into a migraine and there's no way I'll be well enough to go out for dinner.

* * *

They leave just before seven. I can hear them through the open window, Theo wheeling Ada's chair down the ramp and Daniel calling for Polly to hurry up. I'm sorry not to be going with them. I've always wanted to eat at Fleur de Lis – I've walked past it loads of times and wondered what frogs legs taste like. But the chance of having the house to myself is too good to miss and I know I'll regret it if I don't make the most of the opportunity.

I wait for five minutes in case anyone's forgotten something and then head straight for the downstairs bedrooms. I'll give Theo's a miss, but I have to search Polly's. And I didn't get round to Emma and Daniel's bathroom last time so I need to check there. And I'll look at Emma's phone again to see if she's made any more calls.

Polly's room is immaculately tidy so I have to be super-careful to put everything back exactly where I find it, but I know from experience it's easier than reproducing a mess. She's not got much stuff, and I suppose most of it is back in London. There's a collection of cuddly toys which probably aren't cool enough for college, and a few items of makeup on the dressing table. Polly's not a great one for dressing up, but there's a gorgeous long dress and a smart linen sheath hanging in her wardrobe alongside her trademark baggy shirts. They must be the dresses she was going to wear for the festival. Maybe she's got another one on now for dinner. I'm tempted to try them on but I tell myself to be professional. They should be gone for at least two hours but I can't take any chances. I turn towards her little en-suite shower room and freeze. There's a noise outside. The scrunch of tyres on gravel.

It could be another delivery for Emma, but I'm sure she'd have mentioned if she was expecting one, and Sunday evening's not a likely time anyway. I have to assume it's Daniel returning for something. Or Emma. I can't risk staying here. What if it's Polly who's forgotten something? They'll come in here, and there's nowhere to hide and no patio door like in Emma and Daniel's room. I cross the room like lightning and go into the hallway and half way up the stairs before turning round so that I'm walking down them again. I've got my foot on the first step when the front door opens and Daniel comes in.

'Oh! Scarlet! You gave me a shock. What are you doing down here?' He's heading towards the stairs as he speaks, not waiting for an answer. 'Mother forgot her purse and she's insisting on paying for the meal. I told her I could pay and we'd sort it out later, but you know what she's like.'

'I'll get it for you,' I say, turning round and heading up again. 'I know where she keeps it.'

'Oh, yes, thank you,' he says, but I'm already heading up the spiral, slowing my speed as I remember that people with migraines don't like to rush. Ada's purse is sitting on the side table, ready for her to put in her bag. It's not like her to forget it, and I'm not surprised she made Daniel come back for it. I walk back down with care, keeping my head as stiff and still as possible.

'Thanks, Scarlet. Hopefully, I'll get back before the first course arrives.' He grins. He's almost out of the door when he turns. 'What did you say you were coming down for? I thought you'd be asleep.'

'I woke up and needed a drink of water,' I say, rubbing my forehead and doing my best to look pale. 'I heard the car and thought it might be a delivery, and I didn't want anyone ringing the bell and making my headache worse. I'll go back to bed now. Have a good evening.'

'We will. Feel better soon, Scarlet.' He's gone. I sit on the bottom step and count to ten, listening to the car pull away. That was far too close for comfort. What if I'd given in to temptation and tried Polly's clothes on? I might have got away with hiding in her bathroom, but I can't even remember if I shut my bedroom door upstairs. What if he'd gone up and seen it open and an empty room? I have to be more careful. And fast. Daniel's not likely to come back again, but I shouldn't bank on it.

I stand up with a renewed sense of purpose and go into Polly's bathroom. There's nothing of interest there; it's not much different from mine. I don't really expect Polly to use the same hiding place as Emma, but my fingers are crossed in my head as I start on the bedside table. The top drawer contains nothing more exciting than headache tablets and tissues, and there's a pile of old birthday cards in the second. I check through them, just in case, but there are no love letters lurking amongst them. People don't write them these days; if I want to read Sam's sweet nothings I'll need to get hold of her phone.

It's the bottom drawer that yields a surprise. It contains her 'ladies' products', as Ada would call them, and underneath – and I almost laugh, despite my shock, at the irony of her keeping it here – is a pregnancy test. It's still in the box, so I have to open it to see if it's been used or not. It has. Two narrow blue lines sit in judgement on the little stick. I've seen these on the telly. I know what it means. Polly's pregnant. My hands are shaking as I take a photo and put it back in its place. She lied. She doesn't want to get back to London to split up with Sam. It's to tell him she's pregnant. Or to get an abortion. My brain is pleading with me for the chance to think about what it means, but I can't. I've got to look in Emma's room before they come home. Polly will have to wait. I take three deep breaths, count slowly to ten and leave the room, closing the door softly behind me even though there's no one to hear it. It restores my sense of control, and I go to have a look at Theo's room next, thinking it will be light relief before Emma's.

I peep inside Theo's room and retreat swiftly, deciding there's no need to venture any further. It's a classic boy's room, at least it looks like what I've been told is a classic boy's room – messy and with a whiff of sweat. I can hardly see the colour of the carpet, and I feel a pang of sympathy for Emma having to nag him about it. Emma. It's time for Emma's phone and Emma's bathroom. This is where I'm most hopeful of finding evidence, and I feel a tingle of excitement. Please, please, let me find something.

Emma – or Daniel – must have been in a rush because the door's not closed as it usually is. I take a small piece of paper from my pocket and fold it to fit into the angle, leaving it ready on the floor for when I'm finished. It's a trick I thought of myself, and I'm proud of it. The room looks exactly as it did before, and I guess Polly must take after Emma in the tidiness department. I go to Emma's side of the bed first and open her bottom drawer. The mobile's there, in exactly the same position. I know this because I check the photo on my phone. Maybe she photographs it too, although that would be too weird even for Emma. I turn it on and check the call log. There have been six calls since the last time I looked. Who *is* this man? There's no point in worrying about it, and I replace the phone. I've satisfied my curiosity but I haven't learned anything from it. Time for the bathroom.

The bathroom is as modern as the rest of the room, looking like something straight out of a catalogue. It's sparkling clean, and I know that must be down to Emma. My bathroom's pristine too, but only because I do it every morning. A cleaner comes in once a week, but you need to do it every day to make it look like this. It's the biggest bathroom I've ever seen, bigger than any bedroom I've had, and more than twice the size of most. I suppose you can have whatever size rooms you want when you design your own house.

There's a massive freestanding bath with taps in the middle so they don't dig into your back when you lie down, and a rack stretching across with a stand for a book and a little holder for a wine glass. I've always fancied one of those – for the book at any rate, never mind the wine. The walk-in shower is huge, with a shower head the size of a dinner plate, and there are upmarket products on a built-in shelf. There's a toilet, of course, and a bidet – I know what it is because I've seen them on the telly – I'm not so ignorant as to think it's something to wash your feet in. And there are two washbasins, each with its own mirror. The basins are set into a marble-topped unit with little drawers and cupboards underneath to hide all the clutter. There's not much on the surface. An expensive-looking soap dispenser sits in the centre and toothbrushes and toothpaste are positioned symmetrically on each side of the basins in heavy crystal glasses – it literally looks like a showhouse. It's unreal.

I get out my camera to take pictures and head straight for the unit. It doesn't take long to work out which is Daniel's side, and I don't bother looking through his aftershave and toothpaste. Emma's drawer is neat and tidy, as expected. There are contraceptive pills, painkillers, cotton wool and makeup remover. It's a shallow drawer so I don't need to move anything to check what's underneath. I crouch down and open the cupboard. This looks much more interesting. Emma's stuff is in four little woven baskets; in contrast to the fancy fittings, I reckon these are budget items, probably from Ikea. I'll need to photograph each box separately before looking at the contents, and it's going to take time. I pause, wondering if I should take the boxes elsewhere. No, I'll have to risk it; I'm not likely to get another opportunity like this. I sit on the floor to save my knees seizing up and settle in for a good snoop.

Before long I realise – unsurprisingly, perhaps – the baskets are themed. The first and smallest one is for teeth, containing spare toothpaste and brushes, floss and mouthwash. Next is body stuff – some little soaps, maybe for the guest toilet, a big bottle of soap for the dispenser and spare shower gel. There's also a half-used bottle of body lotion and some sun cream. The biggest basket appears to be for general body care. Emma's got a flat, spoon-shaped implement for rubbing dry skin off her feet, a manicure set, verruca cream, face masks and hand creams. I wonder where they keep medicines, and this distracts me for a moment. I get up and look in Daniel's cupboards. Here they are, in a big basket behind his shaving stuff. I get it out and rummage through a wide range of ointments for different skin complaints, plasters and burn treatments. There are two different kinds of painkillers, but nothing of interest, not like Ada's mini-dispensary.

I return to Emma's last basket. It's hair products, and I'm beginning to feel a sense of deflation. I've not found anything out of the ordinary, and my mind is already half way out of the room, thinking where I'll look next and wondering if it's difficult to get the loft ladder down when you're on your own. Emma uses a high-end brand of shampoo and conditioner, and now I can look more closely at the spare bottles I see it's for dry hair. Her hair always looks glossy enough so it must work. There's an oily serum as well and a pair of hair scissors. Emma goes every six weeks like clockwork to a smart salon in town, so they must be from lockdown when she was cutting her own fringe. I'm putting the baskets back in position when I realise the two at the back – hair and body – aren't in line. I push the hair box further back, but it won't go. Something's stopping it from sitting right at the back of the cupboard. It wasn't like that when I opened it; something must have fallen out as I pulled it forward. Cursing my carelessness, I take both baskets out again and lie down on my tummy to reach right to the back of the cupboard. My fingers close around a small box, and as I pull it out I realise I'll have to take a guess at where it was in the basket. I hope Emma doesn't use it often and notice if I get it wrong. Box in hand, I straighten up into a more comfortable position and look at it. It's hair dye. Blonde hair dye.

* * *

I make myself replace everything meticulously, checking time and again against the pictures on my phone. A last look round confirms

215

I haven't left a trace and I ease the door into position against the scrap of paper, confident that when they return neither Daniel nor Emma will suspect what I've been up to. Checking my phone for the last time I see I've been down here for over an hour. I walk slowly upstairs and stand at the sink, drinking two big glasses of water to calm myself down. Now I'm out of the room and in a place where my presence won't arouse suspicion I can feel my shoulders relax and I find my hand is trembling. I guess snooping is one thing, but finding important evidence is another, and more stressful than I had imagined. I go into the living room and look out of the window. I'm jittery now, as if I've drunk too much coffee. I feel a sudden urge to move, walk, run, anything to release the tension, but I can't go out now – not if I'm supposed to be in bed with a migraine. I decide to try using my relaxation techniques. If they can stop my mind jumping around from one thought to another I'll be a lot better off.

My curtains are still drawn and a light evening breeze is drifting in through the open window. I listen to my breathing, relax all my muscles and imagine myself in a woodland glade carpeted with bluebells. After a while, my mind stills and I realise there's no need to work anything out after all. It's all perfectly clear. Emma's Phoebe Johnson. Or, to be more precise, Phoebe Silento.

* * *

I must be getting better at the relaxation strategies because I drift off to sleep, only waking briefly when the others get back. I'm roused by the sound of the lift door opening and Theo and Ada's quiet voices as they come out of it. I look at my phone and see it's nearly ten o'clock. They must have eaten the full three courses, and I can feel my tummy rumbling at the thought of food. I forgot to eat anything before coming to bed but I can't get up now; it will be much more convincing if I appear to have slept through.

I listen as Theo takes Ada to her room and then goes back downstairs. It's not long before I hear Emma's footsteps on the stairs followed by the low rumble of their voices as she helps Ada with her bedtime routines. I can't hear the words, but their tone is calm; they're not arguing tonight. I'll wait until later before getting up for food and use the time to process what I learnt earlier. I took a photo of the hair dye before leaving the bathroom. It must have been out of habit, as there was no real reason to do so, but looking at it on my phone helps me to focus. Now that I've had time to calm down, I need to unpick my absolute certainty that Emma's Phoebe Silento. The thought popped into my head as soon as I saw the hair dye but I need to be careful not to jump to conclusions. I remind myself that behind every gut feeling is a logical explanation; if I can work out what this one is, it will be much easier to know where to look for more evidence.

Emma's never let it slip that she dyes her hair. It's not something she'd necessarily share with me but I've lived here for years now and I'm sure Polly or Theo would have said something in that time, if only when reminiscing about lockdown and the excitement of getting back to hairdressers. Plenty of people dye their hair, but even though she always looks immaculate, Emma's not vain. And she's been blonde since Polly was a baby – I know that from the photos I've seen around the house. Thinking of photos, I remember Ada showing Theo some pictures of herself when she was young when he was learning about the war for his GCSEs. They ended up looking at all her family albums, including from when Daniel was little. Theo asked Emma if she had any photos from when she was younger and she didn't. Not even of her teenage years. She said her parents had them all in Australia, but who doesn't have photos of their teenage years or their twenties? Emma had nothing at all. She has to be hiding something from her past, and if she *is* Phoebe, she's connected to Max, and all I have to do is come up with a reason for her to murder him. I realise this won't amount to much more than making up a story, but it will help to pass the time.

Emma and Max must have married in haste and repented at leisure, as Ada would say. Maybe she was pregnant with Polly? Or perhaps it was a whirlwind romance. Then she decided to leave. Perhaps he was violent, or a criminal – the reason's not important right now. Emma didn't want him to find her so she changed her name and her appearance and moved away from London. She met Daniel and made a new life for herself. Then Max found her – I'll think about how that happened later – and threatened her in some way. Maybe he wanted a divorce so he could marry Hayley. Perhaps he wanted to make contact with Polly. Neither sound like reasons for killing him to me, but I know people can do strange things where their children are concerned.

I need to write all this down in my book. I've had good ideas in the middle of the night before and forgotten them by morning, and I don't want that happening now. The book is under my pillow and I slide it out, reaching for the pen on my bedside table. By the time I've finished it's nearly two o'clock and I've not heard a sound for more than an hour. I reckon it's safe to creep into the kitchen and make a sandwich now. Even if I am discovered, it would be plausible for me to have woken from a post-migraine sleep and need something to eat.

I stand beside the sloping Velux kitchen window and look at the stars while I eat. It's weird being the only person awake in the house, and the quiet helps me to think. I know there are gaps in my theory, but there's enough which makes sense to me for now. I don't need to know all the details of what happened between Emma – or should I say Phoebe? – and Max. The crucial question is how did she do it? I think back over the past two weeks and consider Emma's behaviour in the light of what I've discovered. Ada knows something, but I don't think she suspects Emma of anything. I'm sure she'd be less confident in a verdict of natural causes if she did. But she's hiding something, and it could be the knowledge of Emma's marriage.

Which leads me to Daniel. Could the cause of his argument with Emma be his finding out about her and Max? Theo certainly didn't know, and my bet is Polly doesn't either. If Emma wanted to keep her true identity hidden, she'd tell as few people as possible. A secret shared is a secret no more – I've learnt that to my cost –

and this scenario would also explain Daniel's recent impatience with the police. If he knows Emma was married to Max, he has to be wondering if she killed him. As I wipe the crumbs off the counter I realise I'm about to start going round in circles. Thinking this way won't get me anywhere. I'll have to ask outright. I can't ask Ada – if Emma's managed to keep her actions hidden from her I don't want to be the one to reveal them. I'll have to ask Emma herself.

TWENTY-THREE

My eyes pop open at six o'clock, a full hour before my alarm's due to go off, and there's a single name in my head. Polly. What was I thinking of last night? Well, I know what I was thinking of – Emma, and how she must be the killer. That's all very well, but what about Polly? That pregnancy test must mean something. She's lying about something, and it's either Max or Sam. It's weird, but for some reason my instincts tell me that if I challenge Emma I might get the truth out of her, but it would be different with Polly.

I roll onto my back and stare at the ceiling. Does this mean Polly's more likely to be the murderer? Did Max make her pregnant? Were they seeing each other or was it maybe something more sinister? And did it end in murder? I don't want to think it, but, looking back over the past few days and our cosy chats, I wonder if she's been deliberately getting me on her side, grooming me. A crushing sense of disappointment mixed with shame engulfs me. I thought we were becoming closer, like sisters. Who was I kidding? It was all a front, cooked up by Polly – and maybe Ada too – to put me off the scent. I can't believe I fell for it, and anger sweeps in, reddening my face. I reach for my book. Writing it down helps as always, and by the time the alarm goes off I've got a plan. I know what to do and where to look. All I need now is the opportunity.

* * *

'There's a change of plan today.' I help Ada sit up in bed and wait for her to elaborate. 'Ah, that's better,' she says as she takes her first sip of tea. 'Yes, I was talking to Emma last night. She's taken today off; she was going to take Polly out for lunch and then drive her to the station but she won't be doing that now. We thought we'd make the most of the opportunity and go to York for the day. I'd like to get some new books and Emma's always up for a browse round the shops. We'll make a day of it and go for a trip on the river, and to the open-air theatre if we can get tickets. It's ages since I've seen a live performance, and they're doing *The Merchant of Venice* – it's one of my favourites.'

Ada's face has brightened up so much at the thought of her day out that I can't help but smile at her, even though it means I'll have less chance than ever of talking to Emma.

'That sounds fun,' I say.

'Yes, doesn't it? And maybe you can have a restful day. It will do you good. We don't want you going down with another migraine, do we?' A look flashes across her face which makes me wonder if she knows exactly what I was up to last night. But no, surely not. She wouldn't leave me on my own in the house if she did, would she?

'What about Polly? Is she joining you?'

'Yes. She needs a distraction. And I might treat her to some new clothes. She brushes up well when she tries. She only needs a little encouragement and a generous budget.' Poor Polly – I can imagine what Ada's idea of a suitable wardrobe for her might consist of; I'd love to be a fly on the wall when they go clothes shopping together, and I reckon Emma could be in for a day as referee. But it means I'll have plenty of time to search the house again, and I hadn't dared to hope for that to happen so soon.

'I'm sure you'll all have a lovely day,' I say. 'And I'll be sure to take it easy while you're gone.'

* * *

I'd hoped to catch Emma downstairs before they leave but Ada keeps me busy, fetching different handbags for her to choose from and bits and pieces for her day out. By the time I've found sunglasses, sunscreen, a hat and a little spray can of misty water Emma and Polly are calling for her to hurry up or there won't be time for any shopping before lunch.

I don't waste any time once they're finally out of the front door. I've tried to put myself inside Emma's head, and Polly's too; where would they hide stuff? Thinking this way has helped me to identify the most likely hiding places, and I've got the whole day to explore them. Emma's obsessive tidiness has its benefits and I know there's no point in looking in obvious places like the study or even the loft. If either of them has anything to hide it will be well and truly tucked away, and I know where I'm going first. The shed.

Emma's funny about the garden. She designed it herself; she told me she needed something to be in charge of since Daniel was designing the house, and it is gorgeous, I have to admit. She's out there every weekend and most evenings in the summer, planting and raking and pruning. She can't do it all herself as it's huge and she has a full-time job so there are gardeners who come in once a week. They bring their own tools so the shed is hers and she won't let anyone in, in case they mess with her stuff. There's a separate shed for the chairs and croquet set and so on which any of us can go into, and everyone knows Emma's shed is private. I've always thought it weird but no one else seems to, and now I know why she's so secretive about it. She's got secrets hidden in there and I'm going to find them.

The shed's securely locked with a big padlock, but a padlock's no use if you've got a screwdriver to remove the fittings with. I know where to find one of those, and it doesn't take long for me to remove the metal ring from one side of the shed door. I'll be able to put it back without it showing, although I'm beginning not to care if Emma does find out what I've done. I know no one will be home for hours but I still look behind me and around the garden before going inside; I'm not taking any chances after what happened last night. Once I'm happy there's no one nearby, I go inside.

One step is all I take, and I stand on the threshold in shock. It's a big shed and Emma's the tidiest person I know so I was expecting an organised set-up, but it's hard to think of anything less orderly than this. There are garden implements stacked anyhow along the walls, shelves loaded with wooden and cardboard boxes, mounds of plant pots, and a huge wheelbarrow I've never seen Emma use in the middle, filling almost all the available space. Once I've got over the shock, I realise this confirms my suspicions. If I were Emma and I had something to hide, this is where I'd put it. Surrounded by chaos and confusion and behind a padlocked door. And if I was Polly, I might use this place too. The question is, where do I start?

There's no way I'll be able to look through all of this at once. I'll focus on Emma for now and proof of her being Phoebe Silento. I think myself into her head and try to work out where to begin. Where would she choose to hide something? After some thought I decide it will be in either the most or least obvious place. Emma might go for the 'hide it in plain sight' approach, given she's gone to so much trouble to make a mess. Although nothing's in plain sight here, apart from the wheelbarrow. I tell myself to think. Calmly. OK, if it's evidence of a former life I'm looking for, it won't be something she looks at often so there'll be dust. And the container won't be new. If it's papers – and I assume it will be – she'd need something like a box, or an envelope. I scan the shelves with fresh eyes and take some photos while I'm thinking; it will be impossible to replace everything precisely without them.

The shelves near the door contain items I've seen Emma using – gloves, a trowel, a kneeling pad. It won't be there. I squeeze round the barrow towards the darker end of the shed. There are pots of paint and other liquids on the lower shelves, with boxes and crates above. I pull out a dusty old crate and find it full of cracked plant pots. Another's got some old, musty overalls, and a third has ski clothes in it. That's weird – Polly told me Emma hates flying so they never go abroad. I take them out and see they're very bulky, not like modern ski wear. They're about my size, so Emma's size too. Maybe I'm getting closer. I pull out more crates and boxes, finding I can sift through them quickly without disturbing their contents too much. It's hot in the shed, and I think I might go back to the house for a cold drink when I find it.

The crate's no different from the others; she's hidden it cleverly, I'll give her that. No bigger or smaller than the others and covered with dust on the outside. You'd never find it if you weren't looking for it, and I heave a sigh of relief as I pull out a manila file, soft with age and curling at the edges. Even before I open it, I know this has to be it. What else could it be? I hesitate, holding it in my grime-covered hands. Do I look now or take it inside and examine it at my leisure? I look at my watch and find it's half past one. My stomach realises it's not had any lunch yet, and Theo could be home soon if he gets a lift from a friend – I'll take it inside.

* * *

I make myself replace the crate, adjust the barrow and check the shed against the photos on my phone. I keep my hand steady as I replace the padlock and its fittings and tuck the screwdriver into my back pocket. I walk slowly into the house and upstairs, clutching the file to my chest, and set it down on the table before pouring myself a glass of water from the tap. These actions keep me calm, and I tell myself that having come so far, I can wait a few more minutes if it means nothing can interrupt me. I take a long drink of water and open the file.

I thought I'd figured out Emma's story but it's different when it's all laid out in front of me. I arrange the documents in what I think must be chronological order, imagining the events behind them, and it all comes alive in a completely different way. I imagine Emma – or Phoebe, as she was – rummaging through a desk, finding the papers she needed – or the ones she didn't want Max to have. She was in a hurry, packing a case and grabbing what she could before he got back from wherever he was. She didn't want to leave any part of her behind, and I find myself wanting to congratulate her – she must have been around my age at the time, and I can imagine the panic she was feeling, the fear of discovery.

The first document in my timeline is Phoebe's birth certificate. It says she was born in 1978 and her parents were called Barbara and Neville Johnson. They lived in Surrey; he was an accountant and she was a primary school teacher. There's nothing suspicious about it, and I wonder when they moved to Scotland, and then Australia. Next is a marriage certificate. It's between Phoebe Johnson and Maximilian Silento. He was living in London and she was still at the address in Surrey, which I don't understand. Perhaps her parents kept the house on when they moved so she could use it later? Their ages are on the certificate – twenty and twenty-four. It seems very young to me, but I guess people get married later these days. This must be the document the police found – or a copy of it. I wonder why Emma took this, as it would be easy for Max to have got a replacement, but maybe she wanted all traces of herself out of his house.

I'd thought I might find a birth certificate for Polly, but there isn't one. I suppose Emma needed it when Daniel adopted her and she changed her name to Rosewood. What I do find is a letter about changing a name by deed poll. It confirms that Phoebe Johnson has changed her name to Emma Stevens. It's dated November 1999, a year after the marriage and a few months before Polly's birthday. It's easy to remember when hers is because Daniel teases her about being a millennium baby. So Phoebe left Max, changed her name to Stevens, registered her baby with the same surname and then met Daniel, when they both became Rosewoods. Which explains why no one reacted to the name Phoebe Johnson. They all think Emma's surname was Stevens.

There aren't many more documents in the file, but there are a few photos. They're mostly of Phoebe and a younger version of Max, including one on some steps where she's holding a bunch of flowers and he's wearing a suit, which must be from their wedding. I'm more interested in the single small photo of a teenage girl with her parents. They're standing in a garden, wearing smart clothes as if they're going out somewhere. It's hard to make out the facial features so I get up and fetch Ada's magnifying glass from the desk. She uses it for some of her magazines, the ones with small print. I keep telling her she should get new glasses but she says she likes the glass – it makes her feel like Sherlock Holmes. I hold the magnifier over the photo and I can't help gasping. It's no surprise to see a girl who looks like a dark and younger version of Emma, but there's no mistaking her father. It's the man on the bench.

* * *

I need some time to work out what this means so I put everything back in the envelope, tuck it under my mattress and go out. I don't want the busyness of town and I need to let off steam, so I dig out some running gear and go onto the Westwood. It's a beautiful late afternoon and there are picnic blankets scattered all over the place filled with mums and children on the way back from school and teenagers hanging out with their friends. The after-work dog walkers are beginning to put in an appearance and there are joggers and horse riders, making the most of the longer days. It's a comfort to be around people who don't know me, who don't ask awkward questions or look at me with lies in their eyes, and I smile at everyone I pass, saying hello and yes, aren't we having a lovely summer, and isn't it good to have such a wonderful space on our doorstep. I head past the racecourse, careful not to get in the way of the golfers, and find a quiet bench on the edge of the trees. The exercise has done me good, but I don't run very often and I'm ready for a rest.

As my breathing returns to normal, I realise I may have been closer to the truth than I thought when I assumed Ada was being blackmailed. Max must have wanted something, but from Emma, not Ada. My guess is he wanted a divorce so he could marry Hayley, but why would that be a problem? Surely the only thing stopping Emma from getting one herself would have been the danger of Max finding her, and that danger was long past. Which leaves only one possibility – Polly. I try out a new story to see if it fits. Max comes across Polly by chance at the college and sees a resemblance – Polly doesn't look much like Emma so the resemblance would have been to someone on his side of the family. And maybe there was more – if Phoebe was a string player like Polly, there could have been something in the way she held her viola that triggered a memory.

In my story, Max comes to see Emma. He tells her he wants not only a divorce but also contact with his long-lost daughter. Maybe money as well – who knows? He comes back again before the festival and Emma says no, he can't see Polly, but Max has already forced her hand by coming to Beverley. She arranges to come to the hotel and when she gets there she kills him to stop him from ruining her – and Polly's – life. Daniel's too, I guess, if he didn't already know about Max. Although I'd guess he does now – it would explain their argument last week. I think it all through again and it still makes sense. I imagine Emma telling Ada about it all and Ada telling her to leave it to her, she'd sort it out. Emma must have panicked, though, and I don't blame her – I can understand her doubting Ada's ability to change Max's mind.

The final detail is Emma's father, the man on the bench. I realise she only called him because of me. He's not important, I'm sure. Maybe her parents don't live in Australia at all, and it's all part of her big cover-up. If Daniel didn't know either, that could be what their argument was about. If I'm right about this, it would explain Emma's phone – it's how she keeps in touch with her parents. When I called Neville's number it registered as a missed call and Neville told Emma about it. They panicked and he came to Beverley to calm her down. Then after she told Daniel everything, he wanted to see Neville too. I don't blame him – I'd have wanted an explanation myself as to why Neville wasn't living in Australia after all.

I'm proud of myself for working it all out, and get up from the bench, thinking it's time I went home. I go over it all again as I walk; it all fits, and that's good, but it is just a story. And I can't help wondering if it's a strong enough motive for Emma. Maybe Polly would have liked to get to know her father. She's a grown-up after all; shouldn't Emma at least have asked her what she thought about it? And even if it is true, what's to prevent Polly having been Max's girlfriend too? And I still don't know how he was killed, whoever it was that did it.

* * *

They're back from York when I get home and no one's in a good mood. Ada's cross because the theatre had tickets but Polly refused point blank to go, saying she didn't want to watch a play about anti-Semitism and had Ada actually read the play?

'I told her not to be so silly, of course I've read it,' Ada fumes. 'But there was no persuading her. She was muttering about minority rights all through lunch. It was all most unpleasant.'

'Did you get any new books?' I ask, trying to find a bright spot in her day.

'Yes, I did.' She brightens up immediately. 'Emma put them in my room and we'll have a good look at them after supper.' I don't ask about the clothes shopping; from the sound of things, I don't suppose it went well. I leave Ada with her Russia book while I cook the meal, my mind busy with plans of what I might say to Polly. Ada carries on with her shopping saga through supper, and it's a relief to be able to clear the dishes and have a bit of peace and quiet in the kitchen. I'm finishing the washing-up when I hear Daniel's measured tread on the stairs.

'Mother? Scarlet?' I come out of the kitchen, wiping my hands on a tea-towel, and Ada rests her book on her lap as he comes into the sitting room.

'Can you come down?' he says, a frown creasing his face. 'It's the police. They want to talk to us all.'

'Now?' Ada's outraged. 'At this time of night?'

'It would appear so.' Daniel's face looks tired, which is to be expected at the end of the day, but there's something else there too – is it fear?

'I can't imagine what could be so important that it can't wait till the morning.'

'I don't know what it is, but I could hardly send them away. That wouldn't look good, would it?' He's trying to be upbeat but it's not working very well.

'Very well.' Ada lets me help her into her wheelchair and we go down in the lift to find DI Twist and Sergeant Carter sitting in their usual places with the family gathered around. I take Ada to the space that's been left for her and sit on the dining chair by her side. DI Twist is back in her heels and smart shirt today. Her hair's looking less wispy than usual, styled in a sleek French plait, and I wonder if it's for a particular reason. She looks perfectly groomed even at the end of what I guess is a long working day, and there's something about her that reminds me of Hayley, although I can't imagine DI Twist scouring the fashion pages for tips.

'We're sorry to interrupt your evening,' she begins, although none of us believe this for a minute, and there's a clipped tone to her voice which I've not heard before. 'Some evidence has come to light today which has opened up a new line in the investigation. We thought it best to come now rather than in the morning when some of you will be out.'

'I suppose that makes sense.' Ada appears to be taking over from Daniel as the voice of reason; he's uncharacteristically silent and I can't help thinking he's hiding something. Does he know about Emma?

'What do you need to know?' Ada asks. 'I'm sure none of us want to hinder your work, Inspector.'

'Thank you.' DI Twist manages not to look surprised at Ada's helpfulness, which probably has more to do with her wanting to get back upstairs to her glass of port and spy series than anything else.

'It's very simple, really,' she continues. 'We need to ask each of you for details of any medications you may be taking.'

'Well, that shouldn't take too long,' says Daniel, a look of relief flitting across his face. 'It's only Mother who takes anything regularly – the rest of us are a healthy bunch. Would you like us to make a list?' DI Twist doesn't return his nervous smile, however, and it would appear she hadn't finished her sentence after all.

'No, that won't be necessary. We'd prefer to confirm the details by looking in your bathroom cabinets. That will save you writing lists and it will provide more secure evidence. We'll need your permission to do so – are you all happy for us to go ahead with the search?' She looks around the room, seeking confirmation and getting nods from everyone, accompanied by bemusement from Daniel and Theo and blank stares from the others.

'Thank you, that's very helpful. We'll get onto it straight away and then we can leave you in peace. And we'd like a look round your garage as well – would that be possible?' It's presented as an afterthought but I know what those mean and so does Ada. There's no change in anyone's expression, though, and Daniel says he'll unlock it for them when they're ready.

'Are you finished with us now?' Ada asks. 'I'd like to get back to my own room if I may, and I'm sure Theo has homework to do.'

'We are finished with you but I'll have to ask you to remain here until we've looked in your bathrooms. I'm sure you understand.' DI Twist gives Ada a polite smile, but we all know what she means. She doesn't want us tampering with evidence – or whatever else she'd call it – before she gets to it. It wouldn't surprise me if they widened the search to bedrooms and the rest of the house, and I suppose she's starting small in the hope of encountering less resistance. 'We'll go upstairs first, Mrs Rosewood; you'll be able to go into your rooms once we're done. We'll try not to keep Theo from his work any longer than necessary.' I'm sure Theo has no problem at all with being prevented from doing homework, but he produces a polite smile. DI Twist rises and turns to Daniel.

'Perhaps you could show us where to go, Mr Rosewood[...] welcome to remain with us. We'll just be taking an inven[...] medications, nothing sinister.'

'Of course.' Daniel gets up and leads the way to the spiral stairs, leaving the rest of us to our own thoughts. It's ages before anyone speaks, and it's Theo who breaks the silence as usual, speaking in a low voice, as if afraid they'll hear him.

'What would they have done if we'd said no? To looking round the house? Would they have got a search warrant?' He looks at Ada, assuming this is something she'll know.

'And will it only be the bathrooms?' Polly asks before Ada can reply. 'They can't look anywhere else without asking first, can they?' Her voice is tight with tension, and I'm not surprised. That pregnancy test would raise a lot of awkward questions.

'No, they can't,' Ada replies slowly. 'And in answer to your question, Theo, they'd need good cause to ask for a search warrant. They may have what they think is sufficient evidence to get one, but it could easily have been a bluff. If I were DI Twist, I'd have bet on us agreeing to the search. It wouldn't look good if we refused, would it?'

'No,' Emma agrees. 'And why should we? After all, we've nothing to hide.' Her chin's in the air and her tone is defiant, and I'm reminded of that song about whistling a happy tune – the one where the woman doesn't want people to know she's afraid.

'Quite right, dear,' says Ada. 'Now, we need something to distract us. Polly, turn on the television, would you? There must be something we can watch.'

* * *

It's ages before they're done. Ada waits until they've finished before asking me to take her upstairs, not wanting to leave Emma before Daniel gets back. The bathrooms don't take long but there's the garage to be searched too, although goodness knows why they want to go in there. I'm thinking furiously about that, blocking out the adventure film on the telly from my mind in order to do so. Daniel finally returns and goes straight to the fridge, where he gets himself a beer.

'Are they finished?' Emma asks, anxiety written all over her face now the police aren't here to observe her.

'Yes and no.' Daniel sinks onto the sofa beside her and holds her hand. 'They were still poking around the garage when they got a phone call and said they had to go and they'd be back tomorrow. I don't know what it was, but they left quickly enough. I don't know how much longer they can spend at it – there's not much in there.'

'Well, they're gone for now, that's what matters,' Ada says. 'And I'm ready for bed after all that excitement.' I wheel her to the lift and the others say goodnight. Although I can't imagine anyone will sleep well tonight.

TWENTY-FOUR

They're getting closer, I know they are, and I toss and turn all night, waking up sweating from dreams of being chased or trapped in a cage. It's no better when I'm awake, my thoughts tormenting me throughout the dark hours of the night. DI Twist will be back tomorrow; what if she extends her search? She'll find Emma's papers, still hidden under my bed. And there's the morphine. Ada said it was somewhere safe, but what if it isn't? An even worse thought creeps into my brain. What if Ada lets them find the morphine? Lets them arrest me? Lets me take the blame for everything? She and Emma have been thick as thieves recently and they were out with Polly all day yesterday. Ada's been telling me not to investigate, but what if she's known all along that it was one of them? What if they find out what I've been doing? Will they do something to me? Put poison in my tea? I don't sleep until dawn, and I wake with a jolt when I hear raised voices downstairs.

It's Emma and Daniel, arguing in the kitchen. I look across at my alarm clock to see the hands stuck at five o'clock. I turn on my phone to see that it's nearly eight. I only turn it off at night because Ada told me it was bad for my health to leave it on, and I wish I'd never paid any attention to her. I scramble into some clothes; Ada will be expecting her morning tea any minute now and I don't want her to be cross with me today. By the time I open my bedroom door there's silence below. Emma and Daniel must have gone downstairs; they both leave the house soon after eight o'clock. I'm relieved not to have heard anything from Ada's room; perhaps she's tired after her busy day yesterday. I'm just about to fill the kettle when I hear the doorbell. It must be DI Twist, back to finish searching the garage. It seems a bit early to me, but perhaps they've got a lot to do today, and I tiptoe down the spiral so as to hear what she says.

'Good morning, Inspector.' Daniel answers the door almost immediately. He was probably about to open it himself to go to work.

'Good morning, Mr Rosewood, Mrs Rosewood. I'm sorry for the early call.' DI Twist's voice floats up the stairs. 'We wanted to be sure to arrive before anyone goes out.'

'Well, you've done that all right,' says Daniel. 'I'll get the garage door open for you.'

'Thank you, Mr Rosewood. Sergeant Moss will be overseeing the search this morning. I'm here for another reason.'

'What do you mean?' Daniel's voice is tense and tight. My stomach feels as if the bottom's dropped out of it and I sit down on the stair to stop my legs from collapsing.

'We need to ask Polly, Scarlet and you, Mrs Rosewood, to come to the station.'

'The station?' Emma can't keep the panic out of her voice. 'What for? Are you arresting us? All three of us?'

'No, but we need to take fingerprints. For purposes of elimination.' I'd love to believe her but I know it's for more than that and I'm sure Emma will too.

'Should we call our solicitor?' Daniel asks.

'There's no need for that at present, Mr Rosewood. Although you're free to consult one if you wish.' It doesn't sound good to me, but maybe it's what they always say in these circumstances.

'Polly's asleep,' says Emma, distractedly. 'Do you want me to wake her? And what about Scarlet? She's got my mother to look after.'

'It would be helpful if you could all come as soon as possible.' DI Twist's trying to keep Emma calm but she's not giving an inch. As I expected, it's Daniel who takes the lead.

'Can you give us a few minutes, please, Inspector? We'll get Polly up and tell Scarlet what's happening. Once she's seen to Ada I can drive them both to the station on my way to work. We can be with you in – what – around an hour? Would that be acceptable? Someone needs to help my mother with her morning routines and I wouldn't want to keep Theo off school.' He makes it all sound very sensible and reasonable, and I hear DI Twist agree and leave. It won't hurt for me to stay where I am, so I wait for Daniel to come up and explain what's happening while Emma rouses Polly.

Ada takes a while to wake up properly in the mornings and it doesn't help that she had a late night, but it doesn't take her long to understand what's going on. By the time she's in her bath she's got a grip on the situation and is bombarding me with instructions.

'Just deny everything. Everything. And don't be afraid to say, "no comment". They've got no proof of anything and they'll have to release you after twenty-four hours if they can't charge you. If the worst comes to the worst, and I don't see why it should, you've got plan B. Maybe we should have gone over it again. Are you sure you remember it all?'

'Yes, I've got it off by heart. I've been going through it in my mind every night, even though you kept saying I wouldn't need it.'

'Good girl,' she says approvingly. 'And don't ask for a solicitor. It would only complicate matters.'

'Yes, Ada. I know.' What else can I say? She'd be right if everything had gone to plan, and it's not her fault that it hasn't. But it is her fault that I don't know who's really to blame. And if I don't know that, what chance do I have of defending myself? I have to try one more time – if I end up in jail I'll never forgive myself if I haven't made a final attempt to get her to talk.

'Ada, it would all be so much easier if you'd tell me what really happened between you and Max Silento. Please. Surely you can see that, now it's come to this. You know I'd do anything for you, but I never thought I'd be hauled off to a police cell. What if they don't believe me? I have to know why you wanted him to die in the first place. In case I have to make up a new story.'

'I'm sorry about the police, Scarlet. I didn't expect this either, but I'm not telling you anything more. There isn't time, anyway. You'll just have to stick to the plan.'

'But what about afterwards? When it's all over and they've gone away. Will you tell me then?' She looks at me for a moment, and I tell myself that if I keep quiet for a moment she might at least agree to this.

'All right. I'll tell you everything once it's over. That's a promise.'

'I'll hold you to that,' I say, and I turn to take her blouse off its hanger. There's a very real possibility this will be the last time I do this, and Ada's promise won't be worth anything if I end up in jail. If they don't believe my story I'll have no alternative. I'll have to tell them the truth.

* * *

I'm ready before Polly and Emma and I sit on the bench in the hall, looking at my feet and wondering if the others have been able to eat anything; my stomach's in knots and all I've managed is a cup of coffee. They come down in silence with Daniel close behind and we travel to the police station without exchanging a word. Daniel says he'll leave the car and walk into the office so Emma can drive to work afterwards. He makes it sound as if we're off for a shopping trip and this only adds to the unreality of the situation.

Once we're in the station they take each of us off in different directions. Emma looks panicked all over again and Polly's face is thin and pale, but there's nothing in either of them to help me work out which of them did it. A woman in uniform takes me to an interview room and tells me to make myself comfortable. She says I might have to wait for a while and would I like a coffee. I reckon police station coffee's awful so I say no and she goes away. There's a table with two plastic chairs on either side of it like I've seen in police dramas, and its strange familiarity helps me to stay calm. I sit down and make myself look at my phone in the hope that it will distract me while I wait. I suppose they can't talk to us all at once, but who will they be interviewing first – Emma or Polly? And when will they take my fingerprints, or was that just an excuse to get us here without a fuss? It's more than an hour before DI Twist comes back, followed as always by Sergeant Carter.

'I'm sorry we've kept you waiting, Scarlet.' This doesn't seem to require an answer, so I don't give her one. Sergeant Carter turns on a tape recorder and says the date and time, we all say our names, and then DI Twist leans forward and tells me I'm here for questioning about the murder of Max Silento and I can have a lawyer if I want.

'Do I need one?' I ask.

'That's for you to decide, Scarlet.'

'Can I say no for now and change my mind later?'

'Of course. We can call the duty solicitor for you at any time.'

'And can I leave if I want to?'

'Yes, you're here voluntarily.' She doesn't say it will look suspicious if I get up and leave but I know she's thinking it. There's nothing I can do – I'm trapped.

'OK.' There's a pause, but I'm not going to ask. Let them tell me why I'm here.

'We've asked you to come in today because we think you have more to tell us about the night Max Silento died.' DI Twist is back to her gazing around the room habit. There's not much to look at on these walls so I can't imagine she'll keep it up for long.

'Well, I haven't. I've already told you. I was in the house with Ada all evening.'

'We have reason to think otherwise,' she says, fixing her eyes on the window behind me.

'Oh?' I'm not giving in without a fight. If she's got evidence, fine, but if she hasn't I don't have to say anything.

'Yes. We've acquired new video footage from near the Beverley Arms. It's from a shop which has been closed for a fortnight's summer holiday, so there was a delay in our getting hold of it. It shows a person walking towards the hotel. A person who looks like you.'

'Lots of people look like me. Emma and Polly for starters, as you've already pointed out.' I cross my arms and lean back in my chair. It might make me look like a hardened criminal but that can't be helped – it makes me feel safer, although I don't know why.

'This person doesn't look like them. This person has your face. Luke?' She turns to Sergeant Carter who produces a laptop. He taps a few times and turns it to face me. I lean forward to peer at the screen and there I am. Walking down the pavement outside Pizza Express, with a backpack on my shoulders. It's remarkably clear, and I reckon the shop owners must have spent a lot of money on their camera. I can see a little date and time showing in the corner. It's the date of the murder, and the seconds on the clock are ticking upwards as we watch. I can't deny it's me. I sit back in my chair again, lips pressed together and thinking furiously.

'Would you like a solicitor now, Scarlet?' asks the inspector.

'No.' I didn't want it to come to this but a corner of my mind knew all along that it might, and I'm prepared. Ada's plan of denying everything isn't going to work but I've got plan B, as Ada calls it, and she'd be furious if she found out I'd asked for a lawyer. 'Can I have a drink of something, please?' I ask, thinking it will give me time to gather my thoughts.

'Of course. I daresay we could all do with a coffee,' she says, and Sergeant Carter leaves the room. I close my eyes while he's out, and by the time he returns with three cardboard cups I've gone through it all again, confident I'm ready. I open my eyes and wait until I'm sure I've got their attention.

'I want to tell you something,' I say, and as the words leave my mouth I feel a surprising sense of relief; I'm finally going to be able to talk to someone about that night, even if it isn't a completely truthful version of events. The detectives exchange glances but neither speaks.

'I was there. In Max Silento's room. I did go to see him, but I didn't kill him.'

'All right.' DI Twist's voice is quiet as always, and I can hear a sigh in her voice. A sigh of relief? Exasperation? 'So you admit going to see him and being in his room?'

'Yes.'

'But not to killing him?'

'No.'

'All right. Tell us what happened.' DI Twist relaxes back in her chair and I don't like it. She looks more like someone getting ready to listen to a fairy tale than a confession, and that can't be good. I can't do anything about it, though, I have to follow the plan.

'It was for Ada. I mean, Ada asked me to go.'

'Did she now? And why was that?' There's a tone in her voice that sounds like we're sharing a joke. I'm suddenly sure that she's not going to believe me, but as long as she can't prove any different, I'll stick to my story.

'She wanted me to ask him – Mr Silento, that is – for a favour.'

'A favour?'

'Yes. She wanted him to help Polly. In her career. She knew he was famous and that he had lots of contacts in the music world. She thought he could help her – Polly, that is – in her career.'

'What did she want you to do?'

'She asked me to go to see him. Late in the evening when he'd be alone. And to take some champagne as a present and a note from her asking him to help Polly.' It sounded fine when we first thought of it, but now I'm saying it for real it's beginning to feel a bit far-fetched. I stick my chin in the air like Emma did yesterday in the hope that it will give me the confidence I need to convince them.

'Why didn't Ada ask him herself? Or Polly? Or her parents? Why did you need to go sneaking around at night on her behalf?'

'Polly would never have asked him herself – she'd think it unprofessional. And Emma and Daniel wouldn't have had the nerve. Ada's different. She's never been afraid to get what she wants. And she knew how much it would mean to Polly. You've got to be ruthless in the music business, that's what Ada says. Anyway, I wasn't sneaking. I wasn't hiding from anyone.'

'You were wearing a hat – that suggests you didn't want to be recognised, don't you think?' I knew she'd ask questions like this, and I'm ready for her.

'I didn't want to attract... unwelcome attention. It was a Friday night, there were bound to be lads around who might have bothered me. I wanted to keep a low profile.'

'All right, so Ada asked you to go to see Max Silento late in the evening when he'd be on his own. She told you to take a bottle of champagne as a gift and a note asking him to help Polly in her musical career. Is that correct?' DI Twist sneaks a look at her sergeant to check he's keeping up. I don't know why he's writing it all down when there's a tape going, but perhaps they don't want to risk the machine breaking or something.

'Yes.'

'Apart from the cap, you were smartly dressed, weren't you? We can see that from the latest CCTV footage. Was that for a particular reason?'

'Yes, we thought he'd be more likely to let me in if I looked nice.'

'If you looked nice,' she repeats slowly. 'Were you planning on drinking the champagne with him?' I know what she means. She can't put words in my mouth, and I don't want to be arrested for entrapment, if that's even possible now he's dead, but the more detail I give them the more convincing my story will be.

'I thought I might do. If he asked me, that is. Ada said it might be helpful if he opened the letter while I was there and we got talking. I might have been able to persuade him to help Polly.'

'I see.' DI Twist sits up in her chair now, and I know this means we're getting to the part of my story that interests her most. Her eyes aren't looking at the wall or the window. They're looking at me.

'What time did you leave home, Scarlet?'

'It was ten forty-five. We hoped he'd be in his room by eleven. If he wasn't, I was going to wait for him in the corridor.'

'Did anyone see you leave? Apart from Ada, of course.'

'No, I used the fire escape.'

'So you don't know if anyone else was out of the house?'

'No.' I allow a puzzled look to cross my face, knowing that I should be wondering why she's asking.

'How long did it take you to get to the hotel?'

'About ten minutes. I put my heels on just before I reached North Bar, so I was a bit slower after that.' DI Twist looks across to her sergeant, who nods.

'Yes, that fits with the CCTV footage,' he says.

'Carry on, Scarlet,' says DI Twist. 'You arrived at the hotel. What happened next?'

'I went in at the main entrance and walked through to the rooms. We'd gone online and looked at the plans from when the hotel was refurbished so I knew how to find the right one. Ada had called the week before to arrange it. She said she was his agent and he wanted one of the downstairs rooms with its own terrace. We thought it would be easier for me to get to a ground-floor room.' The real reason was so I'd have an alternative means of exit, but I can hardly admit to that.

'I found the right room and knocked on the door. He didn't answer so I waited for a bit and knocked again. There was still no answer but I knew Ada would want me to use my initiative so I went round to the terrace.' She nods again, encouraging me to go on without interrupting the flow of my story.

'I knocked again and there was still no answer, so I tried the handle; it wasn't locked so I opened it.'

'And what did you find?'

'I could see him straight away. Lying on the bed, asleep, I thought. He was dressed and there was a light on so I thought maybe he'd just nodded off.' My story's been more or less true up to this point, and I pause, focussing on what comes next.

'But he hadn't just nodded off,' DI Twist prompts me.

'No. I called his name, softly at first and then a bit louder, but he didn't move so I went over to the bed and shook his shoulder. When he didn't wake up I looked more closely and I could see how pale he was, and his chest wasn't moving. There was a pair of reading glasses on the table and I held them over his mouth and his nose. They didn't steam up and I guessed he must be dead.'

'What did you do next, Scarlet?'

'I put the glasses back and left. It freaked me out, finding a dead body like that. I wanted to get away from it as quickly as I could.'

'Did you touch anything else in the room?'

'No.'

'And what did you think had happened to him?'

'I didn't think he'd been murdered, if that's what you mean. It looked like he'd died in his sleep. I was hardly going to start examining him for a cause of death, I just wanted to get out.'

'It didn't occur to you to tell someone? A member of hotel staff, perhaps?' For a moment, DI Twist sounds just like my old English teacher Miss Waters, always asking why something hadn't occurred to me when I got into trouble. I thought it was a stupid question then and I still do now.

'No. At least not until I was half way home, and it was too late by then. And I didn't want people asking questions about why I was there. It would have made Ada angry. I wanted her to think I'd done what she asked.'

'Yes, Ada. What did you tell her?'

'I said it had all gone to plan. I told her he'd said thank you for the champagne and read the letter and then he said he'd help Polly.'

'So you didn't tell Ada the truth?'

'No. I didn't think it would make her any happier. And I didn't want to have to talk about it. Like I said, it had freaked me out. I wanted to try and forget about it.'

'What about later? Didn't she have any questions for you once she knew there was a murder investigation underway?'

'No, I made a joke to her that the champagne must have been too much for him and let her think he'd died after I left. She still doesn't know.' At least that's true. There's a pause and I'm hoping it's over. They've not challenged me yet, so perhaps they're going to let me go. DI Twist leans over to look at Sergeant Carter's screen, and once he's finished typing she turns back towards me.

'You didn't think that what you've just told us could have been helpful to our investigation?' Her tone's been calm and quiet so far, but it's hardened now, and I realise she's not finished after all.

'No, I didn't. I never believed he'd been murdered. I thought he'd had a heart attack or something and you were only checking because his fiancée told you to. What difference would it have made, anyway?' I try to adopt an innocent tone but it's not working very well. And I don't suppose she liked the suggestion that Hayley's been telling her what to do.

'I don't need to explain to you how it could have helped, Scarlet, but trust me, it would have done. It's obvious that your statements so far have been false and they've led to a waste of police time and potentially a perversion of the course of justice. And I see no reason to believe what you've told us now. We'll have to get your story checked out in detail before we take this interview any further.' I open my mouth to speak, but she doesn't let me. She's up and out of her seat and telling me I'm under arrest and anything I say may be used in evidence and all the other things they say on police dramas that I'd never expected to hear said to me.

* * *

They have to take me to Hull because there's no cells at the Beverley station. Two constables in uniform drive me there in a police car but they haven't put cuffs on me which makes it feel better, I don't know why. When we get there a custody sergeant writes down my details and takes my bag away. They take me to a room with a machine in it a bit like a photocopier where they take my fingerprints. I'd expected an ink pad and paper like I've seen on the telly, but I suppose things are different now. Then I get taken to a cell. It's a shock because I thought I'd go to another interview room, but the sergeant says it'll be some time before DI Twist gets to me and I'm to wait here.

'How long will it be? Will I be here overnight?' It's feeling a lot more real now, and I have to fight down the panic inside me in order to sound normal.

'I can't say,' she says. 'But you should be prepared for it. These things take time.' I expect she's trying to be nice but it doesn't help much.

The cell's just like the ones I've seen on the telly. They've taken my phone and my watch so the only way I have of marking time is by when they bring me food. It's not long before someone gives me a sandwich and a bottle of water, and I find I'm hungry despite everything. Once I've finished eating there's nothing to do except sit and listen to the noise coming from the other cells. I try to stay calm but my thoughts are skittering around like a rat in a trap. I tell myself to calm down and think positively. They won't be able to disprove my version of events, and that's what matters. There's still a chance they'll find no evidence of anything sinister and then they'll have to settle on natural causes after all. It's only me that knows about the messed-up room and the two whisky glasses. I wonder what the punishment is for wasting police time or perverting the course of justice. It can't be that long, and Ada would still be pleased with me for trying my best to do what she wanted. Maybe I'll just have to pay a fine and everything will go back to how it was. I could even manage a few months in prison if Ada sticks to her promise when I come out.

An hour or two after my lunch I'm taken back to the interview room. Sergeant Carter comes in first with a recorder and notebook, followed by a constable I've not seen before. They settle themselves in the chairs opposite and plug in the recorder. We go through the names and time routine again and I confirm I don't want a solicitor, thank you very much. I wonder where DI Twist is. Maybe she's with Polly or Emma; perhaps one of them was on the shop CCTV too. Whichever of them did it could have taken a different route to the hotel, but even if they didn't, the police would hardly be likely to tell me, would they? My thoughts are in danger of running away with themselves again and I tell myself to stop wondering what else might be going on. Whatever this is about, I need to give it my full attention.

'I need you to go through part of your account again, Scarlet,' says Sergeant Carter. He's got a folder open in front of him and he's looking at a sheet of paper. I'm good at reading upside down but it's too far away for me to see what's on it.

'All right.' I knew this could happen. They like to make you tell your story lots of times, trying to trip you up. I'm ready for this.

'When you arrived at the terrace door you opened it yourself, is that correct?'

'Yes.'

'So we'd expect to find your fingerprints on the door handle.'

'Yes.'

'I've got a transcript of your interview this morning,' he says, pulling out another piece of paper and pushing it towards me. 'I'd like you to read this page and confirm that it's accurate.' It's the bit about me checking to see that Max was dead. I read it through and can't find anything to worry about.

'Yes, that's what I said.'

'You went to the bed, you realised that Mr Silento wasn't asleep and you checked to see if he was breathing.'

'Yes, that's right.' I can't work out why it's so important, but I don't like the feeling that this is heading in a bad direction.

'You looked at his chest and then you picked up the glasses by his bed.'

'Yes.'

'And you held the glasses over his mouth and nose to see if they steamed up.'

'Yes, but they didn't. That's when I knew for sure that he was dead.' Maybe this is about the time of death, but Sergeant Carter doesn't give me time to think about it.

'Which hand did you hold the glasses in? Left or right?'

'I don't remember… I suppose it must have been my right hand. I'm right-handed.'

'Based on what you've told me, we'd expect to find your fingerprints on the glasses, don't you agree? And Max Silento's too?'

'Yes, I suppose so.'

'There are fingerprints on the glasses: Max Silento's. They're a bit smudged but clear enough for a match. None of them match yours.' My brain freezes. The gloves. How could I have forgotten? I put them on before entering the room. I was pleased with myself, thinking there'd be no trace of me there, but now all it's done is ruin my story.

'Scarlet?'

'What?'

'Your fingerprints aren't on the glasses which you said you picked up to check Max's breathing. How do you explain that?' I can't think. My brain won't work. All I can do is ask myself: what would Ada do? What did she say this morning? It feels like an age ago, but it's only a matter of hours since I was helping her on with her clothes.

'Scarlet? How do you explain it?'

'No comment,' I say, remembering just in time.

'Were you in the room at all?'

'No comment.'

'Or is there another reason your prints weren't on the glasses?' He's not allowed to put words in my mouth, but I know he's wondering if I was wearing gloves, and that's the last thing I'm going to tell him.

'No comment.' It gets easier each time I say it, and it's helping me to feel safe for now. Sergeant Carter closes his folder and sighs.

'All right. We'll leave it there for now. I'll be back tomorrow with the inspector. And Scarlet…'

'Yes?'

'When we come back… you might want to think about telling us the truth.'

* * *

I'm in shock when I get back to my cell, but it quickly turns to anger at myself. How could I have been so stupid? As soon as they mentioned fingerprints this morning I should have worked out what they were doing. Now they'll either be thinking I didn't use the glasses after all or that I was wearing gloves. I couldn't even know the glasses were there unless I was in the room, and what reason could I have for wearing gloves if I'd only gone to give Max a letter and a bottle of champagne? It's all I can do not to hit the walls and yell with frustration; I can't sit still, and I resort to pacing the cell like a caged animal in the zoo.

After what seems like hours I'm given another meal. I have to sit down to eat it and once I stop pacing I realise that I'm exhausted. I suppose it's a good thing – at least it will help me to sleep. I lie down when I've finished and make myself relax in the hope of being either able to sleep or come up with a plan. I don't know how, but when night finally comes I manage to doze off despite the noise from people being brought in and banging about in their cells. A sergeant comes in to check I'm OK and she's not too bad. She says the more noise people make, the less she needs to check on them, which makes me smile. Waking suddenly in the dark at what time I don't know, my mind snaps back to the murder. I have to decide what to say tomorrow. 'No comment' isn't going to work for much longer and I daren't ask for legal advice; I have to work it out for myself.

The police know I was in Max's room the night he died and now they've got my fingerprints on the door handle I can't think of any more innocent explanations. It'd be bad enough to be accused of wasting police time or perverting the course of justice, but if I'm not careful they'll think I'm a murderer too. I've got two options. The easy one is to stay quiet and hope they can't find sufficient evidence. I'm sure they'd have charged me if they could, and they can't hold me here for ever unless they find out more. But what if they do find out more? Do they know about the morphine? And what about the real cause of death? Have they found another poison in his blood in the post-mortem? What if they think it was me who poisoned him with the whisky? It's not enough to hope they'll give up. If they arrest me for murder, I've got to be able to tell them who really did it. And how.

I make myself think back over the past two weeks and everything I've done. I'm sure I'd have found out whether it was Polly or Emma if I'd only had one more day before they brought me in. Going over and over it isn't helping; I need a new approach. I've been able to uncover things the police couldn't, but what have they been able to do that I haven't? They've analysed the contents of the whisky glass for starters. What else? Of course – the search of the house; there must be a clue for me there. It was no great surprise when DI Twist wanted to know about medications, but why did they search the garage? They left before they could finish, perhaps because they got the CCTV footage of me, so they can't have found anything by then. What were they looking for? And was it even there?

I don't know much about cars so there's no point in wondering what Daniel might or might not keep in the garage. If there was something that could have been there but wasn't, it could be because Emma or Polly had moved it. Or because it was never there in the first place. If Max's killer used something that could be in a garage and isn't, it must be hidden somewhere else. And I've already worked out the best place for hiding things at our house. The shed. Why, oh why didn't I think of this before? I could have looked back through my photos for clues, but the police have my phone now.

Cursing myself for my stupidity, I think back to yesterday afternoon. It's quiet for once, and I make myself relax on the hard bed, loosening my muscles, slowing my breathing and letting my mind float back to the shed and focussing on the shelves and their contents. The ones that come most easily are those with the crates on so I start there. The crate with the documents was on the second shelf. The one before it has ski clothes in it and the one beside that one overalls, and then come the plant pots. The bottom shelf has heavy things on it – to weigh it down, I suppose. There's a big tin of undercoat, another of wood stain and some smaller items too. I open my eyes beneath their closed lids, visualising the shelf. There's stuff for greenfly, slug pellets and a big see-through container with a blue liquid in it. It looks like something Oskar had in his shed. He liked to do as much work on his car as possible for himself so he had oil and brake fluid and that same blue stuff. It's anti-freeze.

If I had my phone I'd look up anti-freeze and check if it's poisonous, but I don't need to. There's no other reason for it to be hidden in the shed and it's definitely something you'd expect to find in a garage. Now all I need to work out is which of them gave it to Max.

TWENTY-FIVE

I don't sleep well after that. I try to relax, knowing I'll be able to think better in the morning if I do, but my mind won't leave it alone. Either Emma was Max's wife and she killed him, or Polly was his lover and it was her. Despite having less proof for Polly, it's easier to imagine a motive for her. I can see him laughing at her, perhaps telling her to get an abortion and informing her he's got no intention of leaving his rich American fiancée. But it's harder to think of a motive for Emma. I get that she wanted to leave him, but would it really have been so terrible if he'd asked to see Polly? My thoughts chase themselves around in circles for ages, and no sooner have I drifted off to sleep in the small hours, than my breakfast tray's being shoved into the cell.

I'm almost fully awake when they take me to the interview room. There's no one there and when the custody sergeant returns it's to tell me that DI Twist has been delayed. I ask for a coffee while I wait and use the time to get my thoughts straight. Being in this room helps me to get my priorities in order. I don't care what Ada does or doesn't do, I'm not going to prison for anyone. Now that I've made up my mind, I want to get it over with, and as the caffeine hits my system it takes all my willpower not to start pacing the room again. Eventually the door opens, making me jump, and DI Twist walks in, followed by yesterday's constable. There are no good mornings today. Once our names and the date and time are on the tape, she's straight in there, firing questions at me before I have time to open my mouth and tell her everything I've learnt.

'Where did you put the champagne?' I don't know what I was expecting her to ask, but it wasn't this, and it takes me by surprise.

'The champagne?'

'Yes.' There's a note of impatience in her voice which I've not heard before, as if she wants to get the question out of the way and move on to more important matters. 'You told us you took a bottle of champagne for Max Silento to drink. And a letter. Where did you put them? There was no sign of them in the room or in your house and you told Ada you'd given them to Mr Silento. What did you do with them?' I'm thinking faster than I've ever thought before. If I tell her I poured the champagne down the sink it will look much too calculated.

'I put the letter in a bin on the way home,' I say, to give myself at least a few seconds to think about the champagne.

'And the champagne?'

'I put it with the empty bottles in the car park. You know, for recycling.' Always stick as close to the truth as you can, Ada says, and she was right. They won't be able to check either of those places after all this time. I let out a breath, thinking there might still be a possibility of my getting away with it after all.

'That was quick thinking,' says DI Twist, a hint of irony in her voice; does she mean then or now? 'It must have been very important to you for Ada to think you'd done what you set out to do.' She's not looking at me; her paperwork seems to be more interesting, and it's hard talking to someone who doesn't look like they're paying attention.

'Yes, it was.'

'How did you find the empties?'

'Sorry, I don't understand. How did I find...'

'The empty bottles. The hotel has a big recycling bin for empty bottles. It's well hidden from the rooms – I don't suppose the guests want to sit on their terraces looking at recycling bins – and it was dark. How did you know where to put it?' I don't know what to say. This isn't at all how I was expecting this interview to go. I thought I'd be telling her about my suspicions about Emma and Polly, but my brain feels as if it's a runaway train, and I can't get off.

'I—'

'Had you planned to put it there all along? When it was empty? So that it wouldn't be found in Max Silento's room?'

'I don't know what you mean.' It's the next best thing to no comment. I know what she's suggesting and it's too close to the truth for comfort. She looks at me briefly and then back at her notes.

'We conducted a full search of the house yesterday,' she says. 'Do you have any idea as to what we might have been looking for?'

'No.' I can't help sounding nervous. Is it now? Do I have to tell her now?

'We found items that indicate very strongly that Max Silento was murdered by someone living in your house. Does that surprise you, Scarlet?' I don't know what to say. Will it make matters worse if I say no?

'Scarlet?'

'I…' I can feel my face crumple and fear wash though me. I can't do it any more. I've got to tell someone the truth. 'No.'

'No, what?' She looks up at me, but I can't tell what she's thinking and I'm too tired to try to work it out anyway.

'No, I'm not surprised. I think you found morphine and anti-freeze. But it wasn't me who killed him. I was supposed to, but I couldn't. He was already dead when I got there.' A silence hangs in the room, and the constable's fingers hover in the air above his keys.

'You were supposed to kill him?' DI Twist finds her voice first.

'Yes. For Ada.'

'For Ada?'

'Yes.'

'Let me get this straight. Ada asked you to kill Max Silento and you agreed. Is that right?'

'Yes. She said he posed a terrible risk to the family and we'd all lose everything if he wasn't stopped. She said the only one who could kill him was me.'

'But why would you agree to that, Scarlet?'

'To protect the family. My family.'

'But you must have known there was a chance of your being caught. Why would you put yourself at such risk? Were you trying to impress Ada? To show her your loyalty? I know you've a lot to be grateful to her for, but it shouldn't require you to carry out a murder for her.' She's trying not to let it show, but I can hear incredulity in her voice, and it's weird, but it feels good to have someone else think it was a crazy thing to do.

'I wanted to. Ada's done so much to help me, and I wanted to protect—'

'Yes, you've said. To protect the family.' She lets the sentence hang in the air, the silence communicating her incredulity more effectively than words could have done. I don't know what to say. She doesn't understand and she never will. Ada *is* protecting me but I can't tell her about our agreement. Not while I can still hope that she'll trust me to go through with it. I look at my feet and wonder what she's going to say next.

'Did Ada tell you what kind of risk Mr Silento posed to the family?' DI Twist looks back at her papers again, and it's a relief not to have to look her in the eye.

'No, she wouldn't. She said I didn't need to know even though I must have asked her a hundred times.'

'But you did what she wanted anyway.'

'Yes. It was a foolproof method, she said.'

'But it wasn't foolproof, was it?'

'It would have been, if someone else hadn't got there first and mucked it up. I was going to give him morphine to drink in the champagne and then inject an air bubble into his vein. Ada said it was the easiest way to do it and no one would be able to tell afterwards.'

'She might have been right about that, but you did it after he was dead so the morphine wasn't absorbed into his system. And what about the anti-freeze? How did that come in?'

'I didn't have anything to do with the anti-freeze. That was the real murderer, not me.'

'Hmm, so you say.'

'You've got to believe me! I had nothing to do with the anti-freeze.'

'So how did you know we'd found it?'

'Because I found it first. And Emma's papers. And the hair dye and—' DI Twist holds up her hand to stop me as the constable leans across to show her his mobile.

'Hold it there, Scarlet. Turn off the tape.' DI Twist reads whatever's on the phone and mutters in the constable's ear. Then she's out of her chair and heading towards the door. The phone must have made a noise but I was so caught up in my thoughts that I didn't hear it. The constable tells the machine that the interview has been paused and we sit in silence, me staring at the table and him peering at his screen. I'm suddenly terrified they won't believe me. The family will close ranks and leave me to take the blame. This is why Ada wouldn't tell me anything; she didn't want me to be able to give away the real killer. She was duping me from the start and I was stupid enough to let her. I can't get up and walk around, not while the constable's in the room, and I sit, twisting my fingers in my lap, willing DI Twist to come back so that I can tell her everything. The hands on the clock only move on by ten minutes but it seems like hours before DI Twist returns. Or at least the top half of her does, leaning around the door.

'I'm sorry for the delay. We're going to have to leave it there, I'm afraid. I'll be back to ask you some more questions this afternoon.' She looks tired, but at the same time her forehead looks younger, smoother, and I realise there are fewer wrinkles there than before.

'But I need to tell you! It wasn't me. And I know who it was, or at least who it could have—'

'There's no need for that, Scarlet. You can tell me whatever you want, but it will have to wait for later.' She's come into the room now, followed by the custody sergeant, who I guess will be taking me back to the cell.

'But why? It wasn't me, you have to believe me.'

'I do believe you, Scarlet. I know it wasn't you. We've already charged someone with Mr Silento's murder.'

'Who? Who have you charged?'

'Emma Rosewood. She confessed to murdering Max Silento this morning.'

TWENTY-SIX

I didn't want to go back to the house; I was scared of what Ada would do and what the rest of them would say, so I told my solicitor not to ask for bail and stayed in jail until my trial was over. By the time I was given my sentence six months had passed, I'd already served the time on remand and Polly's baby had arrived. It had all come out by then, Ada's plan and what I'd tried to do, and even though he was in bits about Emma, Daniel came to the trial and took me home afterwards. He sat me down at the kitchen table and told me I could stay in the house for as long as I wanted.

'You're part of this family whether you want to be or not, Scarlet,' he said. 'We've missed you and we want you back. None of what happened is your fault. Max was a dreadful man, and I can't imagine the stress Emma was under when he barged his way back into her life. I only wish she'd told me about him sooner.'

'She told Ada instead.'

'Yes, Mother had been helping Emma to hide her secret for years. She even bought the house in Scotland so Neville and Barbara could see the children. They were all terrified of Max tracking her down and finding out about Polly.'

'I suppose they were right to be worried about him.'

'Yes, but it doesn't excuse Mother asking you to murder him. I still can't believe she did that. Maybe it was a sign…' Daniel paused, lost in thought. A sign of what? Perhaps he was wondering if it was Ada who'd told Emma not to confide in him. We used to joke that she liked to be in charge, but maybe she'd had more control over his life than he wanted to admit. Emma's too, come to that; I'm sure Ada was behind the pay-as-you-go phone for Emma to contact her father – it was just the sort of spy strategy she loved. With Daniel being so nice to me I thought I could risk asking him to tell me more. I'd been going over and over it in my brain while I'd been in prison, and it was driving me nuts not knowing all the details.

'What did he do, exactly? I'll understand if you'd rather not say, but Ada never explained it properly to me.' Daniel sighed deeply and gave me a sad smile.

'If there's anyone who deserves to know the full story, it's you,' he said. 'It's simple, really. Emma – or Phoebe, as she was – met and married Max while they were at music college. He was older than her and very controlling. It was like those stories you read in the paper where wives kill their husbands after years of emotional abuse.'

'But she didn't kill him. Not then, anyway.'

'No, she got out. It was getting pregnant that gave her the courage to leave. Max had isolated her from her family and friends by then, so she went to a refuge and reinvented herself as Emma Stevens. And after we married, Mother helped her to make contact with her parents again.' Daniel paused, gazing out of the window, perhaps thinking back to happier days. I didn't want to upset him, but I needed to know more.

'And then he found her.'

'Yes. He'd searched for years without success, but he'd never given up entirely. Then he took the post at the music college. There was no reason for him to come into contact with Polly, but he attended a concert one night, and there she was. He told Emma that he recognised her at once – apparently she's the spitting image of his mother. And the frown on her face as she played her viola was just the same as Emma's when she played her violin.' His voice cracked, and he got up to fetch a glass of water, hiding his face as he did so.

'I never knew she played the violin,' I said, hoping the attempt at relatively small talk might help Daniel to calm himself.

'Join the club,' he said. 'None of us did. None of us knew most things about Emma, as it turns out.' He paused, and I let him gather his thoughts again. 'Anyway, Max turned up making all sorts of threats. He was furious with Emma for leaving him, for hiding from him, for keeping Polly from him all those years. It wasn't enough for him to make contact with his daughter; he wanted revenge. He deliberately made her squirm, wanting her to sign divorce papers, arranging to perform at the festival, and then, finally, threatening to whisk Polly off to America with him. He said he'd get her into a top music college over there and tell her "the truth" about her mother. He told Emma that by the time he'd finished, Polly would never want to see her family again. And she believed him. He was very charming and highly manipulative, and Emma believed every word he said. He reduced her to the traumatised state she'd been in when she left him, and she panicked. Even though Ada promised to sort it out for her, she couldn't trust her to do so.'

'So she took matter into her own hands.'

'Yes.' There was nothing more to be said, and we sat for a while in a silence that felt like a relief. It was Daniel who brought us back to the present, with a lighter expression on his face, as if telling the story had given him some respite from his troubles.

'Anyway, as I said, we want you back. Your room's waiting for you; everything's just as you left it.' He was looking at me expectantly, waiting for me to say that was wonderful, but I didn't. I had nowhere else to go, but a prickle of fear was creeping up my spine. I'd had plenty time in prison to think about Ada and I knew what she'd done to me. She'd brainwashed me, sucking me into her world a step at a time, letting me think it was normal not to have friends, normal to never go out, normal to euthanise my employer and even normal to commit murder for her. She knew I had no family, that I'd do anything to get one and to guarantee a secure future. I didn't know if I wanted to risk that happening again, even if it did give me back my family and my home. And there was no way I'd be able to euthanise her now, not after everything that had happened; would she accept that? Daniel could see my hesitation, and I felt as if he were seeing right into my thoughts.

'She's changed, Scarlet,' he said at last. 'It's only a few months since you were here, but you'll find her very different. It's the shock, the doctor says, and the change in routine, different carers coming in and so on. Not having you here – and Emma, of course...' Daniel's voice wobbled, and I waited while he cleared his throat. 'Not having you around has unsettled her more than you can imagine. I do hope you'll stay. Please. Why don't you just go up and talk to her? Maybe that will help you to make up your mind.'

'But she won't want me back, will she? She'll think I've let her down. She'll be furious with me.'

'No, she won't. Go on up, Scarlet. She's expecting you.' My legs were unsteady as I mounted the spiral stairs. I couldn't imagine what Ada would say to me and wished that Daniel had come with me. I paused at the top of the stairs, drinking in the room and feeling an enormous weight lifting from my shoulders with the realisation that I'd never have to go back to the noise and grey of the prison. Ada was sitting in her favourite spot by the window, a mug of coffee and her hearing aids on the table beside her. She wasn't going to hear me, so I walked slowly into her field of vision, picked up the aids and handed them to her. She looked at me carefully as she inserted the little buds.

'Hello, Ada,' I said, and sat down opposite her.

'Have you done it?' she asked. 'Have you killed him?' I should have been shocked, but the delayed recognition on her face had already half-prepared me, and she was in no state to notice my hesitation.

'Yes, Ada. It's all right. He's dead. It's all over now.'

'You took a long time. I've been waiting for you a long time.' The confusion in her eyes was almost too much to bear but I kept my voice even and gently patted her hand.

'I know. But I'm back now.'